DEFINITE
POSSIBILITY

Visit us at www.boldstrokesbooks.com

By the Author

Totally Worth It

Serious Potential

Definite Possibility

DEFINITE POSSIBILITY

by
Maggie Cummings

2017

CREDITS
EDITOR: RUTH STERNGLANTZ
PRODUCTION DESIGN: SUSAN RAMUNDO
COVER DESIGN BY JEANINE HENNING

Acknowledgments

Once again, thanks to Rad and Sandy for affording me this incredible opportunity. I also want to express my heartfelt thanks to Ruth for her boundless patience, guidance, and support. And to the entire team at Bold Strokes Books, thank you for all the work you do to make my dream a reality.

Special thanks to my friends Liz and Amanda whose enthusiasm for these characters has made writing the stories so much fun. Thank you also to my BSB friends, who have become so much like family. And, of course, to my family—Kat, Caleb, and Abby—thank you for the endless love, encouragement and support that makes my life what it is.

Dedication

For Zsa Zsa

CHAPTER ONE

S he's the one."
Meg could barely keep her excitement in check as she gripped the back of a kitchen chair tightly with both hands and bounced on the balls of her feet. She gnawed on the inside of her cheek to keep a smile from busting out.

"Wait a second." Her best friend Lexi held one hand in the air, effectively halting the conversation. "You're sure?" She looked skeptically at Meg. "I thought this was something you were *mildly* considering," Lexi said, turning her attention to the pot of sauce in front of her and giving it a quick stir. "You sound like your mind's completely made up."

"That is because my mind is completely made up."

"Wow." Lexi rested the wooden spoon across the edge of her pot. She blew out a long breath that wasn't in line with the kind of approval Meg was hoping for. Chewing on her lower lip, she looked over at Meg. "Megan McTiernan, this is a big commitment. Are you sure you're ready?"

"You're right." Meg nodded agreement. "But I think it'll be good."

"Your whole life is going to change."

"Hey, don't sound so disappointed. I'm excited about this. Be happy for me."

"I am." Lexi's shoulders slumped. "I'm not disappointed. Honest. I just want to make sure this is really what you want."

"Come here." Meg motioned Lexi over and held up her phone. "Look at her." She tilted the screen and felt a smile forming again. "Is there really even any question?"

"She is cute."

"Cute, she's adorable. I can't wait to hold her and cuddle her, kiss her sweet little face." She inched her phone up, forcing another peek on Lexi, and punched her arm playfully when she caught her friend rolling her eyes.

"Fine," Lexi said through a grin. "You have my blessing." She walked back to tend her vodka sauce. "When's the big day? Wait." She leaned against the granite countertop and folded her arms, nodding with her chin toward Meg's house across the street. "What did Reina say?"

"About what?" Meg heard the defensiveness in her tone and wondered if Lexi would call her out on it.

"You didn't tell her, did you?" Lexi asked. She furrowed her brow as she spoke. "You didn't tell your girlfriend about this major life change. Huh," she said under her breath continuing her inner analysis.

"You're being kind of dramatic," Meg said with a small laugh. "It's not that big of a deal *and* I mentioned I was thinking about it," she said with a wry smile. "She didn't have an opinion one way or the other." Meg put her phone down. "It's not like she's allergic or anything. And she doesn't live with me, even if she was."

"But she stays there a few nights a week. I thought maybe at some point…"

"Yeah, maybe," she said addressing Lexi's gentle press as to where things were headed in her love life. Meg walked to the cabinet and helped herself to a wineglass. "We're light years away from that." She poured herself a healthy serving of red. "Don't take that the wrong way. Things with me and Reina are fine. Completely. But a lot of the time she stays over out of convenience. I mean, she lives forty-five minutes away. Her dental office is practically around the block from here. It makes sense."

"But things are good?"

"They're fine," Meg said as she looked at the picture on her phone again. "And they will stay fine when I bring this furry baby home in three weeks." She enlarged the photo, zooming in on the tiny paws first. Lexi came around her chair to peer over her shoulder.

"She is precious. Did you name her yet?"

"I have a few ideas I'm tossing around."

The front door opened and Jesse came through, decked out in full attorney mode, complete with suit and briefcase.

"Ideas for what?" she asked, diving right into the conversation.

"Meg's getting a kitten."

"No way. Good for you, kid."

Lexi looked at her wife. "How was court?"

"Fine. Just opening arguments today. Nothing to report." She walked over and kissed Lexi, before squeezing Meg's shoulder. "Tell me about your cat, Meg. Where did you find her?"

"My sister's neighbor's cat had kittens."

"Color?" Jesse asked dropping into the seat next to Meg.

"She's a white calico mix." Meg pulled up the picture for the third time. "Are you a cat person?" she said, openly admitting her surprise. "I didn't even know you liked animals."

"Who doesn't like animals?" Jesse took a sip of the wine Lexi gave her. "I grew up with cats—Ginger, Fig Newton, Mr. Snuffles."

"How did I not know this?" Meg laughed into her drink and watched Jesse-the-lawyer shuck her jacket and transform into her buddy as she inched her chair closer and snatched Meg's phone to examine the rest of the kittens together. Lexi came up behind them and draped her arms over her wife's chest as she scrolled.

"Get this, babe, Reina doesn't get a vote."

"Why would she?" Jesse bent her head to kiss Lexi's forearm. "Reina doesn't live there."

"Thank you!" Meg held her glass in an appreciative air toast to Jesse's vocal defense of her decision.

"I guess she's not here?" Jesse asked, not even bothering to look up. "Since we're having this conversation and all."

"She's working until eight tonight. Maybe she'll come by later," she said, but she wasn't convinced. "Unless she goes home to Queens tonight," Meg added under her breath. "She'll text one way or the other."

"Oh, babe," Jesse said, twisting her wineglass, "I meant to tell you before. I talked to Betsy earlier—she and Tracy have plans tonight."

Lexi nodded. "It's probably better this way. Just us, you know. This way we get Sam all to ourselves." She bounced back over to the stove. "I'm so excited she's back."

"Bummer it's because of a breakup," Meg said.

Lexi stirred her sauce. "Yeah, but she didn't seem too busted up about it." She shrugged. "You know, she told me it's been over for a while. Now she's just happy to be home. Ready to move on and all."

Meg looked back and forth between her two besties and decided to go for the easy laugh, even though it was completely predictable. "Well, geez, I hope someone warned the locals."

❖

Sam pulled into the small strip mall parking lot, threw her Tahoe in park, and weighed her slim options as she glanced between the storefronts. It had only occurred to her after she'd driven past at least a half a dozen bakeries and as many liquor stores that she'd completely forgotten to pick up something to bring to Lexi's. It was only day three at her parents' house and she was already losing the ability to form rational thought. Less than a quarter mile from Bay West, she'd pulled into the lot, encouraged by the bright entrance of Angelo's Pizzeria shining a light on the sign of the adjacent store—a florist. But on closer inspection, she was too late. The flower shop had its wrought-iron gate drawn and padlocked.

As far as dessert went, Sam was left with hoping that Angelo's had something suitable to offer or checking out a new place called Lucy's Coffee Bar that definitely wasn't here last winter.

Last winter, when she'd left her friends and the community she loved to follow her girlfriend across country.

It had seemed like a good idea at the time. She'd been in a committed relationship and her job as a graphic designer allowed her to work from anywhere. Just a year later, and it was so obvious that she would have been better off staying put at Bay West. Decisions—she shook her head swallowing a chuckle at the thought—always crystal clear in retrospect. Regardless of the past, she took a step forward, smiling inwardly at the complete faith she had in her choice tonight.

Lucy's Coffee Bar, it was.

Pulling the door open, she was surprised when a bell jingled to quaintly announce her arrival. The shop was empty except for an androgynous chick deep into her laptop in the corner. Light jazz drifted in from the speakers and the smell of fresh coffee and cookies wafted around her. Score. She rested one elbow against the counter as she waited for service. The space had a charm about it. Antiqued couches and worn-out Persian rugs, plus a few small tables and chairs. The walls were fitted with built-ins giving a homey quality. She studied the Old English style font on the glass storefront but her eyes were drawn to a series of decals bordering the large window—the American flag, an NYPD patch, the Human Rights Campaign logo, a rainbow flag, a Bay West emblem. Plus stick figures of two men, two women, and a man and woman. Finally the words *All are welcome.* She loved this place already.

"Sorry to keep you waiting."

"No worries," Sam responded automatically, turning around and giving the woman a discreet once over. Whoa. Petite. Dirty-blond hair pulled up off her face. Flour, or maybe sugar, dusted across the middle of a tight V-neck tee that showcased small perky breasts. Hip-hugging yoga pants stretched over some really nice curves. Lucy? She dragged her eyes back up to the woman's face.

"Can I get you something?"

"I bet you can," Sam responded smoothly. She wasn't subtle, that wasn't her style. This technique had been her forte since college. At five ten, Sam was taller than most women and while she had feminine features—a tiny nose and high cheekbones—she was completely butch. She sported awesomely wavy hair that was cut into a tight fade on the sides. With no real curves, she looked better in men's clothes than her brother. She was never, ever mistaken for being straight and she liked it that way. She found it an advantage when she was flirting, and even in situations like this, when she was working a sort of dude-in-distress act, she felt her straightforward appearance complemented her schtick.

She leaned forward onto the countertop and squinted one eye closed. "I have a teensy problem."

The woman barely bit as she reached for a counter rag and wiped the surface between them clean. "I hope it's something a coffee can fix."

Sam furrowed her brow and ducked her head waiting for eye contact as she laid it on thick. "It may be a little more complicated than that."

"I'm listening."

"So, tonight's my first night back in town. I was away for a while."

"Prison?" the woman deadpanned.

Sam laughed at her fast wit. "Funny. No. I just moved home. And my friend is making me, like, a welcome home dinner. But I forgot to bring something, like wine or dessert. She lives just up the street so I'm almost out of options."

"So I'm your last resort?"

"Hey"—she let the word dangle between them—"I would never say that about you."

"Cute."

"No, seriously, I pulled in here because I realized last minute that there's nowhere left to go, and I was going to get flowers but they're closed. So I could jump into Angelo's pizzeria and maybe get some zeppole, but that's pretty lame."

The woman scrunched up her nose in obvious disapproval. "I mean Angelo makes fantastic everything, but zeppole to a dinner party…" Her voice trailed off leaving no question as to what she thought of that plan.

"Lucky for me I spotted this place and I thought maybe…" Sam tapped her finger on the counter before pointing to a plate of cookies near the end of the counter. "If my senses are correct, there's a fresh batch baking up as we speak." Sam drew her bottom lip in and raised her eyebrows. "I'm kinda hoping you're about to tell me I got here just in time."

"Does this typically work? This"—the woman waved her hand in a circle at Sam—"this, I'm so cute, I can just charm my way into getting whatever I want?"

Sam was about to answer, but the door to the back opened and a girl with jet-black hair peeked her head out. "Lucy, the timer just went off for your cookies. I took them out to cool. I'm gonna head out—" She cut herself off and licked her lips as she overtly checked Sam out. With a look that left very little to the imagination she added, "But I could *definitely* stay."

"Good night, Raven."

"Fine. Keep all the good ones for yourself. Like that's fair."

"Go," Lucy ordered with a playful shake of her head. She turned back to Sam. "Sorry about that."

"No worries. I think she just said something about fresh cookies, though." She scratched her chin dramatically. "Did I hear that right?"

Lucy rolled her eyes but Sam gave a slo-mo fist pump anyway.

"Let me guess. This is the type of thing your girlfriend usually takes care of?"

"Ex-girlfriend. But yes. Only now I suspect she's taking care of it for her new girlfriend."

Lucy grimaced. "Ooh, I'm sorry."

"It's all good." Sam held eye contact and her voice came out smooth, her confidence intact. She saw Lucy blush.

"Are you in a hurry?" Lucy asked. "Those cookies would do better if they cooled for another minute or two. I could get you a drink while you wait."

"I'm fine. There's no rush. I'm only going up the road to Bay West."

"Great."

"Are you familiar with it?" Sam already knew the answer was yes, but she was curious to see Lucy's reaction at the mention of the all-lesbian condo development a quarter mile away.

Lucy's smoky gray eyes twinkled. "I live there."

Sweet. Sam had been hoping she and Lucy were on the same team and her residency at Bay West sealed the deal. Bay West was pretty big as far as condominium complexes were concerned, especially in the suburbs of New York. It was located right on the edge of Staten Island, under the bridge, and it boasted some pretty nice views of Lower Manhattan. But that was hardly its selling point. Bay West was all women, all lesbians to be precise, all the time. Sam still wasn't over the fact that she'd given up her apartment there a year ago.

"I used to live there myself."

"Really? Whereabouts?"

"On Vista, in the rental section."

Lucy nodded acknowledgment. "I'm on Vista now. In a one-bedroom, near the office."

"Excellent. A one-bedroom. Hard to come by, those."

"I've heard that. I was lucky, I guess."

"How long have you been here? And there?" she added, referencing Bay West as she swallowed a grimace, annoyed that her genuine curiosity got the best of her game.

"About six months, for both."

"You like it?"

"Mm-hmm. I'm here at the shop most of the time. It's very convenient."

Weird answer. Usually people went on about Bay West's sense of community, the support, the constant lesbian parties.

Maybe she was married. But no ring. What was she doing? She'd established her priorities before she came back—no relationships, no hookups, no girls, no exceptions. She'd decided that right off when she'd chosen to come home. The focus was work and finding a place to live. She would only last with her parents for so long before they all drove each other crazy. Less than a week and she was already chomping at the bit.

"When did you leave?"

Sam was so deep in her own head that she lost track of the conversation for a second. "Huh?"

"You said you used to live at Bay West."

"Right. I moved a year ago." She saw a question in Lucy's eyes but got the sense she wouldn't ask it. She volunteered the info anyway. "My girlfriend got a job in Oregon. I work from home when I'm not traveling. Either way I'm not tied to any one place." She shrugged. "It seemed like the right move."

"Tough that you broke up then."

"Not meant to be." She looked for hope in Lucy's face but couldn't read her expression at all. "The tough part is that I'm back home with my parents while I'm looking for a place, and let's just say it's not ideal."

"I hear you." Lucy nodded. "Let me get those cookies for you."

Damn, that killed her chances. If she'd even had any. *Note to self: don't mention living with Mom and Dad.* She laughed at herself internally. It didn't matter anyway. She had her agenda, boring as it might be. Finding an apartment was paramount. The time for dating would come once everything else had fallen into place. But damn if Lucy wasn't the cutest woman she'd seen in a good long time. And she had a fantastic body. Sam couldn't help it if she fantasized a little on the spot. Even now as she slipped into the back, Sam watched Lucy's tight ass bounce with each step and imagined what it would be like to come up behind her. Christ, she needed to get laid. While she had a steady piece of action with a coworker—the only exception to her no-fun rule—it was purely because they had a perfect no-strings deal. Even on that front it had been over a month since their paths crossed and there was no telling when they were slated to be assigned together again. And goddamn, was she ready.

"Here you go." Lucy interrupted her X-rated thoughts holding a nondescript white box tied with thin red-and-white string. "There's chocolate chip, oatmeal, and butter horns, which is like a cinnamon-raisin butter cookie. Nothing fancy. Hopefully your date will like them."

"No date." Sam's voice was smooth as she corrected her. "Just hanging with my friends," she added, not even trying to hide her smile. "I'm sure they'll love them." She handed Lucy her credit card and waited while she swiped it through her register. "This is a really nice place, Lucy."

"It was nice talking to you"—Lucy looked at the front of the credit card—"Samantha Miller."

"Sam." Sam held out her hand and watched Lucy smile when she playfully gave her the receipt in lieu of shaking it.

"Have a nice night, Sam Miller. Come back anytime."

Sam grinned into the thin night air as she opened the door, the bell sounding happily above her. "Count on it," she called over her shoulder.

CHAPTER TWO

What was Portland like?" Lexi's question was clearly about the city itself, and if it was possible, Sam loved her best friend a little for not focusing on her failed relationship, which had been both the impetus for the move and the reason she'd come back.

"It was nice. Quirky. Lots of personality. Exactly like you'd expect."

"Did you love it?"

"Yes and no. I think my experience was a little tainted." She surprised herself with her own honesty. Being around her old friends had an immediate impact. She couldn't lie to them. She didn't even want to. She looked around the table at the faces she had missed in the last year and completely relaxed. "I'm glad to be back."

"Well, you look awesome," Meg said, eyeing her closely. "Your hair is on point, dude. And I liked it before, when you had that shaggy hipster thing working. But this is even better. Lean forward, I want to touch the back." Sam indulged her and swallowed a smile when Meg whistled with envy as she rubbed her fingers against the short gradual slope of her hairline.

Jesse put a basket of Italian bread in the center of the table and began doling out pasta. "Lexi tells us that you did a lot of traveling, Sam."

"Oh, yeah," Meg agreed. "Where'd you go?"

"Europe, mostly." Sam pierced a tube of penne with her fork. "I really had no say. It was all work, but I got to see some cool places. Copenhagen, Tokyo, Paris, London, Fiji. Prague. That was my favorite." She heard nostalgia in her own voice. "It was great. Truly."

"And now you're stuck in Staten Island. Is that a buzzkill?" Meg asked.

"Not at all. Being abroad was great. I'm ready to be home, though. I mean, I wish home wasn't my old bedroom at my parents' house, but hey, you can't have everything."

"At least not right away," Jesse offered. "Give it time. Did you see if there's anything available here?" Sam saw Jesse look to her wife for an answer. Lexi's parents were on the board of Bay West. She was always in the know, but tonight she shook her head in response, following Jesse's question with one of her own.

"Would you be open to being in the rental section?"

"Sure, I guess." She washed a mouthful of food down with a sip of wine. "I have no problem with renting in theory, but it will depend on the situation. If there's a unit that's completely vacant, I'm in. But at twenty-eight, I have to be honest, I'm not down with just taking a filler spot and having roommates I don't know. Any chance there's a one-bedroom available?"

Lexi clenched her teeth and looked skeptical. She exhaled. "Doubtful. There's so few of them. I'll find out though. Speaking of which"—she nodded at Meg across the table—"Kam Browne wants us to come by the office sometime this week. What day is good for you?"

"What, now?" Meg asked, choking down her drink. Sam wondered if her surprise resulted from excitement or fear. It sounded like it might be both.

"I told you this, I thought."

"Um, am I in trouble?" Meg covered a grin with her napkin. "Cause it sounds like I'm getting called to the principal's office."

Happy not to be the center of attention, Sam got in on the action. "It kind of does sound like that. What gives?"

"It's nothing." Lexi shook them both off. "Marnie told me the other day that Kam was looking for some new ideas. Ways to make the community appeal to the younger crowd. Mom told her to pick my brain and I guess she decided it was worth a shot."

"Did she ask for me specifically?" Meg asked. "Or did she just tell you to bring a friend?"

"Nope. She asked for you by name." Lexi dimpled as she teased her friend. "You can stop pretending to be cool, Meg. Jess and I already know how obsessed you are with Kam. It's only a matter of time before Sam's in the loop too."

"Stop. You're into her?" Sam asked. "Isn't she way older? And wait, don't you have a girlfriend?"

"Not like that." Meg waved her off. "I mean not at all," she added trying to save her dignity. "I admire her business sense. She's smart and savvy. That's it. Trust me."

"Meg idolizes her." Jesse clapped Meg's shoulder. "We think she wants to be her when she grows up. It's really sweet."

"I don't, actually."

"It's pretty adorable," Lexi added. "I bet she already has an outfit picked out and everything."

Meg narrowed her eyes and shook her head as she played along. "Black button-down, dark jeans, and these awesome new boots I just bought. Casual but trendy, and you guys are jerks."

They all laughed together and Sam watched Meg blush and beam at the same time. She had been around three years ago when Meg had been a complete newbie at Bay West and had witnessed her immersion into the community first hand. It was nice to see her obvious elation at being part of the inner circle now. If she had stayed, would she be part of the in-crowd too? Well, no regrets. Time to focus on the positive. Perhaps between Lexi and Meg she could get a line on an apartment here in the development. Sooner rather than later, with any luck.

Lexi and Jesse didn't allow her to lift a finger during the cleanup, so she sat with Meg, observing the comfortable back and forth between her married friend and her wife. They doted on each other, even when it came to stacking the dishes in the sink and wrapping up the leftovers. It made her heart happy, and she found herself surprisingly envious of their connection. "So, Meg," she said, redirecting her attention. "Tell me about your girlfriend. Reina, that's her name, right?"

"Yep. Reina."

"How come she didn't come to dinner? I was looking forward to meeting her."

Meg swallowed the last of her wine. "She's working. The dental office she works at has late hours some nights."

"How long are you together now?"

"Seven months." Meg nodded in affirmation of her own response.

"Nice. Well, next time, I hope."

"Yeah, definitely." It was silent for a second before Meg added, "Hey, Sam, I was sorry to hear about you and Julie."

"Thanks." Sam drummed the table with her fingers hoping to break the momentary tension. "It's all good." The moment passed on its own when Lexi placed the box of cookies Sam had brought in the center of the table, cutting the tie as she spoke.

"Do you guys care if I just leave these in the box?" she asked.

"Unacceptable. We're very formal, as you know, Alexis," Meg teased.

"Well, Megan...get over it." Lexi reached for a chocolate chip, making a silly face at her friend before she took a bite. "Oh my God, where did you get these, Sam? They're amazing."

Sam peered into the box, eyeing up the cinnamon one Lucy had mentioned earlier. "Some store just down the block. A coffee place," she added. "Lucy's, I think it was called." She saw Lexi's eyes widen as she chewed.

"I should have known." Lexi reached for one more. "Wait. Did you meet Lucy?" She sounded too excited and it made Sam skeptical, but she answered anyway.

"I did."

"Pretty, right?"

Sam paused for a second, not really sure how she wanted to field this question.

"Stop." Jesse came to her rescue. She stood behind Lexi and covered her mouth with her hand. "Don't do it. Fight the urge."

Lexi pulled her hand down but held on to it and leaned back. "What? All I said was she's cute. That's it."

Meg chimed in, "Yes, but we all know where you're headed with this. You love to play matchmaker. And it never works."

"Who are you kidding?" Lexi challenged. "It worked for you."

Meg tilted her head, obviously considering her friend's words. "True...I guess. But it wasn't even you who set me and Reina up."

"Semantics," Lexi quipped.

"Guys"—Sam stopped to laugh at both of them—"I just got back. Really, I don't need a setup. I'm fine. Really." She reached for another cookie and decided she could get away with one more question without sounding too eager. "You all know her? Lucy, I mean."

"Sure, we know her." Lexi rocked a little against Jesse who was still holding her from behind. "She's sort of the reason we got together," she continued sweetly as she laced her fingers with her wife's. "Abstractly, anyway."

"How do I not know this story?" Sam asked.

"You do," Meg answered, before Lexi took over.

"Remember that case that I was working on when I was interning at Jesse's law firm? Before we were together? The one with the cop and the shooting?"

Sam took a second to think back. "Vaguely?" Her tone was full of uncertainty and Lexi brushed her off with a wave of her hand.

"When I was interning for Jesse, there was this cop who was wrongly accused of firing her gun inside the precinct. It was a whole to-do, and Jesse pulled me in to work the case with her. We ended up spending all this time together." She bit her lip, looking shy for a second. "That's how we fell in love." She paused and

Jesse dropped a kiss on her head. "If it wasn't for Lucy, we might not be here right now."

"Wait, Lucy was the cop?" Sam let her confusion show. "Why is she working at a coffee shop?"

"It's a long story. The case didn't pan out." Lexi shook her head, appearing mildly frustrated before moving past it. "But the point is, we owe her." Sam was about to speak but Lexi wasn't done. "So you'll all forgive me if I want to repay the debt by introducing Lucy to one of the best people in the world"—she looked right at Sam—"and seeing if *maybe* you two can't find just one ounce of the happiness that I have. Fucking sue me for wanting a little romance."

Sam couldn't help herself and she felt her smile reach all the way up to her eyes. "Thank you, Munchkin," she said, pulling out a long forgotten childhood nickname. "She is pretty. Lucy, I mean. We talked a little." There was no point in trying to hide it. Not now. "Let's just not get ahead of ourselves."

"Yes." Lexi clapped once, in support or success, Sam wasn't sure. The topic was dropped there for the night, but when she zipped by the closed coffee house on her way home, Sam couldn't stop her mind from picturing Lucy's sweet gray eyes, her tight body, her gravelly voice. What was that caveat about no girls? Tsk, tsk. Rules, made only to be broken, she reminded herself as she sped off into the night.

CHAPTER THREE

Meg flopped next to Reina and pulled the blanket up to cover her naked body from the draft that wafted through her bedroom window.

"You good?" Reina asked, reaching for her iPad before Meg answered.

"Good." Meg let a long breath out, feeling her heart rate starting to regulate. "I came right before you did. You couldn't tell?" She didn't even try to hide her irritation that Reina hadn't noticed, and when she looked over, it seemed her girlfriend was barely listening now. At least it made her feel less guilty that she hadn't exactly been thinking about her when she came. She'd felt bad in the moment, but let herself off the hook with the rationalization that plenty of people fantasized during sex. Probably not about their exes, but thankfully no one could see inside her mind, so she would never have to own up to that particular detail.

The truth of the matter was she thought about Sasha all the time these days, not just during sex. Last week she broke into a full-on smile at her desk when she heard Jane's Addiction pop up on her office mate's music feed, remembering the time that she and Sasha had belted out the lyrics while they were photocopying. Totally random that they both knew all the words to such an old song. Just yesterday, she found herself getting nostalgic when she spotted a *Game of Thrones* ad plastered on the side of a city bus.

The new season would be starting in a few weeks. Would Sasha be watching by herself? Did she even want to know the answer? One thing was certain, Meg would be viewing it solo. Reina had zero interest in anything remotely sci-fi.

But they were good together, she and Reina, Meg reminded herself. Sure, she had some concerns that they so quickly seemed beyond the honeymoon stage. That was probably normal. Maybe she was just being too idealistic. They had a nice time together, they respected one another, and those things were important. Sasha had fucking cheated on her and it would serve her well to remember that. Maybe it would also help with the mid-sex fantasizing. The problem was she *did* remember. But she reminisced the tender moments just as often. The way Sasha curled into her body and held her hand while she fell asleep. How she liked to wake her up with a string of baby kisses across her face. Time was tricky like that. It really wreaked havoc on her memories, allowing her to distort the facts so the past was all roses, no thorns.

If her girlfriend would pay a smidge of attention to her right now, she wouldn't be thinking about Sasha at all. It annoyed her that Reina could downshift so easily from having sex one minute to playing on her phone or iPad the next. Not that Meg needed a whole cuddle session afterward, but a little intimacy would be a welcome change. God, she was such a girl sometimes. She laughed inwardly and shook off the thought as she glanced out the window, eyeing up a six-inch icicle dangling from the eaves.

Mid-March and still no end in sight to the frigid winter. She felt Reina move next to her. She brushed her side, knowing she needed to quit feeling sorry for herself and take stock of the good things in her life. Yes, there was still snow everywhere, but the sun was out in force this morning. It was Friday and she'd just had morning sex. It wasn't mind-blowing, but it wasn't half bad either. And she was working from home today. She could stay in pajamas all day if she chose to. A smile plastered across her face, she grabbed her phone to check the text that had pinged in the middle of her orgasm.

"Hey"—she ran her hand along Reina's forearm—"Lexi wants to go to Roaring Twenties tonight," she said, checking to gauge Reina's interest. "That could be fun."

"That's that roving dance party thing?"

"Uh-huh. Tonight it's in the East Village. Irving Plaza."

"You don't even dance."

"That's not the point."

"It's not?"

"I like hanging with my friends. And I like watching you dance. Doing your sexy little salsa moves."

"And what am I supposed to do about my mother?"

"Bring her." Meg nodded emphatically even though she was teasing. "She's an attractive older woman, I bet she'd do okay there."

"Ha-ha."

Putting her phone aside, Meg turned to Reina. "How about this one Friday you skip the routine?" Seeing the outline of Reina's full breasts under the covers was enough to ready Meg for a second round. Her voice was still husky. "Come on. Hang out with me today." She smoothed her fingertips across Reina's soft belly. "I have, like, two things to do for work. That's it. We can stay in bed all day. Your mother will understand."

Reina widened her eyes. "Not if I tell her like that, she won't."

"Well, maybe leave out this part." Meg moved closer placing a small kiss by her ear hoping the advances would sway Reina. "It's freezing out. Stay. We'll play all day, then go out with our friends tonight. You haven't even met Sam yet."

She could sense Reina wavering. Meg kissed softly along her jawline and inched down her throat, licking and kissing along the way. "Mmm." Reina moaned, fisting Meg's short hair and pulling up. "I can't. I'm sorry, babe. Fridays are important to my mom."

"What about me?" Meg pouted playfully, and saw Reina register her mild disappointment.

She dropped a kiss on Meg's nose and ran her finger along Meg's cheek but didn't change her mind. "Let me get moving.

I'll spend the day with Mom. We'll do an early dinner and maybe even skip the movie if I can convince her that I'll make it up to her during the week. I'll meet you there. I'm sure that party doesn't get going until later on anyway."

Meg sighed at the defeat. She knew from experience that once Reina was with her mother, it was unlikely she would leave. It was sweet, their relationship, and she admired their standing Friday date, even joining them on occasion. But the odds that Reina would ditch her mom and trek into the city alone were slim and she knew it. "Promise me you'll try?"

"I promise," she said, but Meg wasn't convinced.

The club music thumped in Meg's ears. She'd been monitoring her phone all night but it was ten fifteen and there was no sign of Reina. She frowned at the blank screen even though she wasn't overly surprised.

"No word from your girlfriend yet?" Sam squeezed in next to her and placed her drink on the bar.

"Nope." Meg couldn't care less that her aggravation showed.

"Well, it's still early. She's probably on the subway with no signal."

Meg slipped her phone into her back pocket and put her empty beer bottle down. "I got this one." She nodded at Sam's empty glass while they waited for some attention from the bartender.

"Cool, thanks."

"How come you're not out on the dance floor tearing it up with Lexi?" Meg asked over the bass.

"I was out there before. I'm kind of beat actually." Sam laughed at her admission.

"I'm sure we won't be out too late. Particularly since Lexi drove." Meg was pretty sure she had her friend's number on that move. Lexi had talked about wanting a big family even before she married Jesse last summer. Meg suspected they might already be pregnant.

She followed Sam's stare to Lexi and Jesse talking across the way. "Hey, Meg, here's a totally random question." Meg froze for a second figuring Sam was onto them too and even though she didn't know for sure, she wondered if she should lie.

"Shoot."

Sam swallowed a healthy sip of her fresh drink. "Does that Lucy chick from the coffee shop ever come out with you guys?" She kept her eyes on the crowd and took another swig. Meg hid her smile at Sam's failed attempt at casual.

"She hangs out with us sometimes. But more it's us going to her store and chilling with her there. She practically lives at the coffee shop, but she came to dinner at Lexi and Jesse's once or twice. I know Lexi invited her tonight, but I guess she was busy."

"Is she, I mean, does she have a girlfriend?"

"Oh my God, you really are smitten. Where did this even come from?"

"Can you not be a dick about this?" Sam's laugh was strained. "I'm just curious, that's all," she added.

Meg shook her head over the rim of her glass. "Dude, if you think I'm not going to break your balls over the fact that you, Sam Miller, self-proclaimed lady-killer, skirt chaser, flirt to end all flirts, are swooning over a girl you met one time, you are dead fucking wrong." Meg reached up and tousled the back of Sam's hair roughly. "What did they do to you out west? Or was it Europe that tamed the beast? Tell me. I have to know."

"You're an ass," Sam said through a smile. Even in the dim lighting, Meg could see she was blushing. "Forget I asked."

"No way, brother." Meg hit her with a shoulder bump. "P.S., I'm pretty sure she's single." She was about to elaborate, give Sam the scant details she knew, but the sight of the familiar girl one foot in front of her stopped her cold.

"Hi, Megan."

Meg was almost too stunned for words and she felt Sam's stare go back and forth between them trying to place the tension.

"Sasha. Hi." Meg froze for a second, but forced herself to take a sip of her drink, hoping the pint glass hid her shock long enough for her to pull herself together.

"You look really great." Sasha eyed her from head to toe and Meg could swear she saw emotion in her eyes, but before she could be sure, Sasha shifted her attention to Sam. "Hi, I'm Sasha," she said, extending her hand. "Meg and I used to work together." There was a full beat before Meg realized that Sasha thought she and Sam were together. Meg was moved by her discretion, but corrected her right away.

"Sash, this is Sam. Lexi's friend. The one who moved out to Portland last year with her girlfriend. You remember the story."

"Oh, right. I wasn't sure, I mean, I didn't know if…" Her voice drifted and she appeared slightly embarrassed but also relieved at Meg's explanation. "Nice to meet you, Sam."

"Likewise."

Meg wanted to ask a thousand questions, starting with finding out what Sasha was doing at the gayest girl party in the city. What a joke. Less than a year ago Sasha had broken her heart when she couldn't commit—not to Meg, not to being a lesbian, not to any of it. Meg swallowed a snide laugh at the irony. Of course anyone was welcome to partake in the awesome music and top shelf booze, but Sasha's presence felt like fraud and she was tempted to call her out. She might have done exactly that if Sasha hadn't looked so incredibly nervous. Her expression tugged at Meg's heart unwittingly and she let herself feel it, reminding herself that she was better than stooping to such depths anyway. Truth be told, Meg knew, in spite of her anger over how things had played out between them, there was still a part of her heart that belonged to Sasha, as pathetic as that might be. She longed to use this opportunity to feed her curiosity over Sasha's well-being. She couldn't help it. She had loved her once upon a time.

Meg took another quick sip of her craft brew and opened her mouth to be civil, but out of nowhere Reina was next to her.

"Hey, Meg. Sorry we're late."

Meg looked from Reina to Sasha and back again, a deer in the fucking headlights of life.

"Reina, I'm Sam. I've heard so much about you." Meg silently thanked Sam for the save.

"That better mean all good things," Reina joked. She turned to Meg. "Babe, this is my friend Melinda."

Meg hadn't even noticed the pretty girl who'd come in with Reina. "Oh, hi." Meg gave a chin nod and awkwardly offered her hand at the same time. The girl returned a limp handshake and paired it with a lame smile, barely making eye contact. Weird. Meg swallowed the lump in her throat. "Um, Reina this is Sasha." It made no sense, but Meg knew she sounded nervous at the introduction. For a split second she saw a flash of something in Reina's eyes at the recognition of Sasha's identity. Jealousy or anger, she wondered. Either way, the fallout wasn't going to be pretty.

Reina curved her mouth into a fake smile and tossed it at Sasha before giving her order to Meg. "Babe, get me a cosmo. You want one too, right, Mel?"

"I should get back to my friends. Nice meeting you all," Sasha said. "See you, Meg."

Meg wanted more time, even though she hated herself for it. And wait, did Sasha just say *friends* or *friend*? Damn the fucking loud music. There was a huge difference and she was dying for the answer. God, she hoped Sasha didn't have a girlfriend. It made no sense, her jealousy, and she knew it. It didn't matter, she reminded herself. She didn't want to be with Sasha, despite her little fantasy this morning. Their relationship had been a disaster.

Meg took a deep breath, centering herself. She was simply curious about Sasha's life. It was completely normal to wonder about your exes, particularly when you ran into them in a gay club after they'd denounced their lesbianism. Fuck, she needed to stop and get focused. She made eye contact with the bartender and put in Reina's order, adding a quick shot of Jack for herself.

For the rest of the night she found herself searching for Sasha in the masses, but she didn't see her again. What she couldn't stop seeing was the bizarre dynamic between Reina and the friend she'd brought. Getting close on the dance floor was one thing, but they were inseparable off it too. Meg wasn't sure if Reina was reciprocating or if she simply liked the attention, but Melinda was definitely crushing. She should care but she didn't. Despite her internal lecture to the contrary she was more concerned with finding out if Sasha was with a crowd or on a date. She shook her head into her drink. This night was a mess.

"Hey, you ready to head out soon?" Lexi's voice in her ear caught her off guard.

"Sure, whenever."

"Meg, I saw Sasha before. Sam told me you guys talked. How was it?"

Meg looked for Reina as she answered. "Fine. We just said hi, that was it."

"You okay?"

"Yeah, fine," she said, even though she wasn't. She hated that the brief conversation had such a lasting effect on her and she was positive Lexi read the truth behind her stock response. "Let me find Reina and see if she's ready to go. Honestly, I don't even know if she's coming home with me or going back to Queens with her *friend*." She emphasized the word dramatically and Lexi picked up on it.

"Who is that, by the way?"

"Some girl from her building. They've been hanging out a bunch. This is the first time I've met her."

"Oh." She heard doubt in Lexi's voice but didn't feel like dealing with it. She'd seen it too, the way Melinda stared at Reina, dancing just a little too close, following her around like a puppy dog.

Meg spotted Reina a few feet away and grabbed her arm. "The girls are ready to go. Are you coming with me?" Reina was tipsy—Meg could see it in her eyes and her body language.

"Can Mel come too?"

Meg raised her eyebrows at the question, momentarily unsure what Reina was asking.

"Not like that, Meg." She reached for Meg's hand. It was the first time they'd touched all night. "I just don't want to send her home alone."

"Fine. Just...fine."

"What?" Reina challenged.

"You know she's into you, right?"

Reina looked right in Meg's eyes. She was serious, even through her half-drunk haze. "You really want to have this conversation? Let's not forget, I blew off my mother and came all the way in here because you asked me to. Then I get here and you're hanging out with your ex-girlfriend, chatting away."

"It's not like that."

"I'm sure." Reina licked her lips. "The same way Mel's baby-dyke crush on me doesn't mean anything. She knows no lesbians, Meg. That's why I brought her. So she could maybe meet someone. Or at least get out. But I'm not going to leave her here or tell her she's on her own getting home. Plus"—she nodded over Meg's shoulder—"you said Sam is always down to hook up with a cute girl. She's single, right? Invite her back too."

Meg swallowed hard. It was a lot of info to digest from such a short conversation. "Okay. Get Melinda and meet me in front in five."

Less than an hour later Meg, Reina, Sam, and Melinda nursed drinks in Meg's living room, talking easily about the music and the vibe at the dance party. Meg detected zero chemistry between Sam and Melinda, and she tried not to get annoyed every time she caught Melinda checking out Reina. It didn't bother her the way it ought to, but still, she thought it rude that Melinda came back to her house just to ogle her girlfriend, and while Reina didn't quite encourage it, she clearly loved the attention. Meg didn't dare address it, not even when she and Reina were alone. She hoped her disinterest passed for understanding of Melinda's plight, but the truth was she knew any conversation at all would lead right back to talking about Sasha, and Meg wasn't ready to admit the effect that interaction had to anyone, including herself.

CHAPTER FOUR

D ude, wake up."
Sam turned onto her back and registered Meg standing over her. Half a second passed before she remembered where she was.

"We're meeting Lexi at the coffee shop in twenty minutes. I know you want in on that."

"Fuck, my bag is at Lexi's." She sighed heavily, her hangover hitting her full force. "I left it there last night before we went out."

"Nope. She dropped it off this morning before she went to the gym."

"There is a God." Sam rubbed the sleep from her eyes and sat up on Meg's couch. "What time is it anyway?"

"Just after ten."

"Wow. I was really out. I hope I wasn't in your way down here."

"Not at all. I got up when Reina and Melinda left about eight, then I went back to sleep. I only got out of bed like a half hour ago when Lexi texted me." Meg pulled the blanket off her. "Hurry up and get in the shower. I know you're going to need at least a few minutes to primp yourself for Lucy. I remember how you operate."

"I hate you."

"Correction." Meg backed away as she started folding the blanket. "You love me for not letting you sleep through this golden opportunity *and* for waking you up in time to get yourself all jazzed up. Thank me later. Now, go. I can only hold out for so long. I need coffee."

Twenty minutes later, Sam crunched the ice underfoot as they walked the short distance to Lucy's Coffee Bar.

Meg broke the silence. "So I'm guessing since I found you on my couch fully clothed, there was no love connection with Melinda."

"Nah, dude." Sam shrugged. "She's a nice girl but I wasn't feeling it. I don't think she was either, to be honest."

"No?"

Sam heard surprise in Meg's voice and was flattered at the subtle compliment. She shook her head in response. They were quiet for a few more steps before Sam gambled on a dicey subject. "I think that Melinda might be into Reina." She checked a look at Meg's demeanor and was relieved that Meg wasn't surprised at her well meaning heads-up. "You picked up on that, I gather."

"Sure did." Meg tapped at a chunk of ice with the tip of her boot, sending it skittering along the sidewalk ahead of them. "I actually said something to Reina about it," she said. "She blew it off." Meg shrugged. "I'm not even sure how I feel about it, which is the worst part."

"Still hung up on your ex?"

"Not hung up," Meg said.

Sam couldn't help but notice that Meg's tone, while not quite defensive, sounded more than a little uncertain.

"What happened with you two?"

"Me and Sasha?" Meg watched a car whiz past them. "It's complicated," she said, thrusting her hands in her pockets. "Actually, who am I kidding? It's not. I was really into her. Her, not so much."

"No, come on," Sam countered, not quite believing Meg's scarce summary. "She seemed interested last night."

"That's the thing with Sasha. You never know what you're going to get. One minute she's in love with you and the next she's making out with your colleague in the middle of the hotel lobby."

"Ouch."

"Yeah, that's putting it mildly."

"Sorry, dude. How long did you guys date or whatever?"

Meg looked at the empty street as they waited at the crosswalk. "Almost a year, but on and off."

"I'm sensing you guys don't keep in touch."

Meg harrumphed and her breath came out in a cloud against the cold air. "I haven't seen her since we broke up. Until last night. You know, five seconds before my girlfriend showed up. I know that sounds bad and I don't mean anything by it. Honestly. It just might have been nice, I mean…" Sam heard Meg struggling for the right words and felt her frustration. "I guess I would have liked to talk to her a little."

"Fucking timing, though. Brutal." Sam pushed open the door and smiled to herself when she heard the bell ring underneath the music coming through surround sound. The coffee house was warm and inviting, and unlike her last visit, it was packed. She spotted Lexi sitting at the end of a couch, her belongings strewn across several cushions, clearly trying to reserve the real estate for her friends.

"Jesus, I thought you guys were never going to get here." She waved them over emphatically. "These college kids are vultures." Lexi stood up and gave them both genuine hugs.

Shaking free of her winter jacket, Sam turned to put it over the arm of the couch, completely surprised to see Lucy right next to her. "Hi," she said, cringing a little at the enthusiasm she heard in her own voice.

Lucy didn't miss a beat. "Hey there, Sam Miller." She touched Sam's shoulder and gave it a little squeeze, throwing her off her game even more. "Morning, girls," she added, tossing a nod at Meg and Lexi. "Sit down," she said. "I'll bring over some coffee." She looked right at Sam. "Milk and sugar for you, hon?"

Lucy's use of the endearment surprised her, even in light of their spirited conversation the other day. The level of attention was exciting and she knew it showed when she stumbled over her response. "Sure. Actually half-and-half, if you have it. And three sugars."

"I should have guessed." Lucy grinned, seeming to be on the inside of a private joke. Sam knew her confusion must have showed when Lucy clarified her comment. "It's always the tough ones. Hard as nails on the outside, but give 'em a strong cup of java, and they curl up in fetal position." She hung her head and frowned in mock disappointment.

Sam found her footing and got in the game. "I just like my coffee like I like my women."

"Which is...ridiculously sweet?"

"Don't forget creamy."

Sam let her face relax into a smile at her friends' laughter. Her comment was over-the-top and she knew it, but Lucy shook her head and smiled, promising to return with their drinks shortly. Sam didn't even try to hide it as she let her gaze follow Lucy all the way back to the bar.

"I knew you guys would hit it off."

"Settle down, Lex, it's just flirting. Completely baseless. I'm sure it's all just part of business."

"She doesn't flirt with me."

"You're married."

"Meg, does she ever flirt with you?" Lexi challenged.

"No. But thanks for pointing that out. You know, just in case my confidence happened to be on the high side this morning."

"Oh, stop." Lexi dismissed her with a wave. "Like you don't have enough women falling over you right now."

Meg shook her head dramatically. "I'm not even going to pretend I know what that means."

Sam loved the easy camaraderie her friends had. She wasted no time getting into the mix. "Oh, yes you fucking do."

"Nobody was falling over me last night," Meg countered. "Sasha said hello, that's it. And Reina, Christ, I don't know what the fuck is going on with us right now."

"Well, you worked something out when you got home," Sam added with a smirk. "I slept right underneath you, don't forget." She saw Meg's cheeks redden and reached over to clap her shoulder. "I'm just teasing, buddy. But seriously, your mattress springs are shot." She pulled away just in time to beat Meg's playful punch, and in doing so bumped against Lucy's leg just as she arrived with their drinks.

"Whoa, sorry," Sam offered, awkwardly touching Lucy's thigh as she tried to make up for her gaffe.

"It's okay. It'll take more than that to get me on the ground. Maybe after your coffee. Although for you"—she scrunched up her nose—"with coffee that wimpy, it might take two cups." She placed a tray of muffins on the small table in front of them. "The scones are blueberry, the muffins are cranberry orange. They're vegan. Just the muffins, the scones are regular. I'm curious what you think. Enjoy, ladies."

"That was totally flirting," Lexi said, reaching for a scone.

Sam didn't bother to deny it. She loved the chase. Sure, she'd only seen Lucy two times and she still thought this might be part of her schtick with new customers, but there was an energy between them, she'd picked up on it right way. Whether it was just a game or something more remained to be seen. She was thoroughly looking forward to the play by play, but that part she kept to herself.

"Did you guys have your meeting with Kam Browne yet?" she asked, changing the subject.

"Oh my God, I can't believe we didn't tell you," Lexi said as she shielded her full mouth with her hand. "Kam wants us to, like, run some of the socials."

"What does that mean?" Sam asked, giving a muffin a try.

"You know the socials, the parties that are open to everyone. Even people who don't live at Bay West."

"Duh, Lex. I haven't been gone that long. So she wants you guys to work the door and stuff?"

Meg fielded the question. "Kam wants us to be in charge of them. Maybe that includes working the door—I didn't even think about that." She shook her head, obviously considering the possibility, then continued. "We're supposed to come up with themes. She's hoping for some fresh ideas to bring in new blood. Then do the marketing, advertising, stuff like that. Holy shit, you should help us."

"You totally should," Lexi echoed. "You're a graphics genius and Bay West's website could use a serious makeover." She did a tiny cheer with her hands. "Oh my God, would you do that for us? Put in links to different social media platforms and stuff? You are way more tech savvy than me and Meg."

"Sure, yeah."

"We should maybe check with Kam before making any major changes," Meg said, sounding a little nervous.

"Are you kidding, she's going to love it." Lexi rolled her eyes. "We'll run everything by her, Nervous Nellie. But quit being a pussy. She's looking for us to take charge here."

Sam swallowed the last of her coffee. "Any news on a vacancy there, by the way?" She put her empty mug down. "I would hate to miss being part of all this because I'm in jail for murdering my parents."

Lexi responded through her laughter. "No, I'm afraid. Bay West is at full capacity. My mom said she heard some rumors that there may be one or two units on the market soon. I know we talked about renting, but would you ever be able to buy if the opportunity came up?"

She took a second to consider. She'd been traveling on the company dime steadily for almost five months. Given her per diem stipend and not having to pay rent, she'd socked away a nice little nest egg.

"That would be ideal," she said. "But isn't there a waiting list for when units come up for sale?"

"Sam, you know the entire board. And you're going to help revamp Bay West's image. I'm fairly certain you'll jump to the top of the list."

"Politics and nepotism are alive and well at Bay West, I take it?"

"It's not just for rich white men anymore," Lexi quipped.

"To the new lesbian mafia," Meg added, lifting her coffee cup in the air.

Sam felt her smile cover her face. "So I have a shot of getting back in?"

Lexi tilted her head to the side, a full grin emerging as she drawled out her coy response. "Oh, I'd say there's a definite possibility."

CHAPTER FIVE

Three days later Sam stood at the end of the line that stretched from the coffee counter and curved along the interior of Lucy's store. It amazed her that she'd held out this long before coming back, but she'd been bogged down with projects, and while working from home usually gave her the luxury to blaze along quickly, her newly retired parents' constant interruptions were seriously slowing her down. Today she'd decided to set up shop at one of the local public libraries. She'd picked the South Beach branch, telling herself that she liked its proximity to the water, but she knew that the real reason was its location just around the corner from Lucy's Coffee Bar, giving her a perfect excuse to stop in.

There were at least ten people in front of her, but with her height advantage Sam still had a great view of Lucy working the commuter rush. She zipped around in yoga pants, her hair pulled up, smiling from customer to customer. Sam couldn't wait for her turn. Did she flirt with everyone? She told herself she didn't care but felt a twinge of random jealousy anyway. Her phone vibrated in her pocket diverting her attention. Blynn Hughes, her project manager. Huh. It was a bit early for work still and Sam couldn't help but wonder if the call was business or pleasure.

"Slow down, Blynn. I can hardly understand you." Sam jumped off the line and reached for her tablet as she listened. She slid into a seat at a table in the corner, fiddled for a pen and a scrap of paper, signing on and jotting notes while her boss barked orders.

"How much time do I have?" Sam checked her watch as she listened and worked, her attention equally divided. "All right. Relax. I'm on it. I'll text you when I have something ready."

Her coffee sidelined, Sam slipped right into work mode scanning her files and locating the design she knew would work for the client's ad campaign. The artwork she'd created used an image of a blue butterfly, crafted from a picture she'd taken years ago in her grandmother's yard. She still remembered the day, early in the spring, the sky crisp and bright. Sam had been confident in this choice all along, but new clients always thought they knew better. Typical, but it was nothing new making changes in the eleventh hour. She shook her head but smiled to herself, kind of enjoying the rush of pressure as she made some last-minute tweaks before firing off the final version to Blynn.

Waiting for feedback, she opened the company calendar. Dalton Medical was in Connecticut. That meant a definite road trip in the next few weeks. She felt a surge at the thought. She and Blynn—F. Blynn Hughes, when she was being formal—had a fantastic working relationship. One that was outmatched only by their incredible sexual chemistry. Their fling began in Paris after her relationship with Julie had ended for good. In no rush to come home with her tail between her legs, Sam had put her name in the hat for every travel assignment available.

Projects in London, Dubai, Istanbul, and Prague followed, and the mutual attraction held up. The setup was perfect. Strictly business during the day, clandestine hookups after hours. Road trips were spent text-flirting until the sun went down, when they reconvened in Blynn's hotel room for unbelievable, commitment-free sex. Sam never stayed over. Blynn never asked. It was exactly what the doctor ordered. The last thing Sam wanted was a relationship—she was still nursing her ego over her failed romance with Julie. Once or twice she felt a slight pang of guilt over the superficiality of their situation. It was never enough to stop her from coming back, and where the parameters of their arrangement were concerned, surely Blynn had her own reasons, whatever they might be. It hardly mattered. In her mind, they were both winning.

She shifted in her seat. Way overdue, she caught herself getting charged up just thinking about getting laid. With no warning, a vision of kissing Lucy against the coffee counter popped into her head. She blinked quickly, forcing the image out of her mind. She cracked her knuckles and pulled up a project to occupy herself while she waited for Blynn's response.

"Here."

Sam jumped at Lucy's voice.

"Sorry, I didn't mean to scare you." Lucy rubbed Sam's shoulder gently as she placed a lidded paper cup on the table. Sam noticed her checking a look at the line, which was still backed up to the front door. She nodded at Sam's coffee. "I went with the to-go option because I wasn't sure if you needed to be somewhere. Please don't take it the wrong way. You just looked busy—I didn't want to bother you. Stay as long as you like." When Lucy looked at Sam, her eyes were sweet and sincere, and Sam knew she was staring back.

Quickly she pulled herself together and found her manners. "Thank you for the coffee," she said, digging into her pocket for cash.

"Relax, hon. We'll work it out later."

Hon. Two times now Lucy had called her that. On both occasions, it had given her a rush. She was being ridiculous, thinking like a teenager. *She probably calls everyone that,* she thought, reminding herself to keep her libido in check and stop searching for things that were probably not there.

"You need the Wi-Fi?"

"I'm already on it."

"Good." Lucy took a step backward toward the counter. "Back to work," she ordered, adding a quick wink before she turned around.

That was something. Right? She let herself revel in the possibility for a moment before diving back into work.

For the next three hours Sam made real progress on two assignments whose deadlines were still weeks away. She pushed her laptop forward, stretched her arms over her head, and looked around the coffee house. It was quieter now, no lines, the commuters already at work. Patrons still filtered in and out, and a few tables were occupied by people like herself—on their computers, doing work, or writing papers, Sam figured, based on their ages. With her work finished, she looked around but didn't see Lucy anywhere. She played with some pet projects but there was still no sign of the owner, so she packed it in for the day. Putting away her belongings, she took stock of just how much she had accomplished in a short time frame. Working here beat her parents' house by a mile. She acknowledged the thought internally as she set up a plan for tomorrow, as though she needed any convincing to come back.

❖

At ten twenty Sam took a break from a very technical and detailed layout to quickly sketch out an idea in her notepad. She was completely in her own world.

"Hey stud." One of Lucy's workers appeared next to her, a plate in her hand. The dark-haired girl winked and gave her a salacious once-over. "The boss wanted me to bring this to you." She placed the plate in an empty space on the table. "It's her famous banana bread." She rubbed the tattoos lining her forearm. "But, you know, if she's not your type, I'm single. Just so you know."

Sam tipped her head down but was spared a response when Lucy appeared. "That's quite enough, Raven." She dismissed the girl with a pat on her shoulder and took the seat across from Sam. "How's work?" she asked nodding at Sam's things.

"Fine. Good." She reached in her pocket and took out her money clip, fishing through for small bills. "Thank you for breakfast."

Lucy waved her off. "I don't want your money."

"I never even paid you for yesterday's coffee."

Lucy folded her arms and leaned forward. "Yes, you did. With the ridiculous tip you left. You more than paid for your coffee."

"Look, I stayed here for hours, used your wireless, your bathroom, got a break from Mom and Dad. Believe me, I owed you something for your hospitality."

Inching the plate closer to Sam she said, "Come on, eat." She was staring at the sketch. "What's that?"

"Something new I'm playing around with."

"Is it a wolf?"

Sam laughed. "Yes, it is."

"I'm intrigued," Lucy said, clearly waiting for Sam to elaborate.

"I'm friends with these girls, sisters actually, who are just trying to break into the craft beer world. Their last name is Wolfe. I thought this could be a logo or a label or something."

"You're an artist?"

"Graphic designer."

"For a beer company?"

"No." She shook her head. "This is, these girls are my friends." She broke off an edge of the bread. "In real life I work for a global corporation. Tekrant Industries. They're the parent company for a million different businesses whose products you probably have all over your house or here." Sam looked around the shop for emphasis. "But this"—she motioned toward her drawing—"this is just for fun. They're just getting started. They have no money to spend on advertising and design." She popped the piece of bread in her mouth. "I figured if I could help them out, why not?" She swallowed quickly, reaching for another bite right away. "Wow, that's good."

Lucy smiled. "I don't want to keep you from your work. I just wanted to say hi." She eyed Sam's coffee mug. "Refill?"

It was the last thing she needed, more caffeine. She was high on adrenaline from this tiny conversation. "Absolutely."

"I'll bring some right over." Lucy stood and squeezed Sam's shoulder as she passed. It took every ounce of willpower in Sam's entire body not to reach for her hand and beg her to stay.

❖

On day three, Sam stood in front of her vanity for a full fifteen minutes to get her hair absolutely perfect. She smoothed the front of her button-down and tucked it loosely into her perfectly antiqued jeans. She was ahead on all her assignments and barely had any work to do, but she wasn't about to let that keep her from Lucy's.

The store had its regular morning rush, and after she picked up her coffee and settled into her favorite table, she let herself get entrenched in Bay West's website. She did a thorough assessment, making mental notes the whole time. This was going to be a blast to play around with. At almost eleven, she found herself scanning the store in search of Lucy.

"She's at Pilates," Raven said from two tables away, clearing away the garbage of a particularly messy customer.

"Huh, what?" Sam tried to sound as though she hadn't been caught looking.

Raven's dramatic eye roll told her she didn't buy it. "Settle down. She'll be back in a little bit."

Nearly an hour later, Sam was deep in code when the front door bell jingled loudly, grabbing her attention. She popped her head up as Lucy sauntered in. She had on new clothes—jeans and a navy tee—and her wet hair was pulled up in a tight bun. In her hand she carried a brown paper bag. Sam watched as she disappeared into the back momentarily before returning with two plates of food. She had a bottle of water under each arm. With her chin, she nodded at Sam's setup. "Share the table with me?"

"What's this?" Sam asked as she cleared away her laptop and tablet. She checked out the plate Lucy slid in front of her.

Lucy opened her water and took a sip. "Raven told me you haven't eaten a thing all day. This wrap is too big for one person. We can share it." Lucy gave a glance toward her employee currently manning the counter.

"Seriously, her name is Raven?" Sam stole a grape from the small cluster on her plate. "That can't be real. I saw the tattoo on her arm," she whispered. "That's just what she chooses to call herself, right?"

"No. Real name." Lucy lifted her eyebrows as she took the first bite of wrap. She swallowed quickly. "That's who I make her check out to and everything."

Sam watched Lucy's delicate mouth as she chewed. She let her voice lilt showing her suspicion. "Her parents named her Raven? *And* she just happens to look like that, with the jet-black hair, heavy makeup, and goth style." She shook her head. "I don't believe it."

"Well"—Lucy wiped her mouth gently with a paper napkin—"if you ask her, she says she named herself. In the womb." She placed her wrap on the plate. "Her parents are very spiritual."

Sam dropped her chin and looked right at Lucy. "You don't believe that."

"Eh, maybe. What do I know?" Lucy picked at a strand of arugula hanging out of her sandwich, tilted her head back, and dropped it in her mouth, shrugging playfully as she chewed. "All I can tell you is for twenty-three, she's incredibly responsible. And she's a fantastic baker. She teaches me stuff all the time." She nodded at Sam's plate. "Come on, eat."

"I'm not eating your lunch."

"Well, I don't waste food. So if you're not going to eat it, I'll give it to someone else."

"You eat it."

"It's too big." Lucy looked marginally disappointed at her refusal. "I guess I could save half for tomorrow." She looked up and her eyes were begging as she laid it on thick. "Come on, Sam, take pity on me. I just want to have a meal and some nice conversation with another adult for a change. Look around, it's all college kids waiting for their next class." She pouted playfully. "And if you think this is bad, wait until three o'clock. That's when the high-schoolers take over."

"Okay. Okay." Sam reached for the wrap. "One condition. Let me take you for a drink later."

There was an uncomfortable silence and Lucy scrunched up her nose. Swing and a miss. Sam was bummed, but she tried to play it off. "Please tell me it's because you don't drink," she joked.

"I don't."

"You don't what?" Sam asked.

"I don't drink."

"At all?"

Lucy confirmed with a nod as she sipped her water. As much as she wished it didn't, Sam knew her surprise showed. The news shouldn't be that shocking, but truthfully she didn't know anyone who didn't drink at all, even socially.

She tried to recover. "How about dinner then? I know you eat." She peered at Lucy's wrap playfully for emphasis.

Lucy put down her water and looked right at Sam, seriousness etched in every line on her face. "How about this. Lunch again, tomorrow. Here. You buy."

It was not quite the date Sam was hoping for, but it wasn't a total loss either.

"No meat," Lucy added last minute.

"Deal."

CHAPTER SIX

Come on Meg. I don't want to be late." Lexi's voice bellowed up the staircase, but Meg heard her tone soften as she turned her attention to the kitten at the foot of the stairs. "Hello, little Spencer. Do you love your new home?"

Meg came out of her room and looked at her friend below. She held up one finger before disappearing to trade her zip-up hoodie for a light sweater. She took it off immediately and eyed her discarded sweatshirt on the closet doorknob. "How cold is it out?"

"It's fucking cold, what's with you?"

Meg went back into her room and returned with a thick sweater this time. Lexi squinted at Meg's bizarre wardrobe debate. "Why are you stalling? Kam is a stickler for time and so are you. Are you trying to get kicked out of the club?"

"No." Meg stood still at the top of the stairs. "Yes." She futzed with the roll-neck collar. "Maybe," she said, changing her answer a third time. "I don't know."

"What the hell, Meg?" Lexi scooted the cat off her lap and marched up the stairs to guide Meg down by her sleeve. "Leave this on. It looks fine. Now, what's going on?"

"I don't want to talk about it."

"Obviously you do."

Meg stopped on the landing and looked off to the side. "I just…I feel kind of uncomfortable around Kam."

"Like, intimidated? I thought you idolized her business sense." Lexi squeezed Meg's arm. "I know she can be a lot to take, but this is your chance to get an insider's view on this whole place. She trusts us. She trusts you. She wouldn't have asked us to be involved if she didn't. Believe me."

"It's not that." Meg shifted from foot to foot, nervous about the source of her stress. "You're right. I should totally take advantage of this opportunity. It's just—"

"Oh my God." Lexi cut her off. "Did she hit on you?"

"Gross." Meg knew her face showed disgust and she tried to rein it in. "No." She sighed heavily. "Wait, why would you even say that?"

"I don't know." Lexi shook her head. "Sorry."

"No, it's fine. I mean she didn't. But it sort of leads into why I feel weird around her." Meg knew she wasn't making sense. She took a deep breath, knowing she was about to come clean about what she had witnessed. "Here's the thing, Lex." She searched for the most delicate way to put it. "I know some stuff about her. Kam, I mean. It makes it awkward for me to be around her."

Lexi narrowed her eyes and shook her head, clearly waiting for more explanation.

"Okay, so, I don't know how to tell you this, but I'm pretty sure she's messing around with that renter I used to date, Taylor."

"Okay."

Crap, Lexi didn't get what she was saying. She was going to have to spell it out. "Like, I'm not saying I saw them flirting at a social or anything." She tried to read Lexi's expression, but decided to just come out with it. "Last year I saw them full on making out in front of the Bay West office. I never said anything to anyone and I guess I blocked it out or figured it ended, or whatever, but then I saw the two of them the other day in the back of the auxiliary parking lot. They were pretty much all over each other." She reached for Lexi's arm to help her process the information.

"And?"

"*And?* There needs to be an *and?*" Meg was floored. "Lex, do you hear what I'm saying. Kam is cheating on Mary. And I know about it. I'm friends with Mary. Not great friends, but acquaintances. And she's your godmother. And your parents' friend. It's been eating me up inside."

"I know, Meg."

There was a long silence as Meg fully registered what Lexi meant. "You *know?*"

She watched Lexi twist and chew her lip before letting out a big sigh. "That's why I said *and*—because I wasn't sure how much you knew and I didn't want to, like, out them, I guess." She ran her hands through her long hair and shook the curls between her fingers. It was one of her tells. Meg knew she was nervous, but Lexi continued on. "Meg, they have an open relationship. Kam and Mary."

Meg took a step back and held up both of her hands. "So you knew about this? About Taylor?"

Lexi nodded. "Are you mad I didn't tell you? Because Taylor's your ex?"

"Oh my God, no." Meg shook her head, still reeling from the info. "I'm mad you didn't tell me because I've lost sleep over this."

"I'm sorry. I don't know who knows. I didn't want to say anything. It's none of my business, really."

"How long have you known? I mean, how long has it been going on?"

"I'm not sure," she said. "I saw them together too. Kam and Taylor. Not the way you did, but flirting and stuff. I mentioned it to Marnie and she told me about their arrangement."

"Arrangement?" Meg almost choked on nothing. She cleared her throat repeatedly. "You're telling me there's an arrangement?"

"I guess so."

"And you're just fine with this?" Meg was too stunned, both at the confirmation of her suspicions and by her best friend's cavalier acceptance. "Forgive me if I seem completely fucking shocked at your blasé attitude right now."

"It's not about whether or not *I'm* fine with it. It has nothing to do with me."

"But you think it's okay? You think it's normal," Meg challenged.

"No." Lexi paused. "I don't know." She grabbed Meg's arm and led them to the door as she talked. "They've been together since they were, well, since Mary was nineteen. It's a long time."

Meg stopped to face her. "Lexi, come on."

"I'm with you, Meg. Honestly. But I'm trying not to judge. I love them. Both of them. Even despite the fact that Mary once had a thing with Jesse," she said, blinking heavily at the admission. "I want Kam and Mary to be happy. If this is what works for them, who am I to criticize, right?"

"You're a better person than I am."

Lexi huffed out a laugh. "I'm just trying to be open-minded. But let me make one thing clear—I'm not sharing *my* wife with anyone. Ever." She tossed her hair over her shoulders looking resolute.

"Well thank fucking God. I was beginning to think I was the only one who believed in traditional relationships anymore."

"Said the lesbian."

"Lesbian or not, I'm a one-woman girl." She nodded emphatically. "No threesomes, no wife-swapping. Call me boring, vanilla, I don't care. I know what I want and what I don't."

"Speaking of, are we ever going to talk about seeing Sasha at Roaring Twenties?"

Meg bent down to give Spencer one last scratch between her ears before turning the lock and pulling the front door closed behind her. "It was weird, right?"

"What did you talk about?"

"Nothing. She said hi and then Reina was there. There was really no conversation."

"Did Reina say anything about it?"

"Not really. She started to, but we dropped it."

"Meg." Lexi stopped at the corner to let a car pass, but even after it zipped by she didn't move. She waited for Meg's attention before she said, "I have to ask—what is the story with you and Reina?"

"Uh...she's my girlfriend," Meg answered, some zing to her tone. "So, no story."

"Meg, come on. You're not fooling me. As a matter of fact, you gave me this same lecture when I was dating Julie a few years ago."

Meg furrowed her brow. "What lecture is that?"

"When I was with Julie for all the wrong reasons, you sat me down and told me relationships aren't about what makes sense in your head. You said you have to lead with your heart." When Meg laughed, Lexi punched her biceps. "Don't laugh at me, I'm being serious."

"I seriously doubt I ever said *lead with your heart.*"

"Well, you said something like that, jerk," Lexi responded, stifling a smile. "And you were right."

Meg bounced off the curb onto the dark asphalt. "Where are you going with this, Lex?"

"Hey"—Lexi grabbed Meg's arm, stopping them both dead in the middle of the street—"listen to me."

"What?"

"I know Reina was a rebound for you."

"That's not true," Meg challenged. "I liked her." She looked at the ground as she caught herself and immediately corrected her statement. "I *like* her." She knew she could confide in Lexi that her reasons for dating Reina didn't add up anymore. When they'd gotten together, she'd been heartbroken over Sasha. Reina was sweet and attractive and clearly interested. The beginning was all honeymoon as beginnings are, but Meg had felt for a while now that they had no future together. She strongly suspected Reina felt the exact same way. And while she could say all of these things to her best friend, she knew she didn't need to.

Meg stuffed her hands in her pockets and looked up at the dark sky. She moved out of the street toward the path that led to Bay West's rental section, tossing her arm across Lexi's shoulders. "Did you talk to Sasha at all the other night?" she asked.

Lexi nodded. "A little. I bumped into her on line for the bathroom."

"It's funny, Tracy told me she and Betsy saw her a few weeks ago at The Kitchen but they didn't talk to her," she said. "How is she?"

"She seemed good. Different."

Meg tilted her head. "Different how?"

"I don't know. Just different. Relaxed. Comfortable." She pinched Meg's hip. "She asked about you."

Meg chuckled at the contact. "What'd you say?"

"I told her you were into leather now. That if she wanted to get back with you, she was going to have to be completely submissive."

Meg pushed her sideways. "You're an ass," she said, pulling her back in right away. "What did you really say?"

"Nothing. I told her you were fine. Good. Generic stuff." Lexi looped her arm through Meg's. "Meg, she's still in love with you."

"Oh yeah, she told you that while she was waiting to pee?"

"I can tell."

"From the way she was standing in line, or…"

"Make fun all you want but I have an eye for this stuff. You know I do. I also know you still love her." She leaned into Meg, her voice getting more serious by the second. "So you're telling me that Tracy saw her recently at The Kitchen and now we run into her here." She paused, but not long enough for Meg to say anything. "Oh my God, Meg, she's trying to see you. It's so obvious. That's why she was at the club last Friday."

"Or"—Meg met Lexi's sincerity with a syrupy smile—"she was in the mood to dance."

"Then why go to the dykiest dance party in the city, though?" Lexi ushered them in the direction of the office. "Why not go to any one of the hundreds of straight clubs out there?" She nodded in support of her own assessment. "Nope. Not buying it. Roaring Twenties is the gayest of the girl scene, and The Kitchen...need I say more?"

"So what? You think she's a lesbian now?"

Lexi crinkled her forehead. "I think she was a lesbian always. Or at least bi, or whatever. So do you." She stopped two steps from the condo that doubled as Bay West's business office and shook her head. "I don't know, Meg. I know I only saw her for two seconds, but she was, I don't know..." She drifted off quietly for a second, seeming to ponder her own statement. "All I can come up with is *different*." She shrugged as she met Meg's eyes. "What if she's finally ready to be who she is?"

Meg stepped forward and pressed the doorbell. "Like it matters, anyway," she said dismissively.

"Like it doesn't," Lexi countered, full of sass and obvious disbelief, her tone calling Meg's bluff on the spot. Meg knew Lexi could see right through her, but she was spared the effort of coming up with a rebuttal when Kam Browne opened the door and pulled them in from the cold.

❖

"Hey, there." Meg tossed a look at Reina closing the front door firmly behind her. "I was getting worried."

Reina hung her bag off the top of a kitchen chair. "There was a procedure that went long early in the day. All the appointments were backed up after that. I should have called."

"No big. I just got back from my meeting with Kam a bit ago anyway." She wiggled her eyebrows. "I made stir-fry."

"Smells awesome," Reina said crossing the space to wash her hands at the sink. She leaned over to Meg in front of the stove and pecked her cheek lightly. She'd only been in the house for a minute, but there was something in her body language that seemed distant.

"You okay?" Meg asked.

"Long day. Let's eat." Reina smiled, but it looked forced to Meg. She decided to let it go.

"Tell me about your day," Meg said. She enjoyed hearing about Reina's work at the dental office because it was so different from her own job. Plus, Reina loved talking about it, and Meg thought the topic might shift the energy.

"Not much to tell. Pretty routine day." Reina picked up her phone and answered a text quickly. She scooped up some rice and veggies on her fork, but rested it on her plate to continue texting. She typed feverishly for more than a minute. Meg noticed a small grin playing at the corners of her mouth.

Meg nodded at the phone. "What's up?"

"Nothing," Reina answered, finally taking her first bite. "Melinda was just telling me a funny thing that happened at the building."

"Oh yeah? What was it?"

Reina shook her head, swallowing her food. "It's stupid, just this thing with the super." She waved her fork as if to brush off the topic. "Anyway, how was work for you?"

"Fine," Meg said quickly, choosing instead to recap the details of her meeting with Kam. "Lexi and I had our meeting with Kam Browne before. She loved Sam's new design for the website. We told her about some of the ideas we have. We're thinking of doing a singles dating thing maybe and a summer carnival," she added. She looked up at Reina for a reaction, but she was busy texting again. Meg stopped talking to wait for Reina's attention, but it didn't come. Every few seconds Meg watched her read her texts and thumb her responses in rapid succession, making no secret where her head was.

"I don't even know why you want to get involved in the inner workings of this place," Reina said without looking up. Her comment was flip and her tone dismissive. It thoroughly pissed Meg off.

Meg stopped eating and raised her eyebrows in challenge. "Excuse me?"

Reina sipped her iced tea and Meg noticed her eyes darting to her phone as she obviously struggled to resist reading the text coming through. She met Meg's eyes, but barely. "I don't get it. Sorry." She reached for her cell. "You really want to be part of running this place? Bay West is fun, I guess, but it's kind of incestuous. I mean, I would *never* want to live here."

"I guess it's a good thing you don't then." Her response was sharp but she didn't care. This night was starting to annoy her. Reina was barely present and now she was picking a fight. She knew how much Meg loved Bay West—the people, the parties, the community, all of it. She also knew this opportunity was important to her, and a little support wouldn't have killed her. Meg didn't have a clue where the negativity was coming from anyway. Sure, Reina didn't live here, but her cousin lived around the corner and she'd been enjoying the community perks well before she and Meg had started dating. Suddenly, it dawned on her. This wasn't about Bay West at all.

Meg got up from the table and walked the length of the small kitchen hoping for courage for what she knew she was about to do. She turned around to see Reina deep in her phone again.

"Reina?"

"Hmm?" she answered, not bothering to pull her eyes away. It took a minute, but Meg waited until she finished texting and looked up.

"Reina." She swallowed hard. In her heart Meg knew that they were both ready for this, but still she wondered how much of the timing had to do with her conversation with Lexi earlier. She blew out a long breath and convinced herself it didn't matter. "Reina, what are we doing?"

She saw Reina's face drop for a second before her features settled into a relaxed, complacent look. Although she said nothing, her expression spoke volumes. Reina was right there with her, Meg was sure of it, and for the first time all evening, she put down her phone and focused her attention directly on Meg. Finally, she spoke. "I don't know, Meg." She sounded stressed, but not uncertain, despite her words to the contrary.

Meg pulled out the kitchen chair and flopped in it. She put a hand on Reina's knee. "I don't want to fight with you."

"Me either."

"It just feels like we're going through the motions these days."

Reina looked as though she wanted to disagree, but didn't. "It wasn't supposed to be like this, Meg."

"I know." Meg frowned as she rubbed the thin cotton of Reina's scrubs. "But somehow it is." There was a long pause before Meg spoke again. "Maybe it's just because I'm greedy, but I think we both deserve more than this." She watched Reina nod once, seeming to agree. "Maybe it's better to quit while we're ahead." She shrugged, feeling that her words fell short of her sentiment.

Reina reached for Meg's hand, making direct eye contact for the first time all night. "I know you're right," she said. "Is it just me or does this feel like failure?"

"It's not." Meg tucked a strand of Reina's silky black hair behind her ear, the gesture oddly intimate in spite of the conversation. "Reina, we like each other. We just seem not to be progressing. But no one is hurting. It's just not meant to be." Meg held in the ironic smile she felt forming on her lips. "It's funny in a way. On paper we're perfect."

"We do want the same things."

"I'm sure we'll both have them someday." She waited a beat. "Just not with each other."

"That sounds sad."

"It's not, Reina." She gave another small shrug. "It's just life."

"Meg, you should know"—Reina glanced at her phone reflexively—"there's nothing going on with me and Melinda. I'm serious. I would never do that to you."

Meg supposed it didn't matter anymore but she appreciated Reina's sincerity. "Okay."

"Honestly, Meg. I don't want you to think—"

"I believe you."

Reina touched the corner of her eye, perhaps to catch a tear, Meg wasn't sure. "This is, like, the nicest breakup ever."

"Hello? We're fucking awesome people."

A small laugh escaped Reina and it made Meg smile. "You can still stay here tonight, if you want. It's already late. Queens is a hike and I know you're working early tomorrow."

Reina stood and let out a long breath. "You're sweet, but I think I'll just walk around to Teddy's and crash there."

Meg nodded resolutely as she stood up and was pleasantly surprised when Reina pulled her into a hug. They held each other tightly for a long minute, and when they parted, Meg saw real tears streaking Reina's cheeks. Whether they were spurred by loss or liberation, she wasn't immediately sure. But later when she stopped to think about it, the answer was crystal clear—if Reina's emotions at all mirrored her own, it was both.

CHAPTER SEVEN

S am glanced at the time on her phone, even though it had been less than a minute since she last checked. One fifteen. Any minute now. She stretched her neck to see out the storefront window and jumped when she felt a hand settle between her shoulder blades.

"Looking for someone special?" Lucy asked. Her voice had a certain friskiness and her face was inches from Sam's as she crouched down next to her seat. For a split second Sam was sure she looked at her mouth. "I came in through the back," she offered, answering Sam's puzzled look. "You were really craning your neck there." She gave Sam's back a nice rub as she stood upright.

"Hey, I'm starving. And you're late."

"I'm late, am I?" Lucy's smile melted Sam on the spot. "Anyway, what's on the menu today?" she asked, sizing up the clear plastic bowl of greens in the center of the table.

"Baby kale with almonds and quinoa. Some kind of lemon shallot dressing."

"Mmm. Sounds delish." Lucy doled out a serving each on the two small plates in front of them. Raven brought over two seltzers without being asked and placed the glasses down with a coy smile. On this, the fourth occasion of its kind, there seemed a routine developing and Sam idly wondered what Lucy's employee made of these lunches. Honestly, she wasn't sure she had them figured out herself quite yet.

"How was Pilates today?" Sam asked, knowing the routine.

Lucy shook her head. "No exercise today. I had an appointment." It was a vague response but Lucy didn't seem inclined to elaborate, so Sam let it go, inspecting the complementary flat wheat bread that came with their lunch, breaking it in half and giving Lucy her portion before biting off a crusty end. Lucy thanked her with a nod as she took a forkful of salad. "I've been meaning to ask, how's your apartment search going?"

For a split second, Sam contemplated lying. Her focus for the last few weeks had been squarely on work and these lunch meetings. She'd hardly had time at all to deal with her less than ideal living situation. "It's really not," she answered truthfully. She put her fork down and took a sip of her drink. "I haven't done anything at all in terms of looking. I'm basically crossing my fingers and waiting for something to open up at Bay West," she said through a chuckle. "But that could take forever. I could be *slightly* more proactive," she added, considering her own words.

"Why did you decide to go back to your parents?" Lucy picked up the bread, inspecting it. "Sorry if that came out like judgment. It's not. I'm just curious." Without biting it, she put the bread back on her plate.

Sam wiped her hands on a paper napkin, crumpling it up and discarding it in the empty bowl. "Well, when I first broke up with my girlfriend I needed to just be away from all of it. Her, the city, our friends in Portland. So I took a travel assignment." She spun the seltzer can in one hand. "It was fun. Interesting. I did another and then another. It got to where I was gone for months at a time almost."

"Sounds exciting."

"It was. Definitely. But then it got old. It's hard to live on the road." She took a long sip of her drink. "Anyway, I never looked for a new place. There really wasn't time."

"Fair enough." Lucy held a forkful of greens. "Tell me about your ex," she said, turning the subject in an unexpected direction. Sam was quiet for a moment, thinking about the nature of the question and what it might mean. "Unless you don't want to talk about it." Lucy met her eyes, misreading her momentary silence.

Sam frowned and shook Lucy off. "It's fine." It wasn't her favorite topic, but she didn't mind talking about Julie. She'd never been heartbroken over their relationship's demise. On the contrary, what she felt was closer to embarrassment than anything. She'd uprooted her entire life for a relationship that didn't last, one that she should have known didn't have any longevity. It made her feel foolish and slightly naive. She swallowed her pride. "Julie."

"Julie." Lucy narrowed her eyes, echoing Sam with an edge to her tone. "I hate her already."

Sam smiled at Lucy's playful support. "Nah. Don't. She's a good girl. We weren't..." She stopped herself, deciding on the spot to simplify her response. "I should never have gone with her when she moved. It wasn't that serious. Certainly not for her." She twisted her glass between her fingers. "Not for me either, in the long run." She punctuated her explanation with a small shrug, adding at the last minute a truth she didn't often reveal. "She used to date Lexi. Before me. She was still into her when we were together. Then in Portland, she met someone else."

"After you moved across the country with her?" Lucy twisted her face in disgust. "This girl sounds like a piece of work."

"I'm making it sound worse than it was." Sam picked up her silverware and started eating again. "It was over by then. We both knew it." She took a hefty bite. "After that is when I started traveling. Got to see some of the world. It all worked out."

"You're too easy on her, this Julie character. I want to kick her butt."

Sam brushed it off. "It's fine. Seriously." She looked around the coffee shop, circling her fork to indicate the space. "I want to know more about this place." Their conversations to this point had been light and airy—newsy tidbits, current events—this was their first foray into the personal, and while she was hesitant to overstep, she didn't want to miss a moment to learn something real about

Lucy. "So you just quit being a cop to open up a coffee house? I feel confident a girl figures into this story someway or other."

Lucy's gray eyes were suddenly serious and Sam worried she had crossed a line. "Do you really not know the story behind this?" Steeped in Lucy's voice was a mix of disbelief and caution and Sam racked her brain, wondering if she was supposed to know, if she had been told in the past and had somehow forgotten.

"I don't," she answered.

"Really?"

Sam turned up her palms in surrender. "I know that you were involved in some police case that Jesse handled when Lexi was her intern. I know it's the reason they fell in love. Lexi told me that part." She pushed her plate to the center of the table. "That's the extent of it. Oh, wait"—she interrupted herself, holding up one finger—"I know that the case involved a shooting." She looked down, a little mortified at her outburst. "Sorry, I probably shouldn't have gotten so excited over that last bit." She looked across the short distance between them and saw genuine surprise in Lucy's face.

"Wow, you really don't know." She nodded once. "Impressive."

"You don't have to tell me the details," Sam offered, sensing she should let Lucy off the hook. "I just thought it was interesting to go from being a police officer to running a coffee shop. It seems a big change. I'm intrigued, I suppose. That's all."

Lucy seemed to soften at Sam's explanation. "It's okay, I'll tell you." Her voice lowered with the music in the background. "My therapist says I should talk about it more anyway. The road to healing, she says," she added off-handedly. She took a deep breath and began. "I was a cop for nine and a half years. A detective for most of that time. Anyway, one night there was a shooting in the precinct. With my gun." Sam tried like hell to be stoic when Lucy looked up to gauge her reaction. She must have passed the test, because Lucy continued. "It was complicated." She waved one hand somewhat dismissively. "No one was seriously injured and I wasn't even involved, not really, but it became kind of a scandal, so I resigned rather than fight the system."

"Hold up," Sam said, raising one hand. "I'm not following." She felt her face twist in confusion. "Why would you quit if you weren't involved?"

"I meant I wasn't responsible for the shooting. That's what I should have said." Lucy tipped her head to the side. "Although that's not entirely true either. I suppose it's my own irresponsibility that caused it to happen in the first place."

"I am so confused right now."

Lucy's smile was ambivalent as she spoke again. "So here's the deal. I left my gun in my desk drawer. Which is, as you can imagine, not wise. In my absence, my buddies decided to play a prank, like cops do. They used my gun, while I was away from the squad. It was stupid and things got out of hand. One of them ended up getting shot accidentally. He wasn't hurt badly, but it was still a big deal. The guy behind the joke was very tightly connected in the police department. Things got political right away."

"But if you weren't even there, how could they blame you?"

"I wasn't where I was supposed to be either."

"So you get fired for that?"

"I didn't get fired," Lucy clarified quickly. "I resigned. It's very different."

"No, right, I get that. Still doesn't seem fair."

"Sam." Lucy's face was dead serious. "I made a lot of mistakes back then. Bad decisions that were based on, well, mostly other bad decisions," she said, her tone rising slightly at the ridiculous admission. "I loved being a cop. Truly, I loved it." She looked off to the side avoiding eye contact as she continued. "But there's a lifestyle that can go with it, if you're not careful." She toyed with her fork, touching the tines to the edge of her knife as she spoke. "I drank a lot in those days. It affected everything." She put the utensils down and lined them up. "Leaving that job was the best thing I ever did." She licked her lips and took a deep breath. "I stay busy here with the shop. I eat better. I exercise. I don't drink." She rested her cheek in one hand. "So, hopefully"—she ticked her head to the side still avoiding eye contact—"better choices."

She was clearly trying to sound light, so Sam gave her an encouraging look. Lucy seemed calmer now that her story was out, but Sam was still fuzzy on the details. She watched as Lucy touched her thumb to each fingertip, a nervous trait Sam had seen her employ a few times.

"The way things played out, Jesse got me some settlement money. One small business loan later and I set up shop here." Lucy pulled her hair back behind her head and used the ponytail holder on her wrist to tie it up. "I was actually looking for business real estate and happened upon this place"—she waved around the store—"down the block from Bay West. Completely random. I almost passed out when Lexi came in for coffee the first week I was open."

"She must have been shocked too, I bet."

Lucy responded with a nod. "She's a sweetheart. She had me over for dinner immediately. She always invites me to go out with everyone. To the socials, The Kitchen. It was nice to feel like I had friends right away in my new neighborhood."

"You should come." Sam knew she sounded too invested. She didn't care. "Really. Come out with us. Please," she added, furrowing her brow dramatically for good measure.

"You are very cute when you're begging."

"Only when I'm begging?"

Lucy smiled in earnest and Sam saw she was blushing. "Stop. You know you're adorable."

"I know nothing of the sort," Sam flirted back. "However, I accept all compliments readily." She leaned in and tried again. "Will you come out with us one of these nights?"

"Sam, it's not that easy for me." She looked around the half-full coffee shop. "I spend all of my time here. This is my focus right now. I don't have time for a social life at the moment." She drummed her fingers on the tabletop. "Maybe one of these days."

"Is that a promise?" Sam asked.

"No." Lucy smiled. "It's a maybe."

"I'll take it." Sam pounded the table lightly as though her fist was a gavel and a final decision had been ordered.

"Don't hold your breath," Lucy quipped.

"You'll come around." Sam's voice was full of confidence. "I have to say I'm mildly disappointed that your story didn't involve not one scorned ex or broken heart left behind." She nodded. "I thought for sure there'd be a girl behind such a drastic life change." She threw in a snicker to be playful.

"Oh there was a girl all right," Lucy matched her sarcasm. "More than one, I'm afraid." Her face wore an expression that Sam couldn't read.

"Two girls? Now that's a story I want to hear." She was trying for light but Lucy looked suddenly anxious, a strained smile doing nothing to cover her stress.

"Don't get your hopes up. It's not that kind of a story. This is less ménage-y"—she backed to the counter, balancing their plates in her arms—"more...I-fucked-up-my-whole-life and everyone else's in the process. It's that kind of three-way." Her tone was sharp and she forced a laugh but it was all nerves. Even Raven looked over.

Sam could tell she was upset. "Lucy, wait."

"Sorry, Sam." She blew her off with an eyebrow raise. "Duty calls."

CHAPTER EIGHT

Meg stretched her arms over her head and rolled her chair back a few feet. She'd been crunching numbers all morning for a project, and even though she was way ahead of schedule, she liked to get the busy work out of the way so she'd plowed through, even skipping lunch. The payoff would come tomorrow when she could delve right away into the fun stuff—analysis and problem solving. Her client was way over budget and in need of serious cutbacks and fiscal reallocation. She had some cool ideas already. Right now, though, she was going to reward her hard work with a Diet Coke from the company fridge. She was completely in her own world when she stepped out of her office and heard her boss call her from down the hall.

"Megan, come say hello." Anne's voice brimmed with excitement. "Look who stopped by."

Meg felt frozen solid at the sight of Sasha standing next to her boss. The muscles in her legs seemed to have a mind of their own, however, and before she knew it she'd covered the short distance between her office and Anne's. She swallowed the mix of anger and desire she felt, hoping to God that absolutely nothing showed on her face.

"Hi, Meg."

"Hi, Sash."

There was only two seconds of silence but it was awkward. "Are we working on something with Hewlett?" Meg looked between her boss and her ex-girlfriend as she referenced the rival consulting firm Sasha had left Sullivan for. They shared clients on occasion, Sullivan and Hewlett Steele, and Meg wondered at the existence of a joint project she'd missed.

Sasha bit her lip and looked at the ground. "No. I asked Anne to be a reference for my portfolio. For teaching. I need professional recommendations." She raised a manila envelope between them. "I was just here to pick it up."

"And what an easy one to write," Anne piped in. She threw an arm around Sasha. "You are a wonderful person and a solid employee. If I had children, I could only hope they'd get a teacher like you."

"Thanks, Anne." Sasha looked embarrassed and grateful at the compliment.

"So how is the teaching stuff going? You're looking for jobs already?"

It felt strange having this conversation right now, but despite their rough breakup, Meg genuinely wanted to know about Sasha's life.

"I'm still working on my degree. I left Hewlett so I could go back to school full time. So I could finish up quicker."

"Oh." The obvious dawned on Meg. Time had passed and life was different, not just for her. Sasha had moved on too. She saw Anne watching the strained exchange between them, and was about to say good-bye, but Anne spoke first.

"You girls should go catch up. Meg, take the rest of the afternoon off." She waved her hand before Meg could protest. "It's fine."

She knew the surprise showed on her face at Anne's out of character suggestion. "I'm working on the Dillinger thing. I should probably stay and finish."

"Megan, we all know you're ahead of schedule. Go," Anne insisted. "Spend an afternoon with your old friend. Life is short."

She looked at Sasha and saw her eyebrows shoot up hopefully. "What do you think, Meg? Could you sneak off for the day?" She swayed ever so slightly back and forth, and Meg swore she saw hope in her eyes. "I would love to talk to you."

No two ways about it. This had all the makings of an absolute disaster.

"Let me just grab my stuff."

❖

In the brisk afternoon air, they walked for several minutes, crossing Lexington and Park Avenues, snaking across town and south, making small talk as they fought the biting wind, finally ducking in to a cute little gastropub at the corner of Sixth Avenue and Forty-Fifth Street. The place was a welcome refuge from the weather, and quaint to boot, with its antique furniture and a fireplace crackling in the back. They were seated in a cozy corner by a waitress sporting a genuine brogue. "Start you ladies off with a drink?"

"I'll have a glass of cabernet," Sasha said. She rubbed her hands together for warmth.

"Lovely choice on this bitter day." She turned to Meg. "And for you, love?"

"What do you have on tap?" Meg asked before reconsidering on the spot. "Forget it. I think I'll just have water."

"Have a drink with me, Meg." Sasha's face was pleading, even if her voice stayed even.

The waitress tilted her head and offered an encouraging smile. "You heard her, Meg. Don't make the girl drink alone." She covered her mouth with her cocktail pad and pretended to whisper. "You never know, if you play your cards right, you may get lucky," she added with an over-the-top wink.

Meg smiled. "Fine, cabernet I guess for me too."

"Excellent, ladies. I'll be right back with your drinks."

Sasha reached a hand across the table and touched Meg's arm. "Sorry. I shouldn't have done that." She nodded toward the bar. "I didn't mean to pressure you. First, Anne strong-arms you into coming with me. And here I am"—she tossed her head back in obvious distress—"begging you to have a drink." She shook her head back and forth. "I just wanted a few minutes to see you, to talk, that's all. Meg"—her voice was incredibly serious—"you can bail if you want."

She looked from Meg to the door as she waited for her response. She was fidgeting like crazy with the edge of her sweater. Meg recognized the signs of Sasha's stress and felt a surge of hope rocket through her. What the fuck? She pushed back hard against her ridiculous desire and tried to take the upper hand in stride. "It's fine."

"Are you sure you want to stay?"

"Why not?" Meg gave her best reassuring look. "Plus, the waitress sort of implied that you might put out, so..." It was borderline flirty, but it also broke the tension and she watched Sasha relax in her laughter. "So you left Hewlett Steele?" she asked, returning the conversation to PG status.

"I did."

"When?"

"A while ago." Sasha leaned on her forearms. "I had some money from my mom's estate. I know you'll probably tell me it would have made more sense to continue to work while I finish my degree—"

"I don't think that." Meg shook her head. "You want to be a teacher. I think it's great you're going for it. Good for you."

"Thanks, Meg."

"How's your little brother doing? He graduated, I assume."

Sasha nodded, leaning back in her chair as the waitress served their drinks with a broad smile and slid a menu on the table between them.

"Cheers, girls."

Raising her glass slightly, Sasha looked right at Meg. "It's good to see you, Meg."

"Yeah, you too." She cleared her throat unnecessarily before taking a sip. "So, Devon, you were about to tell me about Devon."

"Devon, yes." Sasha wiped the edge of her mouth delicately. "My little brother is getting married."

"What?" Meg knew her shock registered as judgment. She didn't care.

"I know. He's young."

"Young? He's a baby. What is he, twenty-three?"

"Twenty-four next month. But he's happy. Incredibly happy."

"But he's a kid."

Sasha shrugged.

"That's it, a shrug? You're not concerned?"

"I know, like everyone else, you think he's too young, but he's not really."

Meg rolled her eyes blatantly.

"He's finishing up his master's degree and my dad hooked him up with a good job. He's looking for a house. Age-wise he may be twenty-three but he's so much older, Meg."

Careful to control her tone, Meg made sure her voice held the genuine concern she felt. "Still, Sash."

Sasha rubbed the base of her wineglass. "Meg, you don't understand." She paused and licked her lips as though she wasn't sure if she was going to continue, but went on anyway. "My mom dying, it did something to him. To both of us. Forced us to grow up. I can't explain it."

"I know," Meg said, even though she didn't. "Still though, twenty-four is way young to get married."

"You're right. But I'm not going to talk him out of doing what he wants to do. Who am I to give him advice on love anyway?"

The comment hit a nerve even though Meg wasn't at all sure what it meant. She glanced around the bar purely to avoid making eye contact. "What's going on with you?" It was out before she could stop herself. She took a huge sip of her drink, hating the awkwardness of the segue, the flippant way her voice had come out. More than anything else, she hated herself for wanting so desperately to know the answer.

She watched Sasha swallow hard. "Nothing."

"So, Roaring Twenties? That's your scene these days?"

The look of guilt and surprise on Sasha's face sent Meg the message that her subtle accusation was received loud and clear. Meg pulled back, but only a little. "Sorry, it's just that…you know, last I checked, you weren't even gay."

"I suppose I deserve that."

Meg grabbed at a paper napkin and spread it on her lap. "I'm not trying to be a jerk, Sash." Her voice softened as she looked across the small table. "I guess I'm just trying to understand."

"I don't know what to say, Meg." She shifted uncomfortably in her seat. "I wanted to go, to see what it was like." She paused and said nothing until Meg looked at her. "I'm glad I did." Her lips held the hint of a smile. "I got to see you."

Meg was quiet. She had no clue how to respond.

The waitress's return saved her. "Ready for another round?" She looked between them as they nodded simultaneously. "Something from the kitchen?"

"I could eat," Sasha said to Meg before turning to the waitress. "We didn't even look at the menu yet," she admitted through an awkward grimace.

"I can just bring you out a little sampler to share, if you girls fancy that."

"That works for me. Meg?"

"Sure, whatever."

"Any restrictions?"

Sasha winced. "No red meat?"

"Not a problem, love. Be right back with your drinks." As she skipped away with their order Meg looked at her watch.

"Gah, Meg." Sasha covered half her face with her hand. "I wasn't thinking. Do you need to get home to your, um, girlfriend?" Her voice hitched on the word and it caught Meg off guard.

She shook her head. "Nope." She smiled, pulling out her phone. "I do have to get home to this little beast at some point." She clicked on the home screen, a shot of tiny Spencer looking perfectly mischievous and sweet.

Sasha's eyes widened and her mouth fell open as she tilted the phone in Meg's hands. "Oh my God. You have a kitten?"

"I do."

"Get out. She's adorable. Let me see more pics. I'm sure you have a million."

Meg handed her phone to Sasha and watched her scroll through the dozens of snapshots she'd taken in the weeks since Spencer had become her charge. "Are you still volunteering at the rescue place on the West Side?" she asked.

"Mm-hmm. Every Saturday." Sasha continued to swipe.

"Any pets for you?"

Sasha scrunched her nose. "I have commitment issues."

"That, I am completely aware of." Meg's voice was light and she hoped Sasha knew that while it was the source of their undoing, she was just going for an easy laugh.

"Touché." Sasha rolled her eyes but grinned. She gestured to the screen. "What is this precious kitty's name?"

"Spencer." Meg waited a beat. "Carlin."

It took one second, but Sasha was right there with her. "*South of Nowhere*?" It was posed as a question, but she clearly knew the answer. "You didn't?" she finished with a smile and a shake of her head.

"I totally did."

"I was always more of an Ashley Davies girl, but you definitely had a soft spot for Spencer."

"And look at her." Meg selected a particularly endearing picture of her furbaby from the photo gallery. "That head tilt, she's Spencer Carlin all the way."

Meg looked over expecting a laugh from Sasha but there was something else in her eyes. She was half smiling as she chewed her bottom lip. "Do you remember that weekend? It rained nonstop." Sasha ran her middle finger the length of the phone. "I don't think we even left the apartment." Her voice was heavy with an emotion Meg wanted to believe was longing. "We binged that show straight through from Friday night to Sunday afternoon," she added as her voice faded out, making it seem almost an afterthought.

Meg felt her pulse quicken as images of the things they'd done—and where they'd done them—flooded her mind. Teen lesbian drama aside, it had been one hell of a lost weekend.

She found her voice. "It's a great show," she said hoping like hell it wasn't obvious where her mind had really gone.

If Sasha read her, she didn't show it. Her smile was lovely and genuine as she returned Meg's phone. "She looks like a great cat. I'm happy for you."

The waitress broke their moment when she arrived with the food—grilled gruyere on sourdough cut in fours, chicken pot stickers, and truffle fries—placing the items in the center of the table.

Their hands touched as they both reached for the grilled cheese at the same time.

"You first," Sasha said, redirecting to a french fry. She took one bite and closed her eyes slowly. "Oh my God, these are amazing," she said covering her mouth with one hand.

For a second Meg felt as if it was two years ago and they were still together as she momentarily let herself get lost in Sasha's gorgeous expression. At least Sasha didn't notice, as she reached for the serving dish to tilt a few more fries onto her plate. "So, Meg, when did all this happen. The kitten, I mean?"

Meg shook her head, snapping free of her momentary nostalgia and focusing on Sasha's question. "Just a couple of weeks ago."

"Is she adjusting okay?"

Meg bit off a corner of the sandwich. "I think so. She's eating good. Using the litter box, playing with her toys."

"And what about you?"

Meg smiled as she chewed. "It's great. She's sweet, affectionate. Gives me little kisses once in a while. Does this thing where she touches the tip of her nose to mine. It's adorable." She could feel herself smiling like a proud parent. "She sleeps curled up against the back of my knees. It's precious." She let out a little snicker. "You know, until she wants to play at three in the morning." She popped a fry. "Not as precious then."

"Your girlfriend's a cat person too, I guess?" Sasha asked, holding a pot sticker and inspecting it. "Is that what prompted this venture into pet parenthood?"

Meg swallowed her food. "No." As she reached for her napkin, she saw Sasha's confused look. "I mean, I think she likes cats just fine." She licked her lips, oddly nervous about what she was about to say. "We're not together anymore."

"Oh." Sasha paused. "I'm sorry."

Meg shrugged it off. She could tell Sasha felt bad for asking and even though it was ridiculous, she wanted to put her at ease. "It's okay. It was time." She took a sip of wine and decided to change the subject. "How are your friends? Jane-Anne and the gang?"

"They're good. Same old, same old." She reached for a slice of the grilled cheese. "Oh, Jane's cousin moved to New York, though. She's gay. So that's been kind of cool."

"Awesome," Meg managed, even though the news gave her a sudden jolt in the pit of her stomach.

"It's nice to have someone to go out with."

"I'm sure."

"Not as in, like, a couple. Just hang out with. You know."

Of course Sasha didn't owe her an explanation but she seemed to be volunteering some information, and as much as she hated herself for it, Meg wanted to know every last detail. Fueled entirely by her second cabernet, she asked the question she'd wanted to know forever.

"So what's going on with you these days? You dating anyone?"

Sasha hesitated for just a second. She met Meg's eyes. "I went on a few dates with someone recently." She frowned a little. "There was no spark."

Meg hoped she sounded casual. "This someone was a—"

"Kate." Sasha knew what she was asking.

Meg blinked and looked away, embarrassed over her need to know and her unpredictable jealousy that Sasha had dated a woman, even if there was no connection. She knew her emotion showed on her face, but she couldn't resist going one step further. "So girls, huh?" It came out sharper than she wanted. Fuck. She grabbed a fry and stuffed it in her mouth, hoping the simple action would underscore her tone.

Sasha sat all the way back in her chair. She was quiet for a minute and Meg stopped chewing to look at her.

"I want the right person." She held Meg's stare. "Guy, girl"— she lifted one shoulder slightly—"doesn't matter. As long as they get me. I want the *one*, the person I'm meant to be with. Plain and simple."

Meg forced a smile. "Good luck," she said, wondering where those words even came from. Sasha pursed her lips and nodded and Meg wondered at the bizarre expression on her face.

The conversation lightened—it couldn't get any heavier really—and they moved on to discussing Meg's sister and her kids, work and school, the coldest spring on record. When the bill came they split it down the middle, and as they stepped out into the brisk evening air, they said good-bye, complete with a truly awkward hug.

"It was great seeing you, Meg."

"Yeah, you too, Sash."

"Could we do it again?" Sasha asked, backing down the street.

"Sure," Meg responded before turning around. But with no further plans made, it felt like the kind of thing that's said but never done. For the best, Meg thought as she walked down the steps to the subway. Seeing Sasha was nice. Maybe it was exactly what they needed. A kind of closure they never really had.

Of course, it sucked that Sasha looked amazing. With her deep blue eyes, porcelain skin, and long dark hair, she could have walked straight out of a magazine. And that smile, forget it. Gorgeous didn't even cover it. And she'd been as sweet as ever. But that was Sasha, she reminded herself. Sweet one minute, soul crushing the next.

Nope. No more. This chance meeting had given them an opportunity to forge a friendship, perhaps. Nothing more. And that would be okay. It would be fine. Yet, she couldn't erase the image of Sasha's beautiful, strange expression when she talked about finding someone. Not just someone, *the* one. Her heart beat faster at the thought. She blinked hard as she heard the automated recording announce her stop. Pushing through the rush hour crowd she forced herself to think about the rest of her commute, her Sullivan project, the social that she and Lexi were planning. Anything, really. Anything but Sasha Michaels.

CHAPTER NINE

S am looked at her watch, completely frustrated at the time. By ten a.m., the day had gone completely off the rails. Her morning team meeting had been billed as a routine prep session for the afternoon presentation, but Blynn showed up with last-minute changes. The modifications really did amp up the pitch, but the timing had thrown off the rest of the day. The actual sit down with the company was pushed back to two p.m., completely wrecking her chances of lunch with Lucy. It was ridiculous, but she'd kind of been counting on it today, even parking her Tahoe in the coffee house lot in the morning before hopping the bus to Manhattan.

Because her presence at Lucy's was almost a given these days, she'd texted Lucy at one, when she was certain there was no shot of making anything work. Lucy responded right away and she'd seemed to understand, but Sam thought she sounded bummed. It was hard to tell with texts.

Now, hours later, Sam was still cranky her afternoon had been hijacked, even if it was for work. She couldn't even get a rain check tomorrow because there were already follow-up meetings on the schedule. Gazing out the window while the bus cruised the span of the Verrazano Bridge, she caught sight of the rocky cliff that marked the perimeter of Bay West in the distance. Forget waiting two days. She had a better idea.

She looked around the coffee shop as she entered. It was quiet. Six o'clock was an odd hour for coffee, she supposed. Lucy came out from the back with a warm smile spread across her face and crossed her arms as she ogled Sam walking toward her. She let out a low whistle.

"Hello, handsome," she said. "You look…" Her voice trailed off as she took stock of Sam's business look, clearly searching for the right word. "Sharp," she finished. It wasn't exactly what Sam was hoping for, but it was still nice. "Come closer, let me see that tie."

Sam leaned on the counter as Lucy ran her hands the length of the subtle multicolored tie, letting it rest on the surface between them. Lucy fingered the edges. "It's pretty."

"Thank you. I got it at the Metropolitan Museum of Art a few years ago. I think it's supposed to be based on a painting."

"It's really lovely." Lucy continued to inspect it, never letting go of the fabric.

"I'm sorry I missed lunch today."

Lucy shrugged. "It's okay. Work happens."

"I'd like to make it up to you." She saw confusion in Lucy's expression. "Tonight." Lucy looked like she might protest, so Sam spoke quickly. "It's not dinner. Don't worry."

"I'm not."

"I saw that look of panic flash in your eyes. I'm not talking about a date." Sam licked her lips. She was surprisingly anxious as she spoke and she hoped Lucy didn't notice. "There's a full moon tonight. A supermoon, actually. I'm going to go check it out by the ridge over at Bay West. There's a beautiful view there. I may even bring my camera."

Lucy seemed to be considering, so Sam pressed on. "The sight of the full moon beyond the bridge is amazing. Definitely worth seeing, I promise. And it *is* practically in your backyard. What do you say, keep me company?"

"How's the temperature out there?" Lucy asked with a slight grimace.

Sam scrunched up her face and mock-shivered. "Wear layers. I'm going to go home and change. I'll grab some blankets." She lifted her eyebrows optimistically.

"How do you feel about hot chocolate?"

"Fantastic."

"Okay, then. Let's do it."

❖

Two hours later, Sam stood at the clearing of the trees near the path that led to the overlook behind Bay West's rentals. She bounced on her toes trying to keep her blood flowing to stave off the bitter cold. Fifty feet away she spotted the door to one of the units open and watched Lucy stroll casually across the street. She carried a thermos in her right hand and her wave was full of spirit. It gave Sam the chills in a way she didn't expect. She had to clear her throat just to find her voice.

"You are not dressed nearly as warm as you should be," she said, examining Lucy's fleece pullover.

"You said layers. I have three shirts on under this. I'll be fine."

"You sure?" She pinched the sleeve of the thin pullover. "You should go grab a jacket."

"I'm good. Come on, show me this moon you're so excited about."

"Follow me."

Sam led them through the trees along the ridge, walking along in silence against the biting wind. She turned off to the right just before the clearing ended and headed toward a rocky path that led down the side of the cliff.

"Wait, where are we going?" Lucy hesitated, grabbing at the end of Sam's thick sweater.

"Down to the bottom."

"Why? I mean, is it safe?"

Sam smiled and she knew it showed her confidence. She reached for Lucy's hand with her own. "It's fine. Hold on to me. I'll help you down."

Lucy listened and clutched her hand tightly for the short distance. At the foot of the ridge, a base of rocky boulders layered the foundation. Sam stepped across the series of rocks until she found her spot—a large flat stone big enough for both of them. "This is my favorite one." She reached into her backpack and spread a blanket down.

Her sense of routine and purpose was not lost on Lucy. "You come here often?" Lucy rolled her eyes at her own statement. "You know what I mean."

Sam pulled another blanket out of her backpack and sat down, wrapping it around her shoulders. "Lexi and I used to hang out here all the time in high school." She patted the space next to her and scooted over a little so Lucy could sit. "This is where we had all the big talks. Solved the world's problems."

"Were you two ever a thing?" Lucy settled in next to Sam, taking the end of the blanket and winding it around her back and over her knees.

Sam held in her laugh. "A thing?"

"You know, did you date? Make out here under the stars, go to third base or whatever?" She nudged Sam's shoulder playfully with her own.

"Look at you getting all frisky, wanting to know the details."

"You brought it up."

"I did not."

Lucy shifted her eyebrows. "You're avoiding the question. I'll take that as a yes."

Sam couldn't hold her laughter. "No. The answer to your *probing* question is no. Lexi is practically my sister. Besides that, I don't even know what third base is."

It was Lucy who laughed this time. She shook her head at Sam. "Why are people always so confused about the bases?" She reached up and pointed to her lips. "First." Moving her hands between her breasts, she continued. "Second." She waved in the general direction of her crotch. "This whole area, third."

"You seem quite the authority."

"I just know my bases."

"I will be sure to file that away," Sam responded quickly, unable to suppress a grin as she looked at the light of the moon cascading across the channel of water separating Manhattan and Staten Island.

They were quiet for a few minutes, the only sounds the wind and the low tide lapping the small beachhead beneath them. Lucy tilted her head back and acknowledged the full moon. "It's pretty here."

"I told you."

"The moon is unbelievable," she said nearly under her breath. "I never asked, how was work today? What did your customer think of the new artwork? And your boss?"

"Yeah, my boss, well she's not really my boss, just the project manager, she loved it. The client was pleased too. They wanted some changes here and there, nothing major." She looked up at the sky. "It was a good day. Long, but productive."

"You look great in a suit," Lucy said, still studying the stars above them. "Do you always dress like that for work?"

"Only for the big meetings, like today. Sorry I missed lunch—everything got all backed up." She stretched her legs out in front of her, feeling the cold from the rock come through the thin blanket.

Lucy looked right at her, openly studying her face before she spoke. "You looked…really good." She paused briefly before adding, "Sexy."

Sam was both flattered by Lucy's compliment and surprised by her candor. She broke eye contact, glancing at the stars above them, and over at the Verrazano bridge in the near distance, feeling the simple beauty of their surroundings having an immediate impact on her own inhibitions as well. She kept her focus on the elements. "I want to kiss you pretty badly right now."

"Sam." She heard the hesitation in Lucy's voice and held her hand up to keep her from saying anything more.

"It's okay, Luce." She looked at Lucy and gave a small shrug. "I just wanted you to know."

"Sam," Lucy started again. "You don't want to get involved with me. Not like that."

"Why?" Sam asked. She saw Lucy's nerves in the lines on her forehead and the heavy sigh she released. She leaned over and brushed Lucy's arm with her fingers hoping her touch came off as reassuring instead of pushy. "This is because of the girl who made you leave the police department?"

Lucy hung her head for a moment before leaning it all the way back as she stared up at the endless night sky. Despite Lucy's protests, Sam was overwhelmed with the desire to touch her, and somewhere deep down she knew Lucy wouldn't stop her. But she played it safe anyway, rubbing her hand smoothly along Lucy's back as she spoke.

"Tell me."

"What if you don't like me once you know the whole story?" Lucy smiled, but it was obviously forced. She was clearly trying for playful, but Sam heard genuine concern in her tone.

She looked right into Lucy's eyes. "Come on." Sam rocked her head back and forth as she smiled. "Not possible. You know that." She leaned back against the large rock behind them as if to settle in, as she prepared for Lucy to tell her saga. With a nod of her chin she said, "Pour me a little of that hot chocolate and talk to me."

Lucy reached for the thermos and filled the lid that doubled as a cup. "It's not even that dramatic, this story," she started. "And I don't blame Caroline for making me leave. Or Dani. I left the police department because of poor choices I made."

"Who are these women?" Sam asked.

"Caroline was my girlfriend. We were together for three years." She shook her head. "Ridiculous, actually. We should have broken up ages before we did."

"Why?"

Lucy let out a heavy breath. "Caroline was…let's see. How can I say this without sounding like a jerk?"

"Out with it," Sam encouraged. "No filtering. No judgments." She took a sip of the hot chocolate. "Promise."

Lucy reached for the cocoa letting her hand linger against Sam's for a long second. "Caroline cared a whole lot about what people thought. Of her, of me. Of us together." She chewed at her bottom lip clearly taking time to choose her words. "She really enjoyed telling people that I was a detective. It was the strangest thing. It was like she loved it and was mortified by it at the same time." She registered the confusion in Sam's expression so she clarified on the spot. "She liked to show me off to her fancy friends and at her hoity-toity work events. She would always introduce me as *Detective Weston* and make a big deal about whatever case I was working at the time." She shook her head. "It was stupid. And it made me feel like...garbage, really. I hated that she felt like she needed to give an excuse for me. As though it was okay for me to be a police officer because I was a detective. God forbid I had been just a regular dumb cop."

"Was she really doing that? She wasn't just proud of you?"

Lucy's look answered the question, and Sam held up her hands in mock surrender. "Fair enough. What did she do, this Caroline person? For work?"

"She's in sales. Medical equipment." She wound the loose end of her shoelace around her pinky. "She was going to go to medical school, but well, that's another story," she said dismissively. "She's just very smart. Caroline."

"I'm sure."

"The truth is, for all the showboating she did around her friends and her family, anytime I tried to actually talk to her about work"—Lucy frowned—"she didn't want to hear it. Any of it." She looked off in the distance. "And sometimes it would have been nice to talk about some of the crazy things I saw."

"I bet."

"I started staying later and later at work. Hanging out with the guys in my squad. Having a few drinks here and there. I became very close with the patrol lieutenant on the midnight shift. She was having problems in her marriage. At first we just talked. It was nice. Easy."

"The lieutenant is the other woman you were referring to? Dani, right?"

"Yes." Lucy nodded. "I still can't believe it all happened."

"It's okay, Luce. Stuff happens."

"It was a terrible thing I did. Wrong. Hurtful. Whatever problems Caroline and I had, I should have taken the time to work them out." She wrapped her arms around her knees and pulled them in tighter. "Or I should have left."

"Can I ask you a question?" She waited for Lucy to look at her. "Did she try to work on any of the problems you were having together?"

"No, but—"

"Then come on, Lucy. You know this isn't all you."

"I'm the one who brought us down."

"But you just finished saying you should have broken up anyway."

"Not like that."

Sam leaned her arms forward, her elbows resting over the top of her knees. "My experience, Luce"—she added a shrug as she looked out on the water—"is sometimes messed up things happen because it's the only way to move on."

"Sam." Lucy turned her body sideways and put her hand on Sam's forearm. "I need you to know something. I am not that person anymore." She licked her lips. "I know it sounds ridiculous—"

"It doesn't."

"Let me finish." She waited a second. "I'm ashamed of what I did. Whatever the reasons were. None of them make it okay. I know that. Trust me when I tell you I will never do anything like that again."

"It's okay."

"It's not."

"Hey." Sam's voice was stern but sincere. "I'm going to talk for a second." She quickly gathered her thoughts, trying to figure out a way to make Lucy smile again. "I'm going to say two things right now. I want you to listen."

Lucy looked as serious as Sam had ever seen her. God, she was beautiful. Even now, with the weight of the past hanging heavy in her smoky gray eyes, shivering against the cold breeze, the glare of the moon showing the stress on her face.

"Number one. It's time to forgive yourself. Yes, you fucked up. You know it. You *clearly* own it." She punctuated her words with a nod. "Two. You are freezing." She spread her legs wide and patted the space in front of her. "Come here." Lucy looked skeptical but Sam didn't give her a chance to overthink it. She reached for her arm and guided her between her legs. She slipped her arms around Lucy's waist and felt her relax against her body. "Look at me."

"That's three." Lucy turned her head and arched her brow. "You said two things."

"I changed my mind."

Lucy turned to face her and a strand of her hair blew in the wind. Sam tucked it away behind her ear. She leaned forward and placed a small kiss on Lucy's lips. "You are beautiful." She gave her another small peck, on the cheek this time. "And smart." She tipped her head up and kissed her jaw. "Incredibly sexy." She moved along to her ear. "Funny. Sassy," she whispered, continuing to kiss her face. "My heart melts every single day at two thirty when I see you reserve a table in the window for that old lady and her aide, just so the teenagers don't take her spot."

Lucy smiled at the mention of her daily routine.

"I hate when we miss a day," Sam continued. "And God, I love when you flirt with me." Lucy was blushing. "Your story doesn't scare me away." She kissed her on the lips again. "People make mistakes. Even the really good ones." She smiled. "I'm going to kiss you now. For real. I hope you're ready."

She didn't give Lucy a chance to answer either in protest or agreement. Their faces were already close. Just an inch forward and Sam's lips were on Lucy's again. She led strongly but softly, opening her mouth and letting their tongues touch gently. The kiss was nice, sweet and tender at first, and when Sam moved deeper in Lucy's mouth, she heard a little moan. She pulled away slowly, brushing her lips across Lucy's.

"Hi," she said, smiling against Lucy's mouth.

"Mmm. Hi."

She felt Lucy's fingertips lightly along her cheek, her thumb tracing her bottom lip. She kissed the pad of Lucy's finger. "Was that okay?"

"Very."

Lucy bit her lower lip and faced forward, settling her body against Sam's and lacing their fingers together. Sam hugged her tighter in response, dropping a kiss on her neck. Lucy arched, giving her more exposure, and Sam took advantage, her mouth trailing along Lucy's skin. She could feel Lucy's body purring, and in a second, she turned and their mouths met again. It started slow, but this kiss was hungrier than the first and Sam let her hand travel up the front of Lucy's torso, brushing the outline of her breast over her fleece.

Lucy moaned again, and while she didn't restrict Sam's touch, she slowed the kiss. She held the sides of Sam's face, pressed their foreheads together. "Sam," she said. Her voice sounded pained, and Sam hoped to God it wasn't from regret.

"What's wrong?" she asked.

Lucy huffed out a small snicker. "Nothing." She shook her head against Sam's. "Absolutely nothing." She glanced up at the sky and the supermoon above them. "This night is perfect."

"I hear a *but* in there."

"No, not really." Lucy licked her lips. "I just need to not go too fast. Could we do that? Go slow, I mean."

Sam saw real concern on Lucy's face, as though she was worried the suggestion might put her off. "Of course." She leaned forward and kissed her sweetly. "As a matter of fact, I should probably get you home. We both have work tomorrow. And I know you're still cold."

They packed up their few belongings and climbed back up the cliff using the same path as before and when they reached Lucy's front door, Sam was still holding Lucy's hand. She leaned down to give Lucy an innocent kiss good night, but her lips lingered too long and it turned passionate right on Lucy's front stoop.

Lucy was breathless when she broke them apart to speak. "I want to invite you in." She put her hands on each side of Sam's face. "But I honestly don't trust myself if I do."

Sam throbbed at the obscure suggestion, but she found her manners. "Let's just call it a night right here." She kissed Lucy delicately on the lips.

"Are you coming to the coffee shop tomorrow morning?"

"I have meetings in the city all day tomorrow." She swayed Lucy in her arms a little as she twisted her lips in regret.

"No lunch, even?"

"I'm sorry."

Lucy pushed off of her chest playfully. "So you think you can kiss me like that and then make me wait two days to see you again?" She raised her eyebrows. "Uh-uh." She reached up and rushed her hands through the thick waves atop Sam's head, grabbing roughly and pulling Sam's face to hers. "No way," she said, stealing another kiss. "What time will you be back on the island?"

"I have a late client. Probably sevenish."

"Perfect. Come to the store. I'll be closing up—we can grab food at Angelo's next door and bring it back here." She nodded in the direction of her front door. "Would that work for you?"

"Yes." She couldn't resist the urge to tease Lucy. "Dinner, though"—she widened her eyes—"that's like the food equivalent of second base."

Lucy reached in her bag for her keys. "It's third, actually," she corrected, her voice completely nonchalant.

"Third!" Sam shook off a laugh as she stepped off the stoop. "What's first?"

"Oh, Sam." Lucy shook her head and her lively smile was impossible to ignore. "First is coffee."

Well played, Sam thought. But she said nothing, choosing instead to let Lucy win the spirited face-off. "Good night, Luce," she called as she backed down the walkway to the street.

"See you tomorrow, Sam."

CHAPTER TEN

The elevator dinged open, and Sasha took a deep breath, holding her head high and hoping she looked poised as she walked directly to the reception desk ten feet in front of her.

Inside, she was a bit of a wreck. Her plan seemed genius a week ago, when her internet search not only told her which subway to take to the mandated fingerprinting appointment at the Department of Education, but also that the building housed the DOE's legal division. Three clicks later and she'd confirmed Lexi R. Ducane was still employed as an attorney for the city education department, with an office on the third floor. One thing had become clear to Sasha after her impromptu meet up with Meg the previous week—she needed to up her game. She could use an ally. Confident in her new tactic, she'd spent a good part of the week mentally practicing her strategy of imploring Lexi's help. Suddenly in the moment, she wondered if the whole idea was ridiculous.

"Excuse me," she said, finding her courage as she interrupted the receptionist's game of solitaire. "I was hoping to see Lexi Ducane, if she is available."

"And you are?"

"Sasha Michaels."

"Is she expecting you?"

"No." Sasha shook her head, but the woman was already reaching for the phone and pointing toward the spartan furniture in the small waiting area where she clearly wanted Sasha to sit. Less than two minutes passed before Sasha's attention was drawn to the echoing click of heels on the terrazzo tile. She looked up at Lexi walking toward her.

"Sasha?" Lexi waved as she approached from the depths of the beige hallway. "Everything okay?"

"Yes," Sasha answered. She was relieved to hear her voice sound composed. "I'm sorry to bother you at work. I was downstairs getting fingerprinted and I was wondering if you might be able to talk for a minute. If you have time."

Lexi looked over at the receptionist who was following raptly. "Janice, I'll be back in a few minutes." She nodded toward the elevator. "Come."

"Do you want to grab a coat or anything? It's pretty chilly out."

"No, we'll just go across the street. I'll be fine."

They traveled the two floors down the elevator in silence and Sasha followed Lexi out of the old building to a small coffee shop on the corner. Lexi slid into the window seat. Sasha sat across from her.

"Do you want anything? Coffee or tea or something?" Sasha asked, looking around.

"I only have a few minutes." Lexi shook her head. "I'm here all the time anyway. Believe me, they won't care if I don't buy something this once." Lexi's smile looked forced. "This is about Meg, I assume?"

Sasha nodded. "Yes." She picked at her fingernails. "I know I made a huge mistake with Meg. A bunch of them really—"

"*Yeah*, you did." Lexi's tone was fully defensive.

"I know." Sasha sat back in her chair feeling defeated already. "That's why I wanted to talk to you."

"You should be talking to Meg."

"I did. I am." She reached for a packet of sweetener and flattened it on the table in front of her. "I saw her last week." She chewed her lip nervously. "It was nice. But she has a wall up with me, I can tell."

"Can you blame her?"

"No. Of course not. Not at all."

"What is it that you want, Sasha?"

"I want another chance."

"And you think you deserve one?"

Lexi's words were sharp, but Sasha knew they weren't completely unwarranted so she let them resonate a moment before speaking.

"I know you're her friend. That's why I came to you." She spoke slowly, hoping to make every word count. "Lexi, I made a ton of mistakes with Meg. I did *everything* wrong." She registered Lexi's unconvinced look from across the table. "You don't have to believe me, but I want you to know it anyway." She swallowed the emotions that came out every time she let her feelings about Meg come to the surface. "I'm in love with her, Lexi. I have been from the beginning."

"So why are you talking to me?"

"It's not that easy. Meg won't really talk to me. Which I completely understand." She stared out the window at an eighteen-wheeler trying to negotiate the turn onto Broadway. "When I saw her last week at Sullivan, I practically had to beg her to have a drink with me. And even then when we talked, she had her guard up the whole time. She won't let me in."

Lexi leaded forward, closing the space between them. "That's because you broke her. You destroyed her, Sasha." Her voice was low and biting. "And I want to hate you for it."

"I know."

"No, I don't think you do." Lexi clenched her jaw clearly trying to keep her cool. "Meg was so messed up after you guys broke up that she was willing to settle. She rushed into a relationship where she had, like, zero chance of getting hurt."

"She told me they broke up."

"Exactly." Even her nod was fierce in defense of her BFF. "She is just now, a full fucking year later, finally willing to *maybe* put herself back out there. So if you're going to do this, you'd better be dead fucking sure, Sasha."

"I am. I'm going to do everything I can to get her back."

"Because if you start wavering again, with your lame-ass excuses—"

"Look, Lexi, I'm not going to hurt her." She wondered if she should continue, but did anyway. "Gah, Lexi, how do I say this without sounding like a jerk?"

Her question was rhetorical, but Lexi raised her eyebrows in challenge.

Sasha dropped her eyes to the small formica table. "Last year was a nightmare." She drew her bottom lip in, thinking about it for a tiny moment. "I hated my job. I was terrible at it," she said with a strained laugh. "I had just moved to New York. I was a little lost. Nervous all the time. Then Meg came along." She shook her head, feeling her cheeks get warm as she remembered the start of everything. "She helped me at Sullivan. She made me laugh. I couldn't wait to come to work every day to see her." She laughed outright. "I would pick my clothes, not based on clients or what I had going on for the day. Nope. I wore outfits I thought I looked good in. I wanted her to find me attractive." She lowered her brow, still giggling at herself. "I spent so much money on clothes."

Sasha stuffed the sugar packet she'd been playing with back into its holder. "I fell in love with her at the very beginning." She looked up at the ceiling. "It scared the hell out of me. And then my mother died." She sniffled a little, holding back her tears. "I wasn't ready for any of it. My whole world was spinning. I was in no shape to be in any kind of relationship. Let alone a relationship with *the one*." She raised her eyebrows to signify the weight of her words. Lexi looked like she was about to comment, but Sasha stopped her.

"Look, none of this excuses my actions. The way I treated Meg was…not right. I have serious regrets about that. But I needed this time to, I don't know." She shook her head. "*Process* sounds so trite." She licked her lips. "What I'm saying is, I've gotten my life together. I'm pursuing the job of my dreams. I finally feel like *me*." She folded her hands together on the table. "And because of that, everything is clear." She shrugged even as she felt herself smile in the confidence of her proclamation. "I love Meg. I always have. I always will."

Lexi squinted, and Sasha thought she was trying to read her to make sure she was legit.

"You don't have to believe me, even though I think it would help if you did. I came to you because I want you to know I'm for real. Meg trusts you. I wanted to tell you myself, I'm serious. I'm going to try everything to get her back. I do think my odds are better if you're in my corner." She hated that it came out sounding calculated because her intentions had been pure. "Look, I just mean—"

Lexi held up a hand effectively cutting her off. "Stop. I get it." She waved her hand as she spoke. "Here's a tip. If you want this to work, forget about telling me or even telling Meg how you feel." She looked around the small coffee shop they were squatting in. "You have to *show* her. Make it count. And you know what?" She twisted her face in the early afternoon sun. "When she doesn't bite right away, don't give up." Sasha felt her eyes boring into her. "Don't just fade away like you did last time. Get out of your comfort zone. If you would really do anything for her, then do it."

"I will." Her anxiety peaked and her voice cracked. "This is where I could use your help a little."

Lexi raised her eyebrows, clearly unsure where this was going.

"Gah." Sasha dropped her head in one hand. "The thing is...I was lucky enough to bump into Meg at her job last week."

"And Roaring Twenties," Lexi added.

"Less lucky on that one."

"What do you mean?"

Sasha let out a heavy breath. "Yes, I was fortunate enough to see you all that night. But"—she cringed—"my odds haven't been that good. I've been going to The Kitchen pretty frequently. And hitting every lesbian event where I thought there might be even a slim chance of seeing her." She made a small circle on the table's smooth surface with one finger. "With the exception of the socials at Bay West." She shook her head. "That just seemed, well, off-limits."

"Let me see if I understand you." Lexi held both hands up. "You want me to help you stalk my friend?"

"No, I mean…no." It sounded ridiculous when she heard Lexi say it out loud. "I'll figure it out," she added, not at all sure how. "I just need to know—do you think I have a chance?" She heard her own voice shake and hated how pathetic she sounded.

"You and Meg." Lexi rolled her eyes. "You're supposed to be together. I know it in my bones."

"You think?" She felt her spirits lift at the slight possibility.

"I do." Lexi sucked in her cheeks. "Let's get one thing clear. I'm only helping you because I'm a sucker for love." She sat back in her chair. "And because I care about Meg." Lexi leaned forward and grabbed her forearm, holding on to it tightly. "But Sasha, if you break her heart again, even a little"—her stare was cold, and Sasha felt a chill down her spine—"you will deal with me. That's a promise." Lexi released her grip and scooched herself out of the window bench, smoothing her skirt as she spoke. "There's trivia night at Lucy's Coffee Bar down the block from Bay West. Next Wednesday, seven o'clock. I will figure out a way to get you on our team. Do not be late."

Sasha smiled big. "I owe you."

"Yeah, you do."

CHAPTER ELEVEN

How was your day?" Lucy placed the white paper bag containing their dinner on the counter that separated the galley kitchen from the living room.

"Fine. It went fast." Sam took in the space. Even when she'd lived in the rental section, she'd never gotten a personal tour of the one-bedroom setup. Lucy's unit was on the second floor above another single, and it had a nice layout that was both functional and spacious. "Can I get changed?" she asked, grabbing at the lapel of her suit jacket.

Lucy frowned. "Oh, all right. You look so good though." Sam watched Lucy run her eyes from her tie to her wingtips. "Okay, I'm good," Lucy said, biting her lip openly. She nodded past Sam. "You can use my bedroom."

Sam hoisted her backpack over her shoulder and headed down the hall. She slipped into jeans and a Henley quickly, trying not to get caught up in Lucy's scent, which was everywhere. She sat on the side of the bed and reached for a boot when the sight of the moon out Lucy's window stole her attention. It wasn't full, but it was still breathtaking. She stood up for a better look when a light knock broke her concentration.

"Okay in here?"

"Sorry, I got lost in your view." Sam twisted to see Lucy in the doorway. "Come here. Check out the moon. It's amazing again tonight."

Lucy came up behind and hugged Sam. She pressed her lips against Sam's shoulder and must have been on tiptoe when she whispered in her ear, "I knew it. You're a werewolf, aren't you?"

"I wish," she said, stroking her fingertips up Lucy's arms absentmindedly as she stared up at the dark night sky.

"Did you just say you wish you were a werewolf?"

"I did."

"Okay. Weird."

Sam maneuvered Lucy in front of her under the guise of giving her the better view, but secretly she just wanted an excuse to touch her. "Werewolves don't have it so bad. They answer to the full moon. That's kind of sexy, right? I mean, they don't have it nearly as good as vampires, but still."

"This is by far the strangest conversation I've had all day."

"Come on, everybody knows vampires have the life."

"Actually they're dead," Lucy quipped.

"That's just it. Ageless existence. Decadence galore. Plus, sexy as all get-out. Girls melt for them."

Lucy poked at Sam's forearms. "Like that doesn't happen for you now anyway," she teased.

"What?" Sam feigned surprise.

"Shut up." Lucy turned around and swatted her chest playfully. "You can't even fake it."

Sam dropped a sweet kiss on her lips. "I only care about one girl."

"Oh yeah, huh?"

"Mm-hmm."

Lucy leaned in for another kiss and this time it intensified right away. She pushed into Sam, backing them up to the bed. When Sam's knees hit the edge, she let herself fall onto the mattress bringing Lucy down with her. They kissed for several minutes until their hands were roaming, their bodies writhing. It was amazing, hot and passionate. The one thing it was not: slow.

When they rolled over and Lucy was on top of her, Sam found her resolve. She held the sides of Lucy's face and touched their foreheads together gently.

"We should eat before our food gets cold."

Lucy swallowed and licked her lips. "We should." She sat upright and pulled her hair back, still straddling Sam.

Sam propped herself on her elbows.

"Sorry," Lucy said, hopping off to the side. "I guess I let things get a little out of hand here."

"It's okay." Sam sat all the way up and shook her shoulders trying to get rid of the uncomfortable buzz that was coursing through her limbs.

"Are you mad?"

Sam knew her expression displayed her disbelief at the question, but in case it wasn't entirely clear she answered, "Of course not." She touched Lucy's cheek. "Why would I be mad?"

"I don't know. That was kind of intense. And I know I started it—"

Sam cut her off. "Hey." She put her hand on the top of Lucy's thigh and looked right at her. "There's no rush. We wait until we're ready. Okay?"

Lucy leaned into her, gently resting her head against Sam's shoulder. "Thank you, Sam. For being nice."

Sam took Lucy's hand and stood up, pulling Lucy with her. "I kind of like you a little bit." She put her hands at Lucy's waist and let her guide them out of the bedroom. "Now feed me, woman."

❖

They sat at the kitchen peninsula indulging in a decadent helping of pasta primavera that Angelo had whipped up special for them, talking about everything from work to life to Bay West. Sam shared the pros and cons of living with her parents, surprising herself as she listed the number of benefits. She learned that Lucy grew up on Long Island, the third of four girls, and she had come out when she was sixteen.

"Sixteen?" Sam nodded. "That's brave. How were your parents with that?"

"Fine." She cleared their plates into the sink. "My parents are great," she said with a wave of her hand. "My sister's gay too. Emily. The one I was telling you about the other day, who lives in the city. She's a year older than I am. We told them at the same time." She smiled a little. "They were *not* surprised."

"Wow, both of you. That's fun."

"It is." Lucy nodded. "What about you? Brothers, sisters?"

"One brother. Jack. He's not gay." She returned the smile when Lucy laughed at her dumb joke. "I'm curious about you and your sister. Did you both always know? About each other, I mean."

Lucy nodded and smiled at the same time. "We're all close, my sisters and I. But with me and Em, it's different. We're super tight." She shrugged. "So, yeah, we both always knew about each other. Even when we were little."

"Did you go on double dates and stuff?"

Lucy tilted her head to the side, clearly thinking about it. "Not really. We dated some girls from the same circle. Well, really I dated some girls from her circle. She's been with her wife since they were seventeen. They were high school sweethearts."

"That's sweet."

Lucy made a face as though she didn't one hundred percent agree with Sam's sentiment, but said nothing. Sam read her expression. "Not sweet?" she asked with a dramatically furrowed brow.

"I don't know." Lucy leaned her forearms across the counter. "I think they're not in a great place these days. Frankie, Emily's wife, travels a good deal with her job, and I know that's important." She made small circles with her fingertips on the granite countertop. "They have two kids, plus Emily runs a day care. It's a lot. I worry about her, about them, that's all."

Sam slid her hands underneath Lucy's. "You love her."

"I do."

She held both of Lucy's hands and guided her around the kitchen island until she was standing in front of where she was sitting on a high backed stool. "She's lucky to have you." Sam put her hands on Lucy's hips and Lucy stepped between her legs, draping her arms over Sam's shoulders.

"She is, huh?" Lucy's tone was suggestive.

"Yeah," Sam breathed out as she leaned forward to kiss her. It started out innocent, but it didn't take long before their hands were roaming. Sam purposely took the high road stopping things before she was tempted to take them further. She let their kiss soften and settle before she spoke. "I should go," she said in a low voice.

Lucy let out a sad whimper, but nodded her agreement. She leaned farther into Sam's embrace. "You definitely should."

❖

Three dates and exactly three serious make out sessions later, Sam stood on Lexi's doorstep hoping to kill some time before she met up with Lucy for the evening. She pressed the doorbell once, then peered down the street wondering if her buddy was even home.

"Hey, girl." She heard genuine pleasure in Lexi's voice when the door opened and knew she'd made the right call by stopping by even if it was unannounced.

"Busy, Munchkin?"

"Not at all."

"I come bearing treats." Sam held up a thin pastry box. "From Lucy. But hey, still counts, right?"

"Hell, yes. What's the occasion?"

"None, really." She shrugged. "We haven't seen each other much. I had some time to kill before Lucy calls it a day at the store. Thought we could catch up if you were around." Sam looked over and noticed the table set for dinner. "Ah, you guys are about to eat. It's cool. I can wait for Lucy at her place. I should have called anyway."

"Shut up." Lexi pulled her inside. "Jesse's not even home. She went to pick up dinner from Lombardo's. And you're more than welcome to join us. Drink?"

"I'd take a beer if you have one."

Lexi walked to the fridge, grabbed Sam a Heineken, and sliced off a wedge of lime to squeeze into her own drink.

"What are you drinking?" Sam asked.

"Just seltzer." Lexi pulled a chair out. "Fill me in. How are things with Lucy? You two seem to be spending an awful lot of time together." It came out as kind of a sing-songy cheer and Lexi clapped her hands excitedly at the same time. Sam couldn't help but smile at her enthusiasm.

"They're good."

"Hot-and-heavy good?"

"I don't kiss and tell."

Lexi laughed in her face. "Yes, you do."

Sam felt slightly embarrassed knowing the truth was completely tame, but she answered honestly anyway. "We are taking it nice and slow."

"Wait. You haven't had sex yet?" Lexi's mouth dropped open in purposeful dramatic fashion. "Sam Miller, are you wooing this woman?"

Sam twisted her beer bottle in her hands. "She doesn't want to rush into anything." She smoothed out a bubble in the label with her thumb. "I completely respect that."

Lexi leaned forward. "Aw, Sam, that's really sweet." She rubbed her arm. "You must be dying," she added with a frown of mock empathy.

"I have no idea what you're talking about," Sam said, playing along, before turning slightly serious. "I really like her."

"I see that. That's great." Lexi took a small sip of her drink. "What time does she close the store, typically?"

Sam tapped her beer lightly on the table making a design with the moisture rings. "Seven. Seven thirty. Sometimes eight. It depends. If it was me, I would shut down at six. Who fucking needs coffee after that anyway?"

"I guess. But she does some cool stuff at night. Sometimes she shows movies there and tomorrow is trivia night, right?"

"Yeah, that's why she stayed. Wanted to get some last minute prep work out of the way."

"Why don't you call her and have her come here. You guys can stay for dinner. I can call Jess right now and add to our order."

"No, it's fine. We ate a late lunch. She was still baking when I left. I wanted to see you. I miss you, Munchkin."

"I miss you too. I'm so glad you stopped by. Oh, by the way, Kam loved your new icon for the socials. And she went crazy over the website." She smacked Sam's knee. "She also told me that she thinks the Fishers over on Crescent Street are thinking of moving this summer." She raised her eyebrows.

"Where on Crescent?" Sam asked.

"Down a bit." Lexi gestured with her chin. "Near the entrance."

"Definitely keep me posted on that." She swallowed a long refreshing sip of her drink. "So, Munch, what's new with you?" She made a circle with her beer, pointing at Lexi with the neck of the bottle. "Are you pregnant?"

"What?"

"Don't play coy with me. I have known you since grade school," Sam teased. "Since you were ten, you've been talking about getting married and having babies." She put her beer down on the table with a slight thud to emphasize her point. "I haven't seen you take one drink of anything even remotely alcoholic since I'm home." She grinned right at Lexi. "So tell me. When are you due?"

"I'm not pregnant." Lexi let out a small tense chuckle. "But you're not way off. I want a baby. I'm ready. So's Jess."

"Shit, Lex." Sam clenched her teeth. "You're having trouble?"

"God, no." Lexi let out a heavy breath. "I didn't mean for it to sound like that." She pulled her hair off her face. "The only problem we're having at this point is that Jesse and I can't seem to agree on how to do it."

"What do you mean?"

Lexi shook her head and there was frustration in her tone. "Jesse is being completely obstinate."

The door squeaked open behind them and they both got up to help Jesse as she balanced two bags of takeout and the mail. "What am I being obstinate about?" Jesse asked, sounding not the least bit unnerved at walking into a conversation where she was clearly the subject.

"Baby making," Lexi responded without missing a beat.

Jesse rolled her eyes. "I am being pragmatic and logical." She placed their dinner on the table.

Lexi kissed her cheek. "You are being stubborn."

Jesse looked at Sam as she unpacked their takeaway tins. "What's your take?"

"Don't drag her into this."

"Why not?" Jesse looked between Sam and Lexi. "She's here. She's smart, and I think it would do you some good to hear from your friends on this." Jesse crossed the kitchen and got a small serving spoon. "I am not being crazy. I'm being realistic."

Sam snuck a glance at Lexi and clenched her teeth in apology at having brought up the touchy subject, but Lexi shook her head, letting her off the hook right on the spot.

"Fine." Lexi removed the lid from the chicken parm and leaned out of the path of steam pouring out. "I want to use someone we know as a donor. Jesse wants to use a sperm bank."

Sam looked at Jesse first, then at Lexi hoping they didn't actually expect her to weigh in. She didn't have a chance anyway. Lexi spoke again, this time directing her comments right to Jesse. "Your way is cold."

"My way is clean. Straightforward." Jesse doled out Caesar salad for each of them. "I can't believe as a lawyer you don't see the benefits of using an anonymous sperm donor. No prospective legal battles down the line, no fighting over custody or medical treatments should that ever become an issue. It's a method that has been tried and argued and validated in the legal system. I simply cannot understand your objection to it."

Lexi straightened up in her chair, her fork held aloft as she decided what to eat first. "Doesn't that sound cold, Sam?"

Sam shifted uncomfortably. "I mean, she does make some good points, Lex."

"She's extremely glossing over the fact that you really know nothing about an anonymous donor. Other than what he wants to tell you, or completely make up. I'm sure they're all six feet tall with a full head of hair and fantastic pecs. Yeah, okay."

"Also a valid point." Sam made an invisible notch in the air with her beer. "What's the alternative though, Lex? Do you even know any dudes you'd want to use?" Sam asked, reaching across and stealing a crouton off Lexi's plate.

Lexi was quiet for a second. She twirled some spaghetti on her fork. "So, I really want a baby that looks like Jesse."

"Okay. Sounds like Jesse's plan could work for that." She snagged another crouton. "I'm sure someone at least verifies whether the guy has brown or red or blond hair. Right?"

"Unless…" Lexi's voice was so serious Sam stopped mid-chew. She swallowed quickly and gave her full attention. "*I* think"—Lexi ran her hands over her silverware—"we should get Jesse's brother Justin to donate for us. They look exactly alike." She looked at Sam, probably gauging her reaction, before focusing on her dinner as she continued her pitch. "And he's awesome and we know he's not into drugs or a serial killer."

"He's also my brother." Jesse's voice was serious and full of skepticism.

"Which is why he would do it. He idolizes you, Jess. And he's single."

"Right now he is, sure." Jesse waved her fork in the air. "Let's put aside for one second that it's going to take *a lot* for me to get past you and my brother having a baby. I know people do it." Her mouth was a straight line. "I'm just not sure I can. That minor hurdle notwithstanding, you bring up a fantastic point. He's single *now*." She cut off a piece of chicken. "What happens when he gets married?"

Lexi reached for the grated cheese. "So he gets married, so what?"

"What if his wife is some crazy woman who is not okay with me and you raising a child she considers to be his?"

Lexi rolled her eyes. "I highly doubt Justin would marry someone like that."

"But what if he does, babe? Or what if he gets married and they can't have kids, for whatever reason, and then she wants ours?" Jesse shook her head. "Or even if she can have kids but feels like Justin's children should all be raised together. By them. There are too many variables that end very badly. Like in-the-courtroom badly."

"But we would have paperwork in line. We are lawyers."

"I know, and I know we'd win. But the cost on our family, our children. It would be catastrophic."

Sam leaned forward. "Munch, I think she's right. That scenario, I mean it could be great but it could also ruin everything."

Lexi looked defeated and Sam couldn't help but be moved when Jesse leaned forward to squeeze her hand. "Babe, don't look like that. We're going to figure this out. I'm sure of it."

Sam's phone vibrated in her pocket telling her Lucy was on her way home. "Well, glad I could help here ladies." She thumped the table once and pushed her chair back. "I'm just kidding. I am going to go though, let you guys finish your dinner." She zipped her jacket. "Can I just say one thing?" When they looked at her, they were still holding hands. "You're going to be amazing parents. However you decide to do it."

"Tell Lucy we said hi," Jesse said.

"And tell her thanks for the goodies," Lexi yelled after her.

In the short walk down the path to the rental section, Sam thought about Lexi and Jesse and the decisions ahead of them. It was foreign to her in a way. She'd never thought about having kids the way Lexi always had growing up. She wondered what Lucy wanted. She might ask someday. Not yet, they weren't even close to those kinds of conversations. Still, she was curious in a way she'd never been about anyone she'd dated in the past. It gave her a small shiver and even though she was wearing a jacket she felt tiny goose bumps line her forearms.

❖

"I just have to update my inventory," Lucy said opening the door to her living space as Sam followed her inside. "Do you have anything you could work on for a few minutes?"

Sam groaned, grabbing Lucy from behind in the center of the apartment. "I could work on you," she whispered, placing a small kiss by her ear.

"Mmm," Lucy responded. "Sit down. Give me a half hour and I'm all yours."

"Okay." Sam pouted a little but sat at the end of the couch stretching her legs along the cushions as she grabbed her tablet out of her bag. She was just about to pull up a design she was playing around with when Lucy dropped her stuff on the coffee table and wedged her bottom between Sam's legs, taking her arms and wrapping herself into a hug.

"Well, hello there." Sam gently pressed her lips to Lucy's shoulder blade.

Lucy angled her body. "I'm going to get to my work in one second," she said, touching Sam's face with both hands. "But I missed you." She brushed her lips against Sam's. "And I've wanted to do this for hours." She leaned all the way forward, her body language screaming for more. They kissed deeply for a good few minutes, and when Lucy moaned, Sam couldn't help but smile against her lips.

She trailed her mouth down Lucy's neck before coming back up to kiss her again, smoothing her hands over Lucy's abdomen. Because of the way they were positioned on the couch, without realizing it right away, Sam's hand slid down the front of Lucy's body landing squarely between her legs. At the contact, Lucy spread her legs a touch giving her more access. The move surprised her and she groaned uncontrollably in response. She stopped herself before it went any further.

"Sorry," she breathed out.

"It's okay." Lucy brought Sam's hand to her lips and kissed her fingers. "I should get my work done, though."

Sam ushered her forward, kicking off her shoes and putting her feet up on the coffee table as she killed time while Lucy crunched numbers at the opposite end of the sofa. Thirty minutes went by, and Sam flipped the lid of her tablet closed, then slid it into her bag. She swung her legs onto the couch and let her feet make their way to Lucy at the other end. She tapped Lucy's thigh with her toes.

"Hi," she said, her voice playful and frisky.

Lucy didn't look over but her cheeks lifted and her eyes crinkled at the corners. She whacked Sam's foot. "No distracting me." Handing Sam the remote, she tried for serious. "I'm almost done. Entertain yourself for a few more minutes."

"*Okay*," Sam fake whined, taking the remote and pointing it at the flat screen. "I hope that means you're going to entertain me when you're done." She was mostly kidding but Lucy held her gaze.

"It just might."

Sam grinned and shifted her attention to the television, bypassing several action movies that she'd be into, and instead settled on an old black-and-white movie that was well into its plot.

"I love this movie," Lucy said offhandedly, glancing up from her work.

Sam raised her eyebrows. At twenty-eight, Sam took every opportunity to tease Lucy about their six-and-a-half year age gap. This was perfect. "How old are you, really? Come on, you can tell me."

"Not. Funny." Lucy poked the end of her pen into Sam's shin.

She moved her leg away and Lucy shifted toward her slightly, filling the empty space. "Disagree. I think it's very funny and possibly true. Seriously"—she paused for dramatic effect—"did you see this in the movie theater? It's okay, be honest."

"Brat." Lucy smiled, leaning forward as she seemed to search for the best place to land a playful slap. In her hesitation, Sam grabbed her forearm and pulled her close.

"Come here."

She guided Lucy toward her gently, looking in her eyes before kissing her soft and deep. She heard Lucy's pad and papers slide to the floor. "Sorry, babe. I just needed to kiss you. I'll pick up your stuff and let you get back to work."

"No." Lucy moved her whole body over her and her hair tickled Sam's cheek. She shook her head. "It can wait."

Lucy leaned back down and Sam kissed her again. The palm of her hands pressed lightly on Lucy's ass as they moved against one another. Remembering Lucy's pleas to go slow, she focused and held back but Lucy moaned loudly into the kiss. She pulled back and sat upright, straddling Sam's body. She unzipped her thin hoodie and tossed it on the coffee table. Her small breasts curved under the fabric of her T-shirt and Sam was desperate to touch them.

Despite their past conversations, something in Lucy's eyes told Sam it was okay now, so she let her hands drift up, under her shirt, along her smooth skin. She pulled Lucy back down, her hands in her hair as they kissed. Sam indulged every second and she let her lips find the tender spot just below Lucy's ear, drifting down her neck and sucking her soft pale skin, stopping herself before she left a mark. She felt Lucy gasp when she touched her breasts over the lace of her bra.

"Is this okay?" she asked, dragging a kiss along her collarbone.

"Uh-huh." Lucy's voice was low, and she didn't open her eyes.

Sam's kisses were gentle as she worked her way back up Lucy's neck, breathing in the combination of shampoo, soap, and the faint hint of coffee that still lingered on her skin after a long day at the store. Lucy's nipples were hard against her hands and she was writhing a little against Sam's crotch. Sam lifted Lucy's shirt off. She lowered her head and grazed her mouth along the tops of her breasts before pulling down the lace and letting her tongue circle each nipple. Lucy moaned, low and soft.

"I can slow down if you want." It came out like a question, even though Sam was pretty sure she was getting green lights all the way.

"No."

Sam moved from Lucy's breasts to her mouth, touching their lips together gently as her tongue traced the outline of her soft, full lips. "I don't want to pressure you," she whispered. Even though she was dying, she wanted Lucy to know she was sincere.

Lucy's face was completely flushed, her eyelids heavy. "I can't resist you when you move like this."

"Like what?" Sam moved a lock of hair to kiss the other side of Lucy's face.

"Like the way you're moving right now."

"Huh?"

"Oh my God"—Lucy bit her bottom lip—"you don't even know you're doing it, do you?"

"Doing what?"

"Your hips, they move when you kiss me. Every time."

Sam felt her face get hot. "They do?"

"They do."

She pulled back a little. "Do you want me to stop?"

"God, no."

Sam leaned in and kissed her hard and soft at the same time, holding their bodies close before she flipped them in one smooth motion. She moved on top of Lucy and positioned herself between her legs. She was grinding a little, and for the first time, she was completely aware of it. She almost couldn't help it—she was hard as fuck and she could feel her clit pounding through her whole body. Lucy wanted her. It was obvious in everything, from the way she was moving, to her body language, to the way they were kissing. She was ready.

When she moved to kiss her way down Lucy's torso, Lucy held on to the bottom of her shirt and pulled it off. Sam couldn't help but smile at the clever maneuver. She kissed her soft flat stomach, letting her tongue graze repeatedly over a raised scar near her belly button. *What's the story there?* She might have asked but was immediately distracted when her hand brushed the crotch of Lucy's yoga pants. They were wet. She looked up at Lucy.

"I know." She covered her eyes with one hand. "What you do to me."

"That's hot."

"Embarrassing."

"Sexy."

Sam crawled back up Lucy's body, kissing her sweetly at first and then not so sweetly as she inched below her waistline. A quick glance between them told her that Lucy's panties were the same dark red color as her bra. Perhaps this was in the cards all along. Sam swallowed her smile and slipped one finger under the elastic near the thigh, letting her finger drift over to touch Lucy for real. She went nice and slow, knowing it was going to be fantastic.

When she heard Lucy's phone sound with the fourth text in under a minute, she stilled her hand.

"Ignore it," Lucy said.

"You sure?"

"If it was important they'd call." The words were barely out before the phone rang. "Goddamn it." Lucy pulled herself upright. "It's my sister," she said, obviously recognizing the specific ringtone. "Let me just get rid of her. She's clearly not going to stop on her own." Reaching past Sam, she grabbed her phone off the end table. "What, Em?"

For a second Sam watched Lucy listen to her sister. Then she came up behind her, slid her hands under her bralette and covered her breasts with each palm. She felt Lucy's breathing change at her touch. Sam was loving the effect she had on Lucy, who was writhing ever so slightly and seemed distracted from her conversation. Sam leaned forward to continue her onslaught, but Lucy suddenly moved away.

"Wait. What?" There was a pause. "Now?" Lucy stood up and moved across the room snatching her shirt off the floor. "No, it's okay. Let me go. I'll see you in a minute."

Sam's interest was piqued at Lucy's words and she could tell Lucy was frazzled. "My sister is on her way here. Like, now. She'll be here in a few minutes." She put her phone down and fixed her bra, throwing her shirt on over it. "It's a long story. She's having some problems with her wife."

"That sucks." Sam stood up and found her sweater. "Let me get out of your way here," she added, glancing around for her shoes while trying to get her messy hair back in place.

"No." Lucy took two steps closer. "Stay. Please?"

"Don't you want to talk to your sister?"

"Yes, but this is nothing new. They fight a lot." Lucy sighed. "Emily will hunker down and vent for a while and let Frankie put the kids to bed. Then she'll go home." She frowned and seemed to reconsider. "Actually she might crash here. She sounded pissed. But stay anyway. Please?"

"Are you sure?"

"Yes. I want to sleep next to you tonight." She hooked her pinky on Sam's belt loop. "I am begging a little here."

"Hey, it's fine with me. I don't want to leave. I was being polite."

"Well, stop." Lucy reached up and kissed Sam's cheek. "I have to change quick." She darted into the bedroom. "Thank God I answered the phone, by the way," she called over her shoulder. "Emily has a key and that would have made for one very awkward introduction."

A minute later, Sam was standing behind the kitchen island when the apartment door opened and Emily stepped inside, a confused look washing across her face at the sight of Sam.

"Hi." Sam waved. "Lucy'll be out in a second." She nodded toward the bedroom. "She just had to do something." It was a weird statement that didn't really mean anything. She watched Lucy's sister's eyes narrow for a second as she processed, and Sam tried to breeze over it by introducing herself. She extended her hand. "I'm—"

"Sam." Lucy's sister smiled, shaking Sam's hand as she nodded acknowledgment. "It is nice to meet you." She turned around as Lucy came out of the bedroom.

"Hey, Em." Lucy hugged her sister and walked over to Sam, rubbing her back affectionately. "You guys met, I see."

Lucy had changed into worn jeans and a cozy tee with a pretty low V-neck. If it was possible, she looked even better than before.

"Baby sister, you should have told me your girlfriend was here."

Sam checked a look at Lucy to gauge her reaction to the word they had yet to use for each other. Lucy didn't even blink.

"Oh, please, like it would have mattered." Lucy let out a low chuckle. "I know how you are when you get your mind set on something."

"Still, I feel bad. I'm sorry, *Sam*," she said, sticking her tongue at Lucy as she apologized.

Lucy responded in kind and held Sam's hand all the way to the couch where she curled under her arm as they listened to Emily's saga. It was nice being witness to Lucy's interaction with her sister. They clearly adored each other and it was interesting to see Lucy in a completely different environment than the coffee shop. After about an hour, Sam figured she should give them some time alone. She made an excuse about work, grabbed her things, and headed to Lucy's bedroom.

She didn't want to seem presumptuous, but Lucy had made it clear that she wanted her to stay, so she stripped down to her boxer briefs and T-shirt and slipped beneath the covers. The sheets were soft and smelled of Lucy and she could feel herself getting turned on already. This was going to be quite a challenge. She busied herself watching old episodes of *Friday Night Lights* and was almost dozing off when Lucy came into the room.

"How's your sister?" Sam asked through a yawn.

Lucy frowned and made a so-so gesture with one hand. "She thinks her wife is cheating on her."

"Really?" Sam put her device on the night table next to her. "Is she?"

Lucy twisted her mouth to the side obviously considering. "Eh, I doubt it. I just think that Frankie can be a piece of work sometimes." She crossed to the dresser and took off her watch. "I mean, I get that she works a lot, but still. My sister does everything. She takes care of the kids and the apartment and has her own job." She slid her jeans off. "It wouldn't kill her to pitch in more when she's home." She pulled her shirt over her head, sliding in next to Sam in her lacy bra and panties.

"Whoa, whoa, whoa." Sam leaned on one arm and her eyes took in the length of Lucy's body. "This is what you're sleeping in?"

Lucy laughed. "Is that a problem?"

Sam ran her hand along the curve of Lucy's waist up to and over the fabric of her bra. She kissed Lucy lightly and said in a soft, husky voice, "You're torturing me. You know that, right?"

Lucy smiled against her lips. "I'm actually being kind." She let her tongue graze Sam's mouth as she spoke. "This is *way* more than I usually wear to bed."

Sam kissed her good and hard before pulling away with a huge sigh. "Please tell me your sister is not going to be here tomorrow night."

Lucy turned and curled into Sam's body, taking her arm and wrapping it all the way around her waist. She kissed Sam sweetly. "Tomorrow it's just me and you. I promise."

"Will you close the store early?" Sam breathed out. "Like, noon, maybe?"

"It's trivia night. So no." Lucy chuckled again. Sam half laughed, half groaned with her. "Oh my God, I'm not gonna make it." She rested her forehead on Lucy's shoulder in mock defeat.

"I promise, you'll survive. And when you do, I will so make it worth the wait. One more day. Okay, babe?"

Sam smiled into Lucy's hair. The way she felt in this moment, about this woman, she would wait way longer than a day if Lucy wanted her to. But she kept that truth to herself. Instead she whimpered assent, hugged her close, and kissed her bare shoulder. It was going to be an excruciating twenty-four hours. "Good night, Luce."

❖

From the moment her phone woke her with a text from Blynn at an ungodly hour, Sam's day began its slow but steady veer off course. Their client wanted hands-on attention and the whole team was making the two-and-a-half hour journey to Hartford, Connecticut, to give them what they were paying for. At first, she still believed that she'd be back in Staten Island at a decent hour. Now, at seven p.m., hotel rooms had been secured and the prospect of going home tonight was long gone. Tomorrow wasn't looking much better. It should be good news—the customer was pleased and kept adding on to the project. Her bonus would surely reflect her efforts, but right now she couldn't care less about the money. She wanted one thing—Lucy.

She barely ate her dinner or participated in the conversation as her colleagues tossed around ideas for the expanded platform. She drained the last of her Jack and Coke and was pleased when the waiter noticed and brought another straightaway. She was hoping the alcohol would dull the pain she felt over what she was missing tonight. Even when she tried to focus, her mind drifted back to Lucy in her bed, in her arms, in her lacy bra and out of it. The thought made her pulse race.

"Where are you right now, Sam?"

Blynn's voice held more irritation than curiosity and Sam apologized immediately. This was still a working dinner. She should at least try to pay attention.

"Let's call it a night, people," Blynn ordered, essentially dismissing them. "We'll pick this back up tomorrow at nine." The crew gathered their belongings and said good night, but with a nearly full drink, Sam didn't move. Blynn stayed put as well and Sam watched her eyes follow their colleagues out of the restaurant before she faced her.

"Keep your head in the game when we're working, Sam."

"Yep." She shook the ice in her drink. "Sorry about that."

"That's better." Blynn took a sip of her wine and moved slightly closer. "I know it was a long day." Sam felt a hand on her knee under the table and tried to move her chair, but she was backed into the corner against the wall.

"We have the whole night to work out"—she made a small circle with her wineglass—"whatever it is that's got you so completely distracted."

"About that..." Sam started.

Blynn's hand sped up her leg until it hit her crotch. Sam jerked and reached down to grab it. "Blynn."

Blynn frowned dramatically, still dominating the conversation. "Well that's sad." She sulked a little. "I so hoped you'd already be wearing it for me." She licked her lips slowly and suggestively. "No matter." Leaning forward, she whispered, "Finish your drink and go get ready. I can't wait to have your dick inside me."

She hated herself for it, but Sam throbbed hard at the overt suggestion. It was racy and over the top but it embodied the very things she enjoyed about their arrangement. There was no pretense. Blynn was direct about what she wanted, and in the past Sam had always been more than willing to give it to her. The chemistry between them was unbelievable. Maybe it was their circumstance or the shifting of their boardroom to bedroom dynamic. Sam was almost tempted, but when Blynn stood from the table, Sam stopped her. "Wait."

"Is there a problem?" Her voice was completely condescending.

"Sit down for a second."

Blynn looked around and sat back down, obviously annoyed at the need for more conversation.

"Blynn, I can't."

"Can't what?"

"Do this." Sam wagged two fingers between them. "Not anymore. I'm sorry."

Blynn looked up at the ceiling and let out a frustrated sigh. "What's going on with you, Sam? You were out of it all day." She held her hands up, clearly expecting an explanation. "And now suddenly you have a conscience?"

Even though she was confused by the comment, she let it go. "I'm kind of with someone."

"Well, good for you." Blynn smirked. She waited a second, jutting out her chin before she spoke. "We're not dating, Sam. We're fucking. You'll forgive me if I don't really care about the nuances of your love life."

"Jesus, Blynn." Sam shook her head. "That's not what I meant. I like this girl." Sam looked right at her.

Blynn raised her eyebrows in obvious challenge. "And what, you think I don't like my wife? Feelings don't factor in. That's the beauty of it."

"Hold on a second." Sam held up her hand. "You're married?"

"Please, Sam, don't play dumb. It's beneath you."

"I didn't know," Sam admitted in a low voice.

They had never, ever talked about their personal lives. Sam rarely worked at the office, so she simply didn't keep up with the day-to-day the way some of her co-workers did. She liked it that way. Work was work. This tidbit about Blynn's private life threw her for a loop. Even though when she took a moment to process, it made complete sense. Blynn was a beautiful, smart, successful woman in her thirties. Of course she wasn't single. Sam sank into her chair letting the truth resonate. Had she simply avoided the obvious because it was convenient for her? She huffed out a breath, disappointed in herself on multiple levels.

"Look, Blynn." She struggled for the right words. "Obviously I think you're attractive, and I really…have a good time with you." Did that sound insensitive? She cringed inside but held eye contact. "This girl is special. I'm sorry." She paused for a second before continuing. "I hope this won't affect our working relationship—"

"Christ, Sam. Grow up." Blynn flicked her hair off her shoulders. "Just bring your fucking A game tomorrow. You were a goddamn train wreck today." She stood up and backed away. "I hope your little girlfriend is worth it," she added with an obnoxious smile. "But when you decide she isn't"—she tilted her head in subtle invitation—"you know where to find me."

Sam peered through the glass wall that separated the hotel restaurant from the lobby as Blynn sashayed to the elevator. God, she was sexy. But damn, all she could think about was Lucy. Out of the blue it occurred to her they had never discussed being exclusive. She smiled to herself. It didn't matter. She only wanted one person right now. And it was not her persuasive sexy pseudo-boss or the temptation of a sure thing.

She reached for her phone, secretly hoping to steal a few minutes of playful chitchat with Lucy before things got under way at the coffee shop. She chewed the inside of her cheek as her thumbs banged away, excited to hear the tidbits of Lucy's day. But first things first. She missed Lucy's gorgeous face, so she fired off a quick request and crossed her fingers in hopes Lucy would comply.

Show me you.

❖

"Hey, Luce, your phone is blowing up over here," Meg called from the counter of the coffee shop. "Where did you want me to put this?" She lifted a box full of napkin refills as Lucy approached.

"Could you put those in the back for me?" Lucy stopped to read her message. "Thanks, Meg."

"Please tell me you're texting Sam and she's on her way."

"I am, but she's not coming." Lucy held her phone at arm's length above her, angling and smiling as she spoke. "She's away for work."

"Oh my God, are you sending her a selfie?"

"Do you need another assignment?" Lucy said in response.

"When you're done making goo-goo eyes at each other, tell her I said hi, and she fucked us over for tonight."

"Sure," Lucy answered, barely paying attention.

Meg laughed at Lucy, as she watched two more people filter in off the street. Bay Westers. Cool. She nodded at them from across the space. Trivia night was her favorite. For starters, it drew a completely random crowd. Over in one corner she recognized a mature foursome from last month. They'd been formidable opponents, surprising everyone by owning the pop culture questions. The college crowd was arriving in bursts—the students first, then a few TAs by the looks of them. Sometimes a crew of profs even joined the ranks. It was a good time. Lucy and her staff kept the coffee and sweets coming, including bonus cookies or espresso shots for the team that took each round. Overall winners scored free coffee for a week, with the runners-up snagging a four-pack of five-dollar gift cards. Not bad for a night of competitive fun.

Lexi and Jesse arrived and Meg greeted them at the door. "Hey. You guys heard Sam's away?" She watched them exchange a look. "So it's just the three of us." She ushered them over to a table near the counter. "Too bad we didn't know sooner. I would have tried to grab Tracy or Betsy. I mean, it's so not their thing, but you never know."

Lexi smiled. "Well, who knows, maybe we can pick up a solo."

Meg went to the bar and grabbed three lattes and a few peanut butter bars. She turned around and almost dropped her loot when she spotted Sasha in the doorway. God knew how long she would have kept staring if she hadn't been distracted by Lexi waving Sasha over enthusiastically. They got to the table at the same time.

"Sasha, do you have a team already?" Lexi's voice was animated.

"Uh, no."

"Awesome. Play with us. We're short anyway."

Meg put their drinks on the table, still in shock over what was happening. "Do you want coffee or something?" She knew she sounded confused—even she could hear it in her voice.

"I can get it," Sasha said.

Meg looked at her friends' blank faces but said nothing, choosing instead to follow Sasha the short distance to the counter. Catching the end of her drink order, Meg added, "And a peanut butter bar." Sasha looked at her in question. "Trust me."

"Okay. And a peanut butter bar," Sasha said to the girl ringing her up.

There was no way to mask her surprise, so Meg owned it. "What are you doing here, Sash?" She grabbed a few extra napkins while Sasha waited for her change.

"I heard this was a fun thing." She lifted her paper cup with a little whimsy. "I wanted to check it out." A smile played at the corner of her mouth. "Not gonna lie. Based on the location, and how much you love stuff like this, I thought I might run into you." She secured her money in her purse and scooped up her treat. "I hope that's okay."

"Yeah, of course." Meg didn't know how to feel about that statement, so she pushed it right out of her mind and got into game mode. "Have you played before?" She was pretty sure the answer was no, but figured she should ask anyway. Sasha hung out at gay bars now, so who knows what else she might have explored since they'd last spent time together. "Like, at a bar or whatever?"

"No." She winced. "Should I be nervous?"

Meg smiled reassuringly. "Not at all." She pulled Sasha's chair out for her reflexively. "Lucy does a three game cycle. Each game has five rounds with five questions in each. Every time a team wins a round, they get, like, a fancy coffee shot she's got all whipped up and ready to go. It's usually flavored—pumpkin, French vanilla, something like that."

"They're amazeballs," Lexi said, getting her two cents in.

"Sometimes they throw in a cookie too, or whatever else she has on hand." Meg tapped her latte on the table. "At the end of the night whichever team is the overall winner gets a free pass." She waved her hand around the shop. "Drinks on the house all week."

"Great. I'm ready."

"That probably doesn't help you much, huh?" Jesse lifted her cup and gestured to it with her chin. "Free coffee."

"No big." Sasha shrugged and smiled. "I'm here for the company."

"And the competition," Lexi chimed in, raising her coffee.

"You may live to regret this, Sash." Meg held her thumb and index finger a fraction of an inch apart. "We have, on occasion, gotten a wee bit carried away."

"Nope. I'm down." Sasha lifted her drink to meet Lexi's. "I'll tell you right off, I know nothing about sports. Pop culture, music, obscure history"—she pointed her finger at herself—"look no farther, I'm your girl."

"Looks like we have ourselves a killer team." Jesse joined the toast.

Meg was only a half second behind her, meeting the gang in the center of the table with her drink. She could feel the cheesy smile plastered across her face. She didn't care. Even though she wasn't exactly sure what this night would hold, there were games, great people, and coffee. She was in heaven.

❖

Almost three hours later, they walked in pairs along the main road that stretched from Lucy's up to Bay West, each armed with a punch card entitling them to a week of free beverages. Nearing the entrance, Sasha lingered, not making the turn into the development.

"I guess this is where I leave you." Her slight laugh held some angst.

Meg felt it too. Against her better judgment, she wasn't ready for their time together to be over. "Right," she managed.

"Thanks for letting me join you guys." Sasha looked right at Meg. "It was a really great night."

If things had been at all different, if they'd been buddies instead of exes, Meg would have invited Sasha back to her house, insist that she crash for the night in lieu of going back to the city by herself. But they weren't. They'd had a terrible breakup and since then had hung out exactly two times in the last year. That barely constituted friendship. Still, she could be kind.

"Do you want me to walk you up to the bus stop? I can wait with you until the express bus comes."

Sasha shook her head, a thin smile etched across her gorgeous face. "No, thanks. I'm okay." She pulled out her phone. "I downloaded the schedule. The X1 will be here in just a few minutes."

"You sure?"

Sasha reached into her bag and retrieved the coffee voucher. She held it out to Meg. "Here, give this to one of your friends."

Meg frowned, taking it reluctantly. "Sort of blows that you get nothing for the win."

Sasha's smile reached her eyes. "I wouldn't say *nothing*." Meg couldn't help but notice the lilt in her voice when she responded. Sasha stepped forward and placed a small kiss on Meg's cheek. Backing away, she gave Lexi and Jesse each a small wave before she turned and bounced in the direction of the service road.

Meg was still watching her firm bottom sway with each step when Jesse squeezed both shoulders and leaned into her ear. "Now that, my young Padawan, *that* was something."

CHAPTER TWELVE

L exi stood in front of her closet in her bra and thong, contemplating what to wear. It was still unbelievably cool for almost summer. She fanned through multiple pairs of jeans that were all virtually the same. Where would she find room for maternity clothes? That's if she actually needed them anytime in the near future. She tilted her head back, frustrated that she and Jesse were still at a stalemate. She had one theory she thought might work. She brushed her palm against the fabric of a thin knit sweater hanging in front of her, wondering what was keeping her from putting it up for consideration. She heard the clank of the dishes being put away downstairs and decided to just go for it.

"Hey, babe." She leaned her body through the bedroom doorway calling down to the first floor. "Can you come up here for a sec?"

"In a minute," Jesse answered.

Lexi paced the bedroom, kneading her hands and kind of wishing she had given this presentation just a little more thought.

"Everything okay?" Jesse asked, as she bounded up the stairs. She stopped short in the doorway. "Well, hello," she crooned, giving Lexi and her skimpy attire an exaggerated once over. A guttural moan escaped her as she kissed Lexi onto the bed, misreading Lexi's intent. "Don't you have to leave soon?" she whispered in Lexi's ear.

"Yes." Lexi returned her kisses anyway. Even a year into their marriage, Lexi still had a hard time resisting Jesse, even if it meant being late for the first social she was running.

"Oh no." Jesse rolled off her and groaned in frustration. "I'm not going to be the reason you get in trouble with Kam Browne." She made an effort to sit up, but Lexi held her shoulder.

"Wait."

"Babe, you have to get ready."

Lexi turned on her side letting her nails lightly graze Jesse's stomach, from her belly button down under the waistline of her jeans. She pouted playfully. "Are you trying to get rid of me?"

"Never, babe." Jesse kissed her soundly before pulling back. "Especially not when you're dressed like this." She tucked a strand of Lexi's hair behind her ear. "But you and Meg are in charge of the social tonight. It's a big deal. You can't be late." Lexi saw desire despite her protest. "So I'm being an adult and showing restraint."

Lexi felt herself melt a little at the heartfelt overture. She rolled on top of Jesse, smiled suggestively, and kissed her. "I have, like, an hour before the doors even open. And it's around the block." She sat up in a full straddle on top of Jesse. "But I want to talk to you anyway." She toyed with the buttons on Jesse's shirt, opening two more so she could touch her fingertips to Jesse's chest.

"What's going on?" Jesse held Lexi's waist, leaning upright and holding her in place. "Tell me things." She kissed Lexi's chest gently before looking up at her.

"You love me, right?"

Jesse furrowed her brow at the ridiculous question.

"How much?"

Inching forward, Jesse kissed her soft and slow, deep and full. "The most. You know that."

Lexi couldn't help herself—she moved her hips instinctively at Jesse's words and her touch. "I have an idea." She used her body weight to push them down to the mattress, and spread her legs wider, the need to feel Jesse increasing with each passing second. "God," she breathed out, glancing down between their bodies to where Jesse's button fly made contact with her tiny black panties. "I would let you come in me all the time if you could."

Jesse bucked hard in response. She held Lexi tight, her hand moving up to Lexi's face guiding her closer. "That turned me on more than it should, I think."

"I know. The thought of it turns me on too." She kissed Jesse, slowing her movements slightly so she could look in her eyes. "That's the point though. I want to have a baby." She held eye contact. "But it's not just that. Jess, I want to have *your* baby."

"Honey…"

Lexi put one finger over her lips. "Just hear me out." She leaned back a little and watched Jesse's expression soften. "I've given this some thought." Her fingertips squared the outline of Jesse's unbelievable abs. "I get that you don't want to use Justin as a donor."

"Babe, I'm sorry—"

Lexi silenced her again. "No, I mean it, Jess. I get it." She nodded sincerely even as she worried her lip over what she was about to suggest. "What about if you did it?" She saw Jesse trying hard to control her cringe and she was dying to make it easier for her. "I know you don't want to carry, that's not what I'm saying." She spread her fingers wider to feel more of Jesse's body against her hand. "I have the baby. We use your egg." She bit the corner of her mouth waiting for Jesse's reaction. "And ask Nick to be the donor."

"*Nick*, Nick?" Jesse dropped her chin. "My Nick?" She pointed at herself.

Lexi nodded.

"As in my friend, the PI, who goes home with a new guy every weekend? That Nick?"

"Yes. That Nick." Lexi smiled because she couldn't help finding Jesse's complete surprise utterly adorable. "Your Nick. The PI." She added a nod for effect. "Gay playboy Nick."

Jesse narrowed her eyes. "Where is this even coming from?"

"I know it seems ridiculous, but think about it. Jess, you've known him for a hundred years." She sat up a little. "And I know he's not necessarily the settling-down type, but that's okay. Maybe even better, in a way." She read Jesse's hesitation. This was going to be a hard sell.

Lexi leaned all the way forward, edging her finger along Jesse's chiseled jaw. "Hear me out. Nick is sweet and smart and we know him. And"—she paused, hoping to rein in the excitement she heard in her voice—"don't you remember last year when we had dinner with him, he was telling us about his friend who had done this exact thing for a lesbian couple he was friends with? Nick used a term for it. He kept saying his friend had become a—"

"Bio-dad."

"Yes." She smiled. "You remember."

"I do."

Lexi was pleased and touched at the shared memory but she wasn't done. "Jess, he thought it was cool. So did I."

She could feel Jesse's energy changing, however subtly. "Babe, I never knew Anthony. You know, my moms' friend. The guy they used as my donor or whatever you want to call him. He died when I was a baby. And believe me, I wouldn't change a thing. I love my moms. Both of them. Anthony would never have been my father. Not in the traditional sense." She shrugged a little. "Look, I have stories from Chris and Marnie. And pictures, which is great." She smiled and shrugged at the same time. "But sometimes I think it might have been nice to have known him a little. See what he was like, if we have the same mannerisms or laugh or anything." She looked right at Jesse. "We could have that with Nick."

Jesse reached up and touched the side of her face, keeping her hand in place as she moved her thumb over a dimple. "You are so beautiful."

Lexi smiled and turned her face to place a kiss in the palm of her wife's hand. "So are you. It's why I want our kids to look like you." She leaned all the way forward and her breasts touched Jesse's. "I'm just asking you to consider it, that's all."

"We would still need to put something legally binding in place."

"Of course." Lexi kissed her face. It was hard to be this close and not acknowledge her desire. "Two parents. Me and you. Not negotiable." She let her hand drift between Jesse's legs.

"I think we should sit down and have a conversation with Nick."

"For real?" Lexi asked.

Jesse nodded. "My gut tells me he'll do it."

"Mine too." Lexi's smile stretched ear to ear. "Are you okay with it if he's willing?"

"I am."

Lexi pulled back an inch to assess Jesse's reaction and saw with absolute certainty that they were completely in sync. "I love you so much."

"I love you too." Jesse kissed her softly but Lexi was ready for more. She pressed her whole body into Jesse's and used her momentum to flip them so Jesse was on top of her. Jesse's body responded, even if her words belied her. "Lex, you have to go."

Lexi didn't even bother to check the clock on the nightstand. "We have plenty of time." She wrapped her legs around Jesse's waist. "Plus, I can tell you already"—she let out a gasp at the feel of Jesse's hand between her legs—"this is not going to take long at all."

❖

"Well, if it isn't the new Kameron Browne." Sam stepped in front of Meg who was stationed just inside the door to the Commons, ready to check IDs and collect the cover charge. Sam handed over a twenty.

"Never call me that," Meg said, taking her money.

Sam laughed at Meg's deadpan response. "You can keep whatever the change is. My contribution to a community I hope to call home sooner rather than later." Sam moved aside to talk as a small line of people queued near the entrance. "Where's Lex?"

"She's running late or something. She just texted she'll be here in a minute."

"You need help?"

"I think I got it, but come back here anyway."

Sam slipped in alongside Meg, her eyes focused on the party room. "Looks good. Not much different than before. But the new DJ sounds promising."

Meg doled out change to a patron with a wink and a smile before addressing Sam's comment. "Yeah, Kam wouldn't let us make too many real changes just yet." She shrugged. "Other than the social media and marketing stuff." She smirked. "Which is most of the changes that you made." Meg held up her fist for a pound. "So here's to success."

"Fingers crossed." Sam fist-bumped her. "You didn't see Lucy, right?"

"I figured she'd come with you." Meg fiddled with the credit card scanner making sure it was plugged in. "Awesome she's finally going to make an appearance at a social. I can't wait to hang with her. You know, outside of the coffee shop."

"You and me both," Sam said almost under her breath. "She's never come at all, huh?"

Meg frowned. "Not that I'm aware of." A large group of college-age girls crowded the check in table stealing Meg's attention. Sam helped inspect their driver's licenses to make sure they were legal.

"OMG, has this place been here long?" One of the girls craned her head to see past Meg and Sam into the Commons.

"Yeah, kind of," Meg responded.

"We're experiencing a rebirth of sorts," Sam added, taking payments and stamping hands. "You ladies new to the area?"

"We're from Rutgers University over in Jersey. I saw some stuff on Twitter about it, figured we'd check it out."

Meg grabbed a handful of drink tickets. "First one's on Bay West. Have a good time, girls."

Lexi snuck in behind the college party. "Sorry I'm late, guys." She scooted into place with Jesse on her heels. "That was a decent-sized group, huh."

"Compliments of Sam's social media push."

"That's fantastic. Babe, would you get me a drink?" she said to Jesse before turning to her friends. "You guys want something?"

"I'll take a beer," Meg said.

"Why not?" Sam echoed. "I can walk to the bar with you, Jess."

"No, stay," Lexi implored. "I want to hear about your trip. Did you just get back? Where's Lucy?" she asked looking around.

Sam laughed at the barrage of questions. "Settle down, Munchkin." She placed her hands on Lexi's shoulders. "Breathe," she ordered. "Everything okay with you?"

"Yeah, Lex. What's up?" Meg reorganized the table for the third time. "First you're late and now you're frazzled as fuck. What's going on?"

"I'm fine." She looked between Meg and Sam and must have read concern on their faces because she squared her shoulders and took a dramatically deep breath. "Seriously." She checked a look at the bar. "Jess and I were talking and I just lost track of time."

Meg rolled her eyes. "Oh my God, you were totally having sex."

"I wasn't," she answered, but her deep red blush said it all.

"Here Sam and I are holding down the fort at a Friday night social while our *married* friend is getting action. What's wrong with that picture?" Meg looked to Sam for support but corrected herself on the spot. "I don't know why I'm looking to you for help—your girlfriend will be here imminently. I'm the only sad sack in this crowd."

"No one feels bad for you, Meg." Lexi brushed her off good-naturedly, waving her arm at the building crowd. "Lesbian Shangri-la. Go, mingle." She faced Sam. "Where is Lucy? I thought you said she was coming."

"She's supposed to meet me here." Sam looked at her watch and swallowed her jitters. Nine fifteen. Too late for the shop to still be open. Lucy had suggested meeting up at the social, so she could put in some extra time at the store and grab a shower beforehand. Sam had agreed, primarily because she thought if they met at Lucy's first, it was unlikely they'd leave at all. Her body had been counting down the days since she'd been stuck in Connecticut. It would take a lot to keep her libido in check. This social was important to her friends and she wanted to support them. The minutes rolled by and still no Lucy.

"I'm actually going to give her a call," she said, taking her drink from Jesse and thanking her with a nod of her chin before she stepped out onto the balcony. She hoped she sounded chill, even though she could feel the tension spreading through her limbs.

The phone rang four times before going to voicemail. She paced the outdoor space back and forth, checking her phone, for what, she wasn't sure. Finally, a text popped up.

Got tied up at the store. I'm pretty beat. Rain check on the social?

You're not coming?

I'm tired. My day starts early tomorrow.

Sam started typing, but then erased her message. Two more false starts while she attempted to voice her feelings and keep her cool. Another message from Lucy came through while she hesitated.

Please don't be mad. I still want to see you. A second passed. *Come by later?*

You'll be asleep. Early day and all... She wondered if her sharp sarcasm translated or if Lucy read the message as sincere.

I'll wait for you. Or if it's real late, I can leave the door open.

Sam tried to be mature for a second. *Luce, I know you have work in the morning. I only get you for a few hours, please come and hang out with me.*

Just come here after.

Sam rolled her neck in frustration. *Please. For me?* She hated that she was reduced to begging.

There was a long pause. Sam hoped it meant that Lucy was checking herself out in the mirror, internally debating whether she should change or if she looked presentable.

I can't, Sam. I'm sorry.

Why not?

I just can't. Have fun with your friends. We'll talk tomorrow.

She wanted to throw her phone off the balcony. She wanted to scream in aggravation. What the fuck? She looked at her beer but had no desire to drink it. Through the tinted glass façade she watched Lexi and Meg working away. They'd be busy the whole night. What difference did it make if she stayed? She wouldn't relax anyway.

She walked to the end of the corridor, tossed her bottle in with the recyclables, and slipped down the back stairs taking long strides as she made her way through the path to the rental section until she was knocking heavily on Lucy's door.

Lucy held it open wide, not appearing the least bit surprised to see Sam on her step, but she was already on the defensive. "You didn't have to come."

"I kind of did."

"Sam, I don't want to fight. Go back. Hang out with your friends. We can do this tomorrow."

"Why are you trying to push me away right now?" Sam stuffed her hands in her pockets. "Did something happen while I was gone?" The thought hadn't even occurred to her until this moment and she froze waiting for Lucy's response.

Lucy shook her head. "Of course not." She looked offended at Sam's inference. "You were only gone three days."

"I don't know, Luce." Sam shrugged. "Something's different."

Lucy grabbed the sleeve of her hoodie. "Come in here." She pulled her into the vestibule and stood on tiptoe to kiss her gently. "There's no one else." She found her lips again and Sam couldn't resist—she removed her hands from her pockets and held Lucy's waist, bringing them closer. Lucy touched Sam's face gently. Her voice was soft. "I missed you."

"Why wouldn't you come see me then?"

Above them a timer dinged loudly from behind Lucy's apartment door. She frowned slightly. "I have stuff in the oven."

"Of course you do," Sam said.

"Come." Lucy took Sam's hand and guided her up the stairs.

Inside it smelled like a full-fledged bakery, the countertops lined with trays of cookies and muffins. Lucy bent over to remove a tray from the low rack in the oven, and Sam's pulse quickened at the sight of her slim waist and firm bottom on display. Even in pajama pants, Lucy's tight body got her going. As much as she wanted to inch up behind her and slide her hands under her worn tee and dispense with talking altogether, she could sense this was a conversation they needed to have.

Sam leaned back on the counter and watched Lucy set a fresh batch of scones on the stove top.

"Tell me what happened tonight."

Lucy kept her eyes on the tray, using a thin silicone mitt to inch it forward ever so slightly. She opened her mouth to say something, but then stopped. Sam watched her bite her lower lip, tilting her head back and letting out a long slow breath. She kept her eyes on the backsplash. "I panicked."

"Panicked over what?" Lucy turned around and her face held genuine anguish. It completely melted Sam. "Babe, it's okay. Whatever it is, you can tell me."

"You'll think I'm crazy." She lifted a spatula and hovered over the scones. "Maybe I am."

"Lucy, just talk to me. I think you already know how I feel about you." She waited for her to look over. "You stood me up. There has to be a reason. I want to know what it is."

"I don't really go to the socials," she started.

"I know. The girls told me." Sam unzipped her hoodie and hung it off the pantry doorknob. "Do you not like those guys?" It didn't seem likely, but she figured she should at least ask.

Lucy snickered at the suggestion. "Of course I like them. They're my friends. It's not that."

They were both quiet for a moment.

"It's the drinking, right?" Sam asked, voicing a fear she'd had for a while.

"It's not like you think, Sam."

She had been worried about this. It was stupid maybe, but she couldn't fathom how they could reasonably date and socialize with her friends—their friends—and never be around alcohol. Not that she needed to party all the time, but so much of her social life and her friends' social lives involved drinking of some sort that she almost couldn't imagine a life without it. She wasn't even sure she wanted to.

Lucy must have read the stress on her face. "See, I can tell you're freaking out right now. Don't." She turned back to her scones. "I don't really have a hard time being around it. The drinking, I mean." She started moving her pastries to the cooling rack as she spoke. "There's just never been any reason for me to go to a social. They start late. My hours are always early, so I usually just don't go." She looked back at Sam. "Sometimes I feel like I'm missing out but"—she gave a small shrug—"it's a price worth paying to keep my business and my sobriety." She placed the tray in the sink. "It's not a terrible sacrifice. I get to see everyone in the coffee shop."

"But we made plans to meet up there tonight. And we hadn't seen each other in days. If it's not about the drinking, I don't get what happened." She gripped her keys in her front pocket.

"This thing about not going to the socials, there's no reason. I'm not against them. And the other day, when I suggested it to you, I thought it would be fine. Believe me, my whole family drinks, it's not a temptation for me. But tonight…was different."

"Why?"

"Because Sam, it just was."

It didn't make sense. "There's a piece missing." She rubbed her hands on her jeans as she considered the possibilities but came up with nothing. "What is it you're not telling me?"

"It's embarrassing."

"Just talk to me. You can tell me anything. You know that."

Lucy looked up and took a deep breath. Sam thought she was going to unload something heavy, so she planted herself firmly on a stool. She hoped Lucy took the gesture as a sign that she wasn't going anywhere no matter what she was about to reveal.

Finally Lucy turned around to face her. She crossed her arms and leaned against the stove.

"I told you before I drank a lot, too much. I don't know, maybe I had a problem." She was clearly uncomfortable with the topic and her focus drifted across the room as she spoke. "But after everything that happened with the police department, the shooting incident and leaving, I stopped. Completely. I changed my whole life. I started over." She rested the base of her heel against her calf, balancing on one foot. "It's been great. I have no regrets. Truly." She reached for a towel and twisted it in her hands. "I have the store. I live here. I met you." She looked right at Sam, her gray eyes full of emotion. "You are wonderful and sweet and sexy and God I want to be with you."

"But?"

"That's just it. There's no but." She uncrossed her arms and fiddled with the drawstring on her loose PJ's, wrapping it around her index finger. "I just got scared about tonight."

"But, Luce, it's me."

"I know Sam. Believe me, I know." She widened her eyes for emphasis, even as she broke eye contact. "Before you left for Connecticut, we were at a certain point. You know what I mean." She put both feet on the ground but still wouldn't look Sam in the eye. "I think we both know that things were moving to the next level, so to speak."

Sam almost interrupted her, but Lucy wasn't done.

"I got nervous for tonight. Self-conscious about being with you. And then, the more I thought about it, I got incredibly nervous about going to the social, being around the alcohol." She frowned. "That's not happened to me"—she shook her head slowly from side to side—"ever. It freaked me out in a way that I can't even explain."

"You could have told me that. We would have changed the plan."

"Tonight was important to Meg and Lexi. I know you wanted to go. I didn't want to ruin that for you." She held her hair back with both hands looking desperate in her frustration. "Clearly I've failed there too."

"Stop, it's fine. There'll be other socials." She pitched forward a little in her seat. "I am more concerned about me and you." Across the small space, she took Lucy's hand in her own. "Do not be nervous about us." She tugged at her, gently inching her forward, but Lucy resisted. "We don't have to do anything. Honestly." She looked right in Lucy's eyes as she laced their fingers together and pulled Lucy toward her. "I just want to be with you. We can watch a movie, cuddle on the couch or even in bed like we did the other night. That was nice. Believe me." She pressed her lips to Lucy's forehead and held her tightly. "We will wait until you are sure and comfortable and relaxed."

With her elbows resting on Sam's shoulders, Lucy ran her fingers through Sam's lustrous hair. "Why are you so good to me?"

"Because I like you. Like, a lot."

Lucy buried her face in Sam's shoulder and let out a pitiful moan. "Sam?"

"Yeah?"

"I haven't had sex with anyone in three years." Lucy's voice sounded clearly distressed even though it was muffled in Sam's shirt.

It wasn't what she'd expected to hear but Sam took it in stride. "That's okay."

"There's more." Lucy didn't wait for Sam to comment. "It's been way longer than that if we're talking sober. I couldn't even tell you when that was." Lucy sounded like she might lose courage altogether.

"It's okay."

"Is it?"

Sam pressed her lips to Lucy's, putting a hand at the back of her neck and holding her in place. The kiss was more sweet than sexy, but she wanted Lucy to feel how much she meant it. "Yes."

Lucy touched their foreheads together. "The irony is the other night, before my sister did her surprise pop in, I was fine, I was... ready." She looked shy to admit it. "But then you went away and I had three days to totally overthink everything." She moved her head from side to side. "And then, tonight, the social, complete meltdown."

Sam grinned. "So you stayed home and baked a thousand cookies."

"And scones," she added optimistically.

"On the upside, it smells amazing in here," Sam said through a thin smile. "So what happens now?" She turned Lucy in her arms, cradling her from behind, so they were both facing the stove and the mountain of baked goods. "Do we wrap all this goodness up and watch some TV?"

"We definitely pack this stuff up." She brought Sam's hand to her mouth and brushed her knuckles with her lips as she spoke. "Will you stay here tonight?"

"Yes." Sam pushed off the chair. "I want to get my bag out of my truck. I need my toothbrush and everything."

"You do that and I'll clean up here. Then bed?" she said with a question in her voice. "We can talk. I missed you." She kissed the back of Sam's hand a few times. "I want to hear about your trip. Would that be okay?"

"Perfect."

❖

When Sam came out of the bathroom, Lucy was already in bed, the blanket resting on her belly, a lacy bra the only clothing she could see, although she felt confident there were panties too, the same routine as last time. Jesus, this was not going to be easy.

She almost made a quippy remark, but in light of their talk, she held it in. She crossed the room to the window, dropping her bag on a chair that she didn't remember from the last time she'd been in Lucy's bedroom. She undid the top few buttons of her shirt before pulling it over her head.

"Is this chair new?" she asked, her belt buckle clanking loudly as she folded her jeans without removing it from the loops.

"It is, actually. I'm glad you noticed it." Lucy turned on her side and watched Sam stuff her socks into her chukka boots. "My sister was cleaning house this week while her wife was away. She was going to throw it out, but I took it instead." She rubbed the mattress as she spoke. "I put it in that corner so you could sit there and stare at the moon when you're here."

"Are you serious?"

She patted the spot next to her on the bed. "Yes."

"That is so nice."

Lucy shrugged and smiled at the same time. "I like you a little bit." She added a wink. "Do you draw a lot?"

Sam climbed in next to her. "Sometimes when I'm coming up with ideas. On little slips of paper, the back of an envelope, or whatever I can find. Like that time you saw me in the store. Not like on a canvas or anything." She took off her watch and placed it next to her phone on the small night table. "I would never attempt a portrait or anything, so don't get your hopes up," she said, turning back to face Lucy. She looked at Lucy's body and shook her head slowly. "Why am I telling you this, when I have you nearly naked in front of me?" She blinked slowly. "Scratch that. I totally draw, but I need practice on my nudes. You'll sit for me?"

Lucy rolled her eyes as she smiled. "You're such a brat."

"You love it."

"Come here and kiss me already."

Sam followed the instructions precisely, but after a second she pulled away and sat upright. "Sorry, I don't know how I forgot to take this off before. Something to do with the gorgeous half-naked woman two feet from me," she said, expertly removing her sports bra without taking off her undershirt, slipping it through the sleeve and tossing it onto the floor.

Lucy was clearly impressed at her deftness. "That looked like a practiced move."

Sam cozied into her pillow. "I may have done it once or twice before."

"I bet."

"I wish I could give you a great story there, but honestly it's mostly a learned move from high school. I was always getting changed somewhere before or after school or practice, in the locker room or my parents' car." She ran her hands through her hair. "Really unsexy stuff."

"What sports did you play?" Lucy rested her hand on Sam's stomach, but over her shirt. It got her revved up anyway.

"Softball and basketball."

Lucy dropped a kiss on her shoulder. "Positions?"

"Basketball, I was a forward but I hardly played." She touched the ends of Lucy's soft hair, feeling it flow through her fingers. "My team was very good. I was only so-so." She brought Lucy's hand to her mouth to kiss it once before she returned it to its spot on her abdomen. "Softball, I could do anything really, but I always ended up at first, because you know, left-handed." She waved for emphasis.

"Right."

"Did you play sports?" She was sort of surprised this hadn't come up sooner.

Lucy nodded. "Volleyball. That's it."

"Didn't like it?"

"Eh, I was only in it for the girls."

"And how'd that work out for you?" she asked through her smile.

"Not terrible, actually."

"Did you have a girlfriend in high school?" Her hand left Lucy's hair and her fingertips trailed the middle of her back, over the edges of her bra, and then dipping under it to feel the soft skin there.

Lucy was enjoying her touch, she could tell. She moved closer to Sam and she almost purred as she spoke. "I dated a few girls in high school. One on the volleyball team but only briefly. I think she just wanted to say she made out with a girl. But after that, in my senior year I had a real girlfriend."

"Do tell."

"Mmm, God your hands are so soft." Sam smiled and followed the curve of her spine to her waist. It took a second but Lucy got back on track. "Well, I was in high school, but Jocelyn was one of Emily's and Frankie's friends. A college girl," she added with a knowing look.

"Uh-oh," Sam teased.

Lucy smiled. "No, she was great. Took me to prom and everything."

"And how was that?"

"Typical." Lucy shrugged lightly.

"Typical?" She stilled her hand. "What is typical about two girls going to the prom together? Even in New York. Come on, elaborate."

"Fair enough." She giggled again. "It really wasn't that big of a deal though. I mean, Emily and Frankie had gone to the prom together the year before. People were probably like, oh, there go those Weston girls again." She laughed at herself. "What I meant was it was a typical prom. We went to the dance, then out to a club, then to a hotel." She shrugged. "She was sweet, Jocelyn. Like you," she nodded with her chin. "No pressure."

"Wait. That was your first time? Prom night?"

"It was." Lucy made an *eek* face. "I know, ridiculously cliché."

"I am shaking my head at you. So ridiculous." She scrunched her nose up a touch. "But also a little hot."

Lucy swatted at her.

"What? That's a compliment."

"What about you? Tell me about your first time."

It was maybe a strange conversation to be having, but the effortlessness of their back and forth clearly put Lucy at ease and Sam loved seeing her so relaxed.

She faked serious. "Hasn't happened yet. But things are lining up nicely," she teased. "So I'm feeling pretty good."

"Brat." She shook her head at Sam's playful grin. "You won't tell me?" she asked.

Sam rolled onto her back. "I'll tell you." She rubbed her eyes and her face, hating that the week's travel was taking its toll. "It's a moment I'm not really proud of though."

"Oh my God, was it a guy?" Lucy couldn't hide the shock at her own question.

Sam full-on laughed. "No, it was not a guy."

"Have you, I mean, have there ever been guys?"

"No." Sam couldn't contain her smile at Lucy's frank curiosity. "I have known I was gay since I've known I was alive basically." She rubbed Lucy's arm gently, loving the feel of her breasts pressed against her body as she leaned close to listen.

"I was a sophomore at Pratt. The other girl—woman, I should say—was older. Maybe thirty. I'm not sure. She was my TA in an upper-level course. Anyway, I didn't have a girlfriend. Honestly, I'd never had one."

"Really?"

Sam shrugged. "I was shy. Completely gawky." She reveled in Lucy's hand on her again, this time caressing the skin below her belly button, where her shirt had ridden up a little. "I didn't know any lesbians. My softball team in high school was unbelievably straight."

"What about here, though." Lucy licked her lips. "Bay West. You were friends with Lexi, right?"

"Yeah but her living here worked against us, in some ways. We could never sneak in to the parties because everyone knew us, how old we really were, or they knew Chris and Marnie, Lexi's moms," she added for clarification. "So, I was like this nineteen-year-old total dyke with zero experience. I had kissed a couple of different girls—mostly drunk hookups at house parties or bars, nothing more than that." She settled into the cushiony pillow, lacing her fingers together behind her head. "This TA, I could tell she knew I was gay—I mean, pretty much anyone who had eyes could tell. I caught her checking me out in class a lot. Then one night, I saw her at The Kitchen." Sam looked at the ceiling. "We were talking for a while. She lived around the block. I was waiting on the enormous bathroom line, and she told me I could use the bathroom at her apartment." As she remembered it, she was embarrassed at the circumstance and thought she might be blushing. She shrugged a little, trying to blow over it. "Anyway, I got the message. It was pretty transparent. But I took her up on her offer and we went to her place. It really was right near the bar." Sam looked out the window, but there was no moon. "We didn't talk once we were inside. It was a little weird."

Lucy guided her face back to hers and put a small kiss just at the corner of her mouth. "Do you regret it?"

"A little." She gave a small shrug. "I knew she was only interested in sex." She furrowed her brow and Lucy touched the lines that must have formed on her forehead. "I mean, I guess I was too. But there was something about the way she treated me. Both during and afterward. It was so dismissive. I hated it." She frowned. "I remember thinking, even at the time, that her behavior was unnecessary. I didn't think we were going to be girlfriends or anything. But she could have made me feel just slightly less there to service her." She wiggled a little to shift her body weight, hoping she hadn't sounded overly dramatic.

"Well, that's a shitty first time."

"It's not the end of the world. I didn't need therapy over it or anything." She paused for a second trying to put her thoughts into the right words. "I just think you can have consensual sex without being in a relationship, and not make the other person feel like an escort. That's all."

"That's fair," Lucy said, but Sam wondered what she really thought. She could see questions forming behind her eyes and wondered if she had said too much.

Lucy moved Sam's hair aside with one finger and kissed her temple. She cuddled in close and their faces were almost touching. She brushed her lips along Sam's cheek. "Have you done that a lot? Slept with people you weren't dating?" She didn't hear judgment in Lucy's tone, only curiosity. Still, Sam worried about how to answer such a potentially dangerous question.

There was one thing she was certain of. She wasn't going to lie. She took a deep breath. "I don't know what *a lot* is, but I have done it." She looked Lucy in the eye, hoping if Lucy saw her sincerity she might understand. "I've been single a lot. I've had some...flings, I guess you'd call them. More so than serious relationships." She stroked her finger along Lucy's jawline. "I don't know why that is. I'm not afraid to commit." She let her hand drift down the center of Lucy's chest before bringing it back up to her soft lips. "Does that make you not want to be with me?"

"No. Not at all." She pressed Sam's hand to her lips, kissing each fingertip. "It makes you who you are." She opened her mouth to graze her teeth along the tip of Sam's ring finger. "What about Julie, your ex?"

"What about her?" Sam met Lucy's eyes, completely confused about what she was asking.

"Was she the last person you slept with?"

She hated that she had to answer truthfully. "No." She started to explain immediately. "We broke up a ways back. I stayed in Portland for a while, and then, as you know, I was travelling steadily for almost six months." She hoped it passed the litmus test but Lucy looked a little uncertain.

"So...you had, like, a girl in every port?"

This wasn't how she wanted this conversation to play out. While there *had* been some miscellaneous hookups, she didn't feel like that was an accurate statement. She swallowed hard trying to find the line between telling the truth and giving too much information. "It was more like the same woman, different ports."

Lucy furrowed her brow trying to follow. "Someone you work with?"

"Yes."

"So when was—oh my God." Lucy's face dropped. "Was she with you this week?"

Sam hated that this conversation was happening. She tried to stop it but Lucy must have read her face.

"She was," Lucy said, answering her own question before Sam could.

"Yes." There was no point in lying, but still, it felt wrong. "It's not like you're making it sound. Nothing happened. I swear."

"It's fine," Lucy said, but she sounded hurt. "You don't owe me an explanation."

"Um, yes, I do." She swept a lock of hair off Lucy's forehead and looked her dead in the eye. "I'm with you now. So I do owe you an explanation and I'm going to give you one." She kissed her gently on the lips. "Here's some things you should know. I won't lie to you, ever. That is a promise." She licked her lips. "Yeah, I used to sleep with my co-worker. It is what it is." She hoped she sounded straightforward but not cavalier. "It sucks in particular right now, because I have to own up to it with you and I'm scared of what you think of me. But I'm telling you honestly, it's over. I told her I was with someone and that was that."

"That was it? She accepted that, no questions?"

"Yes," she said, underplaying it. She wanted off this topic, not because she had anything to hide but because she had missed Lucy and didn't feel like talking about Blynn. "I told her I had a girlfriend. That's a true statement, right?" Sam felt the corner of her mouth inch up a little. "I mean, if it's not, I guess I could call her," she teased.

Lucy pushed Sam's shoulder with two fingers. "Don't be a jerk."

Sam lay on her back and pulled Lucy to her. "I do have a girlfriend, don't I?"

"A hundred percent yes." Lucy came closer, her hand slipping under the hemline of Sam's white T-shirt as she kissed her. It started slow but before long Lucy's hand gravitated to Sam's chest, then down over her boxers. They kissed for a good long while, but Sam was making no assumptions about where things were headed, so she let Lucy set the pace, trying like crazy to control her own hips as Lucy massaged her through her boxer briefs. She almost stopped her—she didn't know how much more teasing she could really take before she would need some kind of release, but before she could say anything Lucy moved on top of her.

She writhed a little and let out a small moan. Lucy was soaked. Sam could feel her through her panties. Sam watched, mesmerized and ready to burst, as Lucy closed her eyes and moved against her. When Lucy leaned forward, Sam found her mouth immediately and with her hands in Lucy's hair, she kissed her slow, deep and hard.

Lucy broke away, breathing heavily. "Off." Her voice was husky and low in Sam's ear. "Everything, off."

Her hands were already under the waistband of Sam's boxers and Sam reached down to push them off. She slipped her hands inside the back of Lucy's skimpy panties and took them off as well, taking a minute to indulge in the soft skin of Lucy's bottom against the palm of her hands.

Sam was still lying down and Lucy climbed on top of her. Their skin touched and Sam felt the heat radiate between them. She moved hard against Lucy and Lucy moaned loudly in response. Sitting up, Sam rushed her hands under Lucy's bra before dispensing with it altogether in one swift motion. Her nipples were hard and Sam took one in her mouth, pressing the flat of her tongue against it. Lucy's breathing intensified and she grabbed Sam's shirt, pulling it off and tossing it aside. Their breasts brushed against each other and Sam put her hands on Lucy's hips bringing her impossibly closer.

"Sam," Lucy said through a ragged breath. "I want you inside me."

Sam kissed her, stifling her own groan at Lucy's directness. "Yes, baby."

She slowed them down for a second as she reached between their bodies. She ran her fingers along Lucy's skin—God, she was fucking wet—before slipping inside her. One finger first, but two almost immediately as she wrapped her arm around Lucy's waist, holding her in place as she moved inside. She leaned forward and her mouth trailed Lucy's neck, sucking gently as she listened to Lucy's soft whimpers. Sam felt her start to tighten around her fingers and she sucked harder, not caring there would be evidence in the morning. She could tell Lucy was close, so she leaned back and used her hips to drive deeper as Lucy writhed on top. Lucy's back arched, her nipples were hard, and a soft sheen of sweat glistened on her skin as she squeezed Sam from the inside, coming hard before she fell forward against her chest.

They were quiet for a minute as Lucy rested her cheek against Sam's body. "I'm going to need a minute," she said. "That was"— she let out a long breath and kissed Sam's chest—"wow."

Sam smiled and kissed the top of her hair. "It's fine. Rest. You don't have to do anything."

"Why, do you not want me to?" Lucy sounded stressed, and she popped her head up to check Sam's reaction.

Sam grazed her hands along Lucy's back. "No." At Lucy's distressed look, she clarified. "I mean, yes, of course I want you to. If you want." She kissed her forehead. "I just don't want you to do anything you're not ready for."

Lucy's face softened. "Thank God." She put her head back down. "I'm dying to." Her finger traced the outline of Sam's hip. "I just need to get the circulation back in the lower half of my body." She tilted her face up to look at Sam again and then she leaned forward to kiss her. "Sam, I'm sorry about all the drama tonight with the social and everything."

"It's okay. I'm just glad you talked to me."

Lucy shifted her body weight, leaning on an elbow, still touching Sam's abs with her fingers. "How was the social? Were Meg and Lexi nervous?"

"They were okay. Meg was a little stressed." She tucked one hand under her head and brushed Lucy's hair with the other. "There was a decent crowd, though. Even early on, so that's good."

"Good. I'm happy for them."

"Luce?" Sam touched her face. "Would you ever go? To a social?"

Lucy nodded. "Okay." She sat all the way up. "Babe, if it's important to you, I'll go."

Her hand moved farther down Sam's body and Sam spread her legs wider instinctively. "It's not that I care about the social, specifically." She could hardly concentrate as Lucy started stroking her. She was swollen and ready and Lucy was teasing her with the lightest touch possible. "It's just that—" She fully jerked when Lucy moved her hand lower, slowly but all the way down and back, intensifying the experience a thousandfold.

"It's just what?" Lucy could barely contain her playfully smug expression at seeing the obvious effect of her touch on Sam.

Sam tried hard to keep her voice steady, but it was a losing battle. "It would be nice to go places sometimes."

"Agreed." Lucy raised one eyebrow. "Right now, I have somewhere *I* want to go."

Sam shook her head at Lucy's innuendo but smiled just the same.

Lucy kneeled at Sam's side, leaning over to pepper her body with sweet kisses. She started up by Sam's shoulders and moved down over her breasts, her ribs, and her long, lean torso.

Sam leaned back into the pillow, enjoying that Lucy was taking her time, making her feel loved everywhere. When Lucy reached Sam's belly, she bent all the way forward, and used her hands to spread Sam's legs apart. Sam watched as Lucy tucked her knees under her, crept lower, and buried her face between her legs. The buildup of the last week, and the last few months, was in full effect, and she could feel how hard she was against Lucy's soft tongue. Lucy was still next to her, her soft bottom bouncing slightly as her mouth moved against Sam.

Sam reached over and slid her hand between Lucy's legs. Lucy was still wet and Sam slipped inside her easily. Her touch seemed to encourage Lucy, and Sam felt her tongue increase its pace as a muffled moan vibrated against her clit. Suddenly, she couldn't take being this close to Lucy and not tasting her.

She withdrew her fingers gently and reached over to Lucy, guiding her bottom over ever so subtly. There was no protest. Lucy spread herself over Sam's body, never breaking contact as she let Sam guide her to her mouth. Sam swore she felt Lucy's breath catch as Sam's tongue touched her for the first time. She couldn't be sure though, because she was so focused on her own impending orgasm. She loved everything about the feel of Lucy in her mouth, her taste, her sweet smell. It only intensified as Lucy gave her the same sensation. They were touching everywhere and it was mere seconds before she felt Lucy's movements change, finding a rhythm in time with her own. She was almost there. She held Lucy close, sucking her hard and reached down to place her hand at the back of Lucy's head, applying just the added touch of pressure she needed. That was all it took. She bucked into Lucy, her orgasm ripping through her as Lucy came hard and fast in her mouth.

It was sweaty, raw, sexy, and intense. The perfect simultaneous orgasm and they were both breathless for more than a few minutes. Finally, Lucy crawled her way up Sam's body. She let her lips linger as they kissed. "Tell me you're staying over again tomorrow night."

Sam settled into the mattress, one arm around Lucy as she reached for the edge of the blanket to cover them. "I'm counting on it."

"Perfect." Lucy waved her fingers in a semicircle. "Because we will be doing all of this again." She kissed Sam's pecs and buried her face in her shoulder. "Probably more than once."

"Three years is a long time, huh?" Sam didn't even try to repress the teasing in her voice.

"You have no idea," Lucy responded just as playfully, but when she looked up her eyes were unbelievably earnest. "Sam?"

"Yeah, babe?"

"Thank you for being sweet to me."

"I care about you." Sam kissed her delicately before turning Lucy around to spoon her from behind. She took her hand and held it, covering Lucy's heart with their interlaced fingers.

Lucy brought Sam's hand to her lips and kissed it before returning it to her chest. "I care about you too."

Sam smiled into Lucy's hair. It wasn't *I love you*, but it sure felt like it.

CHAPTER THIRTEEN

The smell of morning coffee wafted from the vendors that lined the short crosstown walk from Meg's bus stop to her office on Manhattan's East Side. Back in the day, she and Sasha walked these same blocks a hundred times over. She didn't know why that memory came to her just now, but decided not to stress it. Instead she indulged herself reminiscing all the times Sasha fell prey to this very coffee cart on the corner of Fifty-Third and Third. They had gigantic coffee rolls and Sasha had a sweet tooth she caved to daily. It was amazing Sasha wasn't a thousand pounds with all the junk food she ate.

Reaching into her satchel for her phone, Meg's heart beat fast as she banged away on the keypad. She had been looking for an excuse to communicate since last week's trivia event. This was pretty weak. She went for it anyway.

How are you surviving without the coffee rolls from the stand outside Sullivan?

The response was immediate. *I'm not.*

OMG, you're dying? she typed, but then scrutinized her own words. It seemed insensitive considering Sasha's mother had died only a little over a year ago. She deleted it. *Do you still come over this way to get them?* She was genuinely curious, but as she looked the question over it sounded like an invite. Erasing it, she took another stab. *Should I have one sent to your apartment?* She shrugged. Fuck it. She pressed the send arrow before wimping out.

Um...yes, please. More bubbles appeared before she could respond. *Even better, hand deliver it! I have coffee...*

Meg smiled. *LOL*, she answered. Nice, safe, noncommittal.

So that's a no?

I'm at work sadly.

Boo. Only a second passed before another message appeared. *And who are you kidding? You're not sad. You love it there.*

Sasha knew her too well. *I know. But I have a meeting at Dillinger Pharmco this afternoon and I'm really not ready for it.*

You'll be fine. You always are. The sentence was punctuated with a smiley face and Meg thought they might be done, but then another text appeared right away. *Hey, Dillinger's HQ is right over by Hunter College, right? I have class later. Any chance you're free for lunch?*

Meg frowned even as she tried to mentally juggle her schedule. She'd been balancing a heavy client load in the hopes of garnering a promotion that rarely went to an associate at her level. Today was jam-packed. Preliminary prep work to square away a small project she'd just been assigned, a think tank meeting with the senior staff and Anne at ten, and then the Dillinger meeting at two. She was going to need every free minute between now and then to be a hundred and ten percent ready. There was just no way.

Sorry, swamped today.

Too bad. Oh, well, if you need to kill any time, I'll be over in the library studying away. Good luck today!

Meg racked her brain for a good response but nothing came to her. She scrolled the emoji keypad instead, her eyes drawn to hearts, smiles, and kissy-faces. What the eff? She shook her head at herself for even considering any of them, but let herself slide just as quickly. Yeah, she still thought of Sasha sometimes. Maybe even fantasized they were still together on occasion. That was normal. It wasn't so very long ago she'd been head over heels for this girl. Like, stop the presses, call your mother, rent a skywriter in love. It was completely rational to have some residual feelings, and the other night at Lucy's proved they still had some connection. What did any of it mean? She had no idea. It was entirely likely they were simply friends and what they were doing here, now, was nice and adult and responsible.

Yep, it sure was. She zeroed in on the thumbs-up emoji and stared at its curled fist and bland emotion. It was…utterly platonic. In spite of her gut reaction, she selected and sent it before she could come up with a plausible reason to go with her earlier choices. She watched it bounce onto the thread full of the promise of bright yellow friendship and felt her heart sink at the implication.

❖

Sasha put her feet up on the small circular table two feet in front of her cozy chair in her favorite corner of the library, rolling a few strands of her long hair between her fingers as she scrutinized for split ends.

"Studying hard?"

Meg's voice came out in a sarcastic whisper and Sasha bit her bottom lip but it did nothing to suppress the smile quickly spreading across her face. "What are you doing here?" She shook her head a little. "I mean, I'm so glad," she said holding her palms up in confusion. "But how?"

"The magic of an alumni ID. My meeting ended early. It's too late to go back to the office. A little too early to go home." Meg's smirk looked a touch guilt-ridden. "Thought I'd bug you for a few minutes. I took a shot that I'd find you in here." She looked around the expansive stacks. "It was easier than I thought."

"You know me. I'm going to find a nook and settle in."

Meg fanned her hand over Sasha's personal effects—her bag, shoes, laptop, and various study materials spread over the small corner. "You do have a way of making yourself right at home."

Sasha twisted her mouth to the side. "I spend a lot of time here."

"What are you studying?"

"Just reading for history of urban education. I have class in a little while."

"I can get out of your way. Just wanted to say hi."

"No. Stay." She heard the mild pleading in her own voice but ignored it, leaning forward to move her stuff from the spare seat. "Sit. Hang out with me. Tell me about the Dillinger meeting."

Meg dropped into the cushioned chair and stretched her arms above her head. "It was good." She let out a long breath. "Short but intense."

"Things are good at Sullivan?"

Meg smiled. "They are. Doug Patterson left. Like, retired." She raised her eyebrows. "There's some interesting things taking shape."

Sasha leaned forward and touched Meg's leg. "Oh my God, you're going to get promoted."

"I mean, not to partner, obviously. But there's some movement happening, a senior associate spot that will open up." She clenched her teeth and crossed her fingers. "I'm hoping."

"It's yours." Sasha gave a little rub where her hand was still resting on Meg's thigh. She knew it was gratuitous, but figured it could pass as positive reinforcement. Honestly, she couldn't care less if it didn't. She wanted to touch Meg. "You are the best consultant there. Everyone knows it."

"Thanks, Sash." Meg shifted uncomfortably in her chair. Sasha knew even though she was dead on, Meg would never admit it. And she remembered how much Meg hated being the focus of this kind of conversation, so she moved on.

"How was your social, the one you and Lexi were in charge of?"

"It was great." Sasha felt a tiny flip in her stomach as she listened to Meg's voice fill with excitement. "We didn't really make too many changes or anything, but Sam, Lexi's friend, the one you met at Roaring Twenties—" Meg stopped talking and squinted her eyes clearly checking if Sasha remembered who she was talking about.

"I remember," she said.

"She's in graphics, so she redid the website and linked the announcement to a bunch of social media platforms. We ended up getting a huge showing from some local colleges and even some new people from Jersey and Connecticut."

The enthusiasm Meg had for Bay West made her smile. It was loyal and sweet and honorable, just like Meg.

"You should have come."

That caught her off guard. "Really?" She gripped her pen tighter, feeling sweat pool in the center of her hand. "That would be okay?"

"Sure, why not?"

A million reasons filled her head, none of which she wanted to rehash in this perfect moment where they were together, connecting so nicely. It was the exact thing she needed—time alone with Meg so she could show her just how much she'd missed her, how much she wanted another chance. "Maybe next time," she said, hoping the opportunity would come sooner rather than later. They talked for a while longer until she either had to blow off class or get her butt there in a hurry.

"I should go," she said with half a frown.

"Yeah, of course," Meg said. "What time is your class?"

"Four thirty."

"Wow, are you going to make it?"

She nodded. Her professor was always a few minutes late anyway.

"Why didn't you tell me to shut up? Here I am going on and on about work and Bay West and my friends and you're about to be late for school."

"Stop it. I love talking to you." Sasha smiled. She wished she could stay and play with Meg all night. She didn't want to wait until the next Bay West social to see her. She didn't want to leave it to chance at all. "What are you doing Saturday?"

Meg looked stunned at the question, but not necessarily in a good way, so Sasha clarified immediately. "The West Side Mission is doing a big adoption event. We could use a few extra hands. Why don't you come?" She stood to pack up her stuff. "You can use your adorable charm to sway people into fostering. Plus, as a new pet parent, you have tons of Spencer stories, I'm sure. What do you say?" she asked, lifting her eyebrows as she adjusted the strap of her bag on her shoulder.

"Adorable charm, huh?"

Sasha shrugged playfully. She knew it was over the top, but she wanted Meg to know she wasn't looking entirely for friendship. "I speak the truth." She backed away. "Seven a.m. Saturday morning. I'll text you the address."

"Seven?" Meg groaned loudly. "You do realize how early I'm going to have to get up."

Sasha laughed. *Gah*, she wished she had the nerve to invite Meg to stay with her Friday night. But they weren't there. In fact, they weren't even close. If she wanted Meg, she was going to need opportunities to convince her they were meant to be. This was the first in a series of small steps, but at least it was a start. "It's for homeless animals, Meg," she answered, laying it on thick as she added a syrupy smile. "I'll see you there." She lifted her eyebrows, hoping to God she would show.

CHAPTER FOURTEEN

Sam glanced through the storefront window at the late afternoon sun shining off the midnight-blue finish of her Tahoe parked in a far spot in the lot. "It would've been a perfect day for a hike today. Not too hot yet. But great light." She turned to Lucy, who was perched on the other side of the counter near the register organizing her bills. "Have you checked out the Greenbelt at all? There's some nice trails there. Sometimes you'll even spot a deer or two."

"Haven't been," Lucy answered without looking up.

"You know there's actually some fantastic places just an hour or so north of the city, some in Jersey too."

"You should have gone today." Lucy made three neat stacks. "There was no reason for you to hang out here with me all day."

"I like being with you." Sam reached for a small square napkin and took a pen from the pocket of her jeans. "I just wish sometimes we could go out and do stuff."

"Me too." Lucy let out a heavy sigh. "I'm sorry, Sam." She glanced around the coffee shop making sure none of her customers needed attention. "This is my priority right now."

"I know." She bent all the way forward as she scribbled away. "I'm not trying to pressure you. I want to be with you. I want to be outside. I want it all, I guess."

"What time are we expected at Lexi and Jesse's?" Lucy asked.

It was almost five thirty, and there were only a few stragglers hanging around in the store. "I think the invite was for six but I'm sure anytime is fine." She tapped the end of her pen on the counter leaning forward so she could whisper and still be heard when she spoke. Lucy caught her eye and Sam summoned her over with one finger. She gestured at the coffee shop's customers discreetly with a nod of her head. "Can't you just kick these guys out? Tell them you're closing up or whatever. Then we could go to your apartment first."

Lucy smiled but shook her head. "Babe, I can't." She pointed at her pile of papers. "I have stuff to do anyway. Why don't you go without me?"

"To your apartment? Kinky."

Lucy shook her head. "I meant to the barbecue."

"No." Sam pouted. "I want to go with you."

"But you're getting antsy. I can tell. Go now and I'll catch up." At Sam's questioning look, she reassured her. "I promise, I will come as soon as I'm through here." She leaned in close. "Everything is cleaned up. I'm just finishing my things, and if it hits seven and there's still people here I'll close anyway. I'll be there at seven fifteen the latest." Lucy leaned across and touched the back of Sam's hand gingerly with her fingers. "You have my word." She noticed the napkin Sam was drawing on and turned it toward her for inspection. "What is this?"

"Just playing around."

"I like it."

"I was thinking you could do T-shirts, mugs, stuff like that to sell here. I bet there'd be a market for it."

"With that artwork, I'm sure you're right."

"Luce, you don't have to use this. I was just messing around while I was waiting. Trying to distract myself from what I'm really thinking about."

"Which is?" Lucy lifted one eyebrow suggestively.

Sam's smile was hungry, impish, and full of lust. "You know what it is."

Lucy dropped her glance but Sam saw the color flood her cheeks at her overt implication. She held the drawing with both hands. "Sam, this is really good." She focused her attention on it. "The coffee cup, the bridge in the background. It's perfect." She held it between them. "Can I keep it?"

"Of course." Sam looked right in her eyes. "I'll make you a real one though. Like, not on a scrap of paper."

Lucy nodded, biting her lower lip. "Come here for a second." It came out as a half question, half command, and she followed immediately as Lucy slipped through the double doors to the back area. "You should go to the girls' house." Her back was to Sam as she reached in the refrigerator and took out the cannolis she had made earlier, placing them on the silver workspace next to her. "Take these with you."

Sam walked up close to Lucy shaking her head ever so slightly. "Nope." She leaned forward and kissed her neck, quickly working her way to her lips as she lifted her onto the counter. Lucy made a sexy noise as Sam's kiss deepened. "You bring them. When you meet me there." She ran her hand all the way down the front of Lucy's body and let it slip inside the front of her pants for a fraction of a second. "This…" She withdrew her hand and leaned forward to give Lucy another searing kiss. "This we will pick up later."

"Oh my God, I hope so."

❖

In a way, Sam was pleased to be at Lexi and Jesse's barbecue for a few minutes without Lucy. Not that she didn't want to spend all her free time with her new girlfriend. But it would be nice to catch up with her friends and relax with a drink without feeling self-conscious in front of Lucy. Sam was pretty sure Lucy would be okay with her drinking, but she was happy to not have to worry about it.

"What are you so deep in thought about?" Lexi asked, placing a tray of shrimp cocktail between them as she settled into the chair next to Sam.

"Nothing. Beautiful day, huh?"

"It is."

Lexi furrowed her brow. "No Lucy?"

"She'll be here." Sam reached for a shrimp and dipped it heavily in the cocktail sauce. "She stays open until seven, even on Saturdays."

"I'm surprised. I didn't think she would get much business at night without a specific event."

Sam placed the end of the tail on her napkin as she shook her head. "It makes no sense if you ask me." She took a sip of her lager. "I get it during the school year. I know she gets a lot of students who come in to do work. But now, when it's nearly summer?" She curled her mouth skeptically. "I don't see the point."

Lexi agreed with a frown. "You guys doing okay?" She was obviously picking up on the tension in Sam's tone.

"We're fine. It's just frustrating sometimes." She took her time selecting another shrimp. "I want her to hang out with all of us, plus I want to, like, go out with her. You know, hiking, and on real dates. I want her to meet my family even though they're assholes. The stuff girlfriends do." She washed her food down with a healthy sip of beer. "But everything is the coffee shop. Which I get, but still."

Lexi bumped her leg with her own. "Are you bailing?"

"No." She huffed out a laugh as she put her arm around Lexi's chair. "The opposite. I want more of her, not less. I just needed to vent for a sec."

"Good, because I like to see you happy," Lexi said with a smile. "And you seem really happy these days."

"This is very true." Sam knew she had on a cheesy smile. "With the exception of her ridic hours, which is really small stuff in the grand scheme, we're doing really good. Fantastic, I might even say. I like her. A lot."

"Are you...?" Lexi let her voice trail clearly hoping Sam would finish for her, but Sam wasn't giving in that easily.

"Am I...?" she repeated, mimicking Lexi's tone as she pretended she had no idea what she was asking.

"Sam." Lexi whacked her. "Don't play. Tell me."

"Tell you what?" she teased back, still playing it up. She shifted her attention from Lexi. "Megan!" she called across the small yard as Meg cleared the back sliders. Sam stood up to greet her, completely leaving Lexi hanging. She patted Meg on the shoulder as she passed. "I'm going to hit the head." Without turning back she called over her shoulder, "Yes, Lex. The answer to your question. A hundred percent yes."

"What was that about?" Meg said, stealing Sam's seat.

Lexi shook her head as she reached into the cooler next to her and grabbed a beer for Meg. She held up a Corona for Meg's approval.

"Fine, whatever." She took it from Lexi and popped the top off. "Seriously, Sam just looked like the cat who ate the canary. What did I miss?"

"She's in love."

"Great." Meg's voice came out sarcastic, but Lexi knew it was all envy.

"Stop feeling sorry for yourself," she ordered good-naturedly. "Be happy for her. Her whole last year sucked. And honestly, I've never seen her like this."

"I am happy for her." Meg cracked her knuckles loudly. "Who needs girls anyway." She nodded emphatically. "I am going to throw myself into work. Then I'll get promoted and the ladies will lay themselves at my feet."

"How's that going?"

"The girls?" Meg shook her head in dramatic fashion. "Nil."

Lexi ignored her joke. "I meant your promotion race."

Meg shrugged. "Who knows?"

"Is that where you were all day? I saw you leave your house at, like, six o'clock this morning."

Meg took a sip of her drink to shield her smile. "No, I went in to the city to help Sasha with a thing at the rescue mission."

"I thought that was a while ago?"

"It was." She diverted her eyes. "There was another one today." She used the bottom of her beer bottle to make a pattern of rings on her worn-out jeans. "It was nice. A lot of pets got homes. It made me feel good."

Lexi made a dramatic show of looking around her empty yard. "You know who you're talking to, right?" She wagged her finger slowly. "Do not try to tell me this is about baby cats or puppies or whatever."

"What?" Meg let the word roll out in playful disbelief. "Honestly, though, I enjoyed it in a way I really didn't expect."

Lexi tilted her head to the side and waited for Meg to meet her eyes. "You could have invited her tonight, you know."

"Who?"

"Don't you *who* me," Lexi quipped, shaking her head.

"I'm just kidding." Meg punched her shoulder playfully. "Thank you for letting me know she's welcome. I do appreciate it." She chewed her bottom lip. "I wonder if she would have come."

Lexi gave her a look that was pure disbelief, Meg recognized it right away.

"I know what you're thinking, but I don't know." She shrugged, bringing her drink to her lips. "I have no idea what we're doing, if I'm being honest. Sometimes it feels like friendship. Sometimes not so much."

"What was she up to tonight?"

Meg leaned forward in her chair, frowning as she pushed around a gravelly pebble with the toe of her sneaker. "She didn't mention anything."

"Because"—Lexi waited for Meg to look at her—"she was hoping you would ask her to hang out."

"You think so?"

Lexi rolled her eyes. "Yes, Meg. Obviously."

Meg wasn't convinced. She closed one eye and peered into her beer watching the small foam bubbles dissipate as they came in contact with the sides of the glass bottle. "I don't know."

"She's been texting you. You two spend every Saturday morning together apparently—"

"Just two."

"So far. She came to see you at Sullivan—"

"She came to get a letter of recommendation."

Lexi shook her head. "Not buying that, either." She held up one finger. "Don't even get me started on the night we saw her at Roaring Twenties. And I was with you at trivia night. I saw the flirting first hand."

"There was no flirting."

"There were flirting undercurrents." She held out her hand, effectively stopping Meg from speaking. "Everyone can see she's into you. There's, like, no debate. The only question is how you feel about her."

"First of all, I'm not sure I agree with you. It feels very"— Meg moved both hands in small counterclockwise circles as she searched for the right word—"friends-ish, a lot of the time."

"But not all the time."

"Yeah, but maybe that's just me speculating. Or being attracted to her."

"Or her wanting to be with you and you picking up on it." Lexi pulled her hair into a bun. "You haven't answered the question, FYI."

Meg let out a little laugh. "And what was the question, exactly?"

"Assuming I'm right, which I know I am, how do you feel about Sasha?"

Meg met Lexi's eyes and held her gaze, hoping if she stared long enough she wouldn't have to put such a complex set of emotions into words, but Lexi wasn't letting her off the hook so easily. Lexi raised one eyebrow as she waited, the silent gesture a demand for the truth.

"I don't know." Meg tipped her head back and took a sip of her drink letting herself get lost in the late-day clouds. "Of course I still have feelings for her. But I can't let that get in the way. I mean, she is who she is. A leopard doesn't change its spots, right? And this friendship is…nice."

"That is the second bizarro cliché thingy you've used since you got here."

"What?"

"Before." Lexi pointed at the sliding glass doors. "When you got here, you made a comment about Sam looking like the cat who ate the canary, and now this." She brushed Meg off with a wave of her hand. "And you don't know anyway. Maybe they do."

Meg shook her head not following. "Maybe they do, what?"

"Maybe a leopard does change its spots or whatever that stupid expression is."

"They don't though, it's impossible. Hence, the expression."

"Well, Sasha isn't a leopard. She's a fucking person. And people do change."

Meg rolled her shoulders. "Doesn't matter anyway."

"What doesn't matter?" Sam asked the question as she shuffled into the yard carrying another tray of appetizers. Jesse followed two steps behind, with the chips and guacamole. She was obviously waiting to be filled in as well.

Lexi checked Meg's face for permission and Meg gave it to her holding both arms outstretched and giving over the floor.

"Meg's in a tizzy because she has this new *friendship* with Sasha." She put the word in air quotes as she continued. "Which is nice." She paused to ensure her summation was making the grade. Meg nodded, so she went on. "But Meg's concerned that she may be feeling something more than friendly toward Sasha"—she held her hand up ramping up the drama as she continued—"because of their history and the fact that they were madly in love and had unbelievable sexual chemistry."

Meg almost choked on her drink. "I didn't say any of that." She wiped her mouth stifling a laugh in spite of being embarrassed.

Lexi grinned. "I know, but they deserve to know the truth." She lifted her shoulders and puckered her lips. "And you gave me license to recap it for you. You know I'm gonna tell it like it is."

Sam raised her hand to get some attention. "Let me just make sure I understand this." She settled on the bench seat at the backyard table and grabbed a chip from the bowl. "Sasha, that's her name? This is the one I met a few months back, the night we all went out dancing? The girl who came all the way from Manhattan to play trivia with you at Lucy's?" She scanned their faces. "Same person, yes?"

Meg nodded in response.

"Look, Meg. I may have missed a year and everything. But let me say this. The one time I saw her with you…" She paused and loaded some guac on her corn chip. "She doesn't want to be your friend. You can believe me or not. But I'm good at reading people." She held the nacho ready to devour it. "Girls, in particular. And that girl, she is not looking for friendship."

Meg looked at Jesse, hoping for an ally. "Jess, a little support?"

Jesse simply shook her head. "You know how I feel about this, kid."

Meg nodded, even though she really didn't know Jesse's perspective. Suddenly, this party was starting to feel like an intervention. "Enough about me, what's new with you guys?" Meg asked, hoping to turn the conversation in a completely different direction.

Right away Jesse and Lexi exchanged a look and Meg couldn't help but smile for her friends. If she'd taken a step back from her own ridiculous drama, she would have seen this moment coming and she felt guilty at having dominated so much of the conversation.

Her friends played it off for the time being, waiting until well after Marnie and Chris joined the party and Lucy had arrived bearing her awesome desserts. Glasses were filled and the group was lively and spirited. And finally, when the sun was about to set, Lexi summoned everyone's attention as she stood at the head of the outdoor table.

"So, I guess you're wondering why we called you all here," she said, getting some mild laughter from her moms as she recycled an old family joke. Her smile was enormous and her dimples popped on both sides. "I mean, you've probably all figured it out by now, but just in case..." She looked at Jesse, whose expression was a combination of excitement and pride as she held Lexi's hand. "We're having a baby." Her voice squeaked with excitement as she said it out loud. Her parents were the first to jump up and congratulate them, but Meg was a close second. Of course Lexi was right—no one was truly shocked, but there were smiles and toasts and Meg was touched to be part of something so special.

Even hours later when she was home, tucked under her covers, Meg still felt a buzz running through her limbs. What a great night. Goddamn, if there was only one thing missing. She shut her eyes, willing the thought out of her mind while she clutched the extra pillow tight, certain that in the safety of sleep Sasha would be right next to her all night.

❖

Sam awoke to Lucy's gentle lips on her cheek. She wrapped her arms around her girlfriend's naked body. "I hate your hours," she whispered in Lucy's ear.

"I know," Lucy whispered back. "You tell me every day."

Sam kept her eyes closed but found Lucy's lips just the same. "The worst part is I *love* morning sex." She fake pouted. "And I never get to have it. It's so *sad...*"

"And here I thought"—Lucy slipped her hand between Sam's legs over her boxers—"the worst part was that you wanted to go hiking with me." She rubbed gently. "Now I don't know what to believe."

"Believe that what you're doing there"—she looked between their bodies—"is getting me going." She moved Lucy's hand away but she came right back. Sam let her stay even though it was torture. She moved a lock of hair from Lucy's face. "How about instead of Pilates today, you let me take you to High Rock Park. It's really nice there."

"I would, but I have therapy today. Not Pilates."

"Tomorrow?"

"Okay," Lucy answered in a breathy voice, her fingers getting greedier by the second.

"I'm going to have to stop you." She stilled Lucy's hand with her own.

"Please?"

"I thought there wasn't time."

"There's always time."

Sam flipped them quickly and went straight for three fingers as they kissed. It had been a long night full of sweet sensitive sex. She wanted this to be different. Lucy was already wet, and she slipped in easily.

"Fast, babe. Okay?"

"I know," Sam answered, already fucking Lucy pretty hard. She felt her tighten around her fingers and knew she was going to come. Even though they were pressed for time, she pulled out for a second. When Lucy whimpered at the loss, Sam encouraged her, lifting her legs up so that her ankles were on her shoulders. She slid two fingers inside Lucy, but with her body weight behind her, she went in much deeper than before.

Lucy gasped. "Fuck, Sam."

Sam looked down at her. She could tell it was working for Lucy but she asked anyway. "Are you okay?"

Lucy could only nod as she bit her lip and threw her arms over her head in a kind of surrender. Her breath was fast and ragged until she let out a moan from somewhere deep in her belly as she clenched against Sam's fingers. She stayed that way for several long seconds, her muscles tight and rigid, holding Sam in place until she finally relaxed, her entire body going limp under Sam.

"You should go." Sam brushed her lips against the shell of Lucy's ear, placing a sweet kiss there.

"No way." Lucy licked her lips and appeared to use what was left of her energy to snap into action. She motioned Sam toward her but when she sat up on the edge of the bed, Lucy touched her shoulder urging her back down onto the mattress. Lucy reached for the waistband of her boxers and stripped them off as she dropped to her knees next to the bed.

Sam could already feel Lucy's breath against her and it almost hurt to say the words but she knew her girlfriend had priorities, and she wanted to respect them. "Babe, you're going to be late." She propped up on her elbows and reached down, putting her hand on Lucy's cheek to guide her back up.

Lucy kissed her palm, smiled devilishly, and took Sam's thumb in her mouth. All the way in her mouth, and it caused her to groan. Lucy licked all the way down to the tip and kissed the end, before lowering her gaze. "I certainly am."

CHAPTER FIFTEEN

It was a rare day that Sam chose to work from her parents' house and by three o'clock she couldn't hold out any longer. She hopped in her truck and headed to the coffee shop to get her fix.

"*Psst.* Hey," she stage-whispered, strolling up to the counter and summoning Lucy with one finger. "Come here." Even now, months into dating, her heart pounded when she caught Lucy looking around to make sure none of her customers were paying attention. It was a sure sign she was about to get a sly kiss, and even though she knew it made her a huge mush, it got her every time. "How's your day?" she asked.

"Busy. What about you?"

Sam nodded in response. "My parents were out all morning. I was able to get a lot done." She settled herself onto a stool. "Which means I'm all yours for the rest of the day."

"I like the sound of that."

Lucy poured her coffee and placed the steaming mug on the counter. Sam stirred it out of habit, even though she knew it was already prepared exactly how she liked it.

"I was thinking." Sam placed the spoon on top of a napkin. "Any chance we could sneak away for a few hours this weekend?" She saw apprehension in Lucy's face, so she edited her idea right on the spot. While she'd been set to pitch a night together camping on the beach at Fire Island, she could already see that wouldn't fly. "What I would really love is to go away for a night somewhere. Hike all day. Maybe camp out. I love being outside—you know that. I want some time to experience that with you." She steadied her shoulders. "But I can see there's no way you're letting Raven handle a Sunday without you."

"Sam, I can't. I'm sorry, babe."

"What about Saturday afternoon?" She touched the curve of the spoon's handle. "Cut out early, we can head to the Jersey Shore." She took a small sip of her drink. "Catch some late-day sun on the beach. Walk on the boardwalk. Go out for a nice dinner. I'll have you home in bed by midnight."

"Yeah, you will," Lucy responded with more than a little spirit.

Sam grinned. "Is that a yes?"

"Almost."

"Almost?"

"Cindy is working Saturday afternoon. I would not relax knowing I left my baby in the hands of Cindy Defazzio. Nice girl, but let me just make sure Raven's available to cover as well."

As if on cue, Raven came through the back door and hugged Lucy from behind. "Lucy Weston, you are my hero. I owe you so big-time."

"Well, that sounds promising," Sam said, lifting the mug to her mouth.

"Sorry, Sam. I'm not really groping your girlfriend. Promise." Raven shucked her apron and folded it neatly into a corner. "I feel so much better already. Thank you, boss lady." She skipped out from behind the counter. "Tomorrow when you see me, I'll be a changed woman. But maybe a little sore." She laughed nervously. "Wish me luck," she called out as the door's bell jingled above her.

"Good luck, honey," Lucy called after her.

Sam held up her palms. "Gonna fill me in or what?" She took a big gulp of coffee. "Raven seemed *pret-ty* excited about your advice."

"It was nothing." Lucy wiped the spotless counter out of habit. "Raven's friend was giving her a hard time."

"The girl she's dating, you mean?"

"No, actually. Just one of her friends. But it was about the girl she's seeing."

"A jealousy thing?"

Lucy put the cloth down and took two steps closer so she was directly in front of where Sam was sitting. "No." She checked a look at the only person present with them, a man finishing up his coffee by the window and whispered, "Her friend was giving her crap because Raven's girlfriend wants to use...toys." She licked her lips. "Like, you know, a dildo." Her voice had dropped another octave.

"I'm familiar with sex toys, babe," Sam whispered back. She watched Lucy blush as she held her hand up, offering a good-bye to the shop's sole customer as he left. "Let me guess. Her friend said using that stuff makes her not gay enough or some shit like that?"

"Exactly."

Sam shook her head into her drink. "That's ridiculous."

"I know. I told her that."

"You obviously made her feel better. What did you say?"

Lucy toyed with the edge of Sam's spoon. "I told her she should do what she wants and to not let anyone come into her bedroom and judge her." She touched the tip of Sam's thumb with her index finger. "What happens between her and her girlfriend is for them. No one gets to weigh in on that."

"Wise words." Sam let her fingers drift all the way up Lucy's forearm. "Sounds like she's going to go for it."

"I don't know. She's nervous. Afraid it's going to hurt."

"What did you tell her?"

"I didn't." She pushed off the counter and then came back in slowly. "I would have had to admit I didn't honestly know. So instead I emphasized that our bodies were designed for all sorts of things—"

"Hold up." Sam twisted her coffee cup by the handle. "Are you saying…" She let her voice trail off, uncharacteristically shy about finishing the question.

"What?"

"Luce?"

"Sam?" She bit her lower lip coyly. "Is there something you want to know?"

Sam could feel her face getting hot but her desire for the answer won out. "So you've never"—she moved her head from side to side—"used, you know, like a strap-on or anything?"

"No."

She focused her eyes on the ceramic cup twisting it back and forth. "And is that, like, something you might be interested in?" Her attempted nonchalance failed miserably but it didn't matter. She watched intently as Lucy examined her short fingernails as she answered.

"Honestly, I never considered it before." She put both hands on the countertop. "It was never really there as an option." She bit her lip, looking both shy and embarrassed at her admission. "Things with you are different. So if you're really asking, a hundred percent I'm interested." They were alone in the store but Lucy spoke low anyway. "I don't think there's anything I wouldn't do with you." Her shrug was almost playful. "So if you're up for it, and judging by the look on your face, I'm going to say that's a yes, let's do it." A small delighted sigh escaped her. "I bet it's going to be unbelievable. I almost can't wait."

Sam was so turned on she could barely talk. This day couldn't get any better. It wasn't yet three thirty on Tuesday afternoon and she'd already talked Lucy into a Saturday date, and they were discussing ramping up their already hot sex life. She glanced over at the door to the kitchen, contemplating whisking Lucy behind it. Lucy would never let things get out of hand, but she would play along for a little bit. Of that Sam was certain. She stood up to go for it when a string of four customers came in together. They were all dudes, dressed in suits, laughing loudly. Literally cock-blocked, she sat back down with a disheartened thud, but Lucy came bouncing out from behind the counter to offer hugs as she greeted them each by name.

Sam looked on from her perch at the bar as Lucy excitedly asked what they were doing on Staten Island. One of them, clearly the mouthpiece for the group, mentioned a meeting at the detective bureau at one of the police stations. Cops. Sam swiveled more to monitor the exchange, half waiting to be introduced. It didn't happen though, and she hardly cared. It was nice to see Lucy so animated at seeing her old cronies. Sam watched as her girlfriend happily hooked them up with complimentary coffee and cookies, clearly proud of the business she had cultivated.

They were standing in a semicircle yammering away in cop-speak when the greeting bells jangled and a woman decked in full uniform strolled in with a younger cop who clearly didn't hold her rank.

"Gentlemen," she said, saying hello to them as a group.

"Captain." They addressed her formally, their laughter dying out. Sam idly wondered if Lucy would be so respectful, seeing as she was no longer part of the force. Sam looked to see for herself, but when she assessed Lucy's reaction, there was neither joviality nor reverence. Only shock.

"Lucy."

"Dani. Hi." Lucy stuffed her hands in the back pockets of her jeans. "You got promoted. Congratulations."

"Thanks." She twisted her eight-point hat in her hands, looking around. "This is a nice place you have."

"Thank you."

"I've been meaning to reach out to you." The officer glanced at the detectives for reference. "I guess you know we had a major case meeting out here today."

Lucy nodded. "The guys filled me in."

"Right."

"Anyway, I was hoping we could talk." Her tone held hope and her eyes did too. "Privately, perhaps?" she added, as though her intent wasn't already clear.

Lucy looked over in her direction, but she clearly wasn't asking permission. Not that she needed to, but it still felt like betrayal when she waved the woman back behind the coffee bar, through the door, and into the kitchen area. Through her anger, Sam listened to the other cops snicker among themselves, making jokes about how some things never changed. One of them turned to her before he passed through the door on his way out. "Hey, tell your boss thanks for the joe." She wasn't sure why she nodded in response.

Her blood pressure began its steady incline as the minutes passed and there was no sign of Lucy. She glared at the lackey cop waiting for his boss even though none of whatever was happening was his fault. He must have felt her ire though because he excused himself to wait outside, crossing his arms over his chest as he virtually stood guard in front of the door.

When they finally emerged, Dani first, Lucy just behind her, they were both silent. Lucy stayed behind the counter but the other woman headed straight for the door. Just before she left, she turned and said, "Think about it, Lucy," before she opened the door and was gone.

Thirty seconds passed and Lucy said nothing. She gave no apology, no explanation. Sam waited until she saw the white-and-blue patrol car pull away before she spoke.

"Are you kidding me?" she asked. When Lucy responded with a blank stare, she controlled the anger in her voice, but just barely. "What was that?"

Lucy took a deep breath and leaned against the prep counter behind her. "It's not as bad as it looks."

"Well, that's good. Because it looks pretty fucking terrible." She didn't care that she was being harsh. Lucy's actions were rude and hurtful. She wanted her to know in addition to taking her by surprise, she'd also upset her. "Care to enlighten me on your private meeting?"

"Calm down, Sam."

"I think I'm being very calm in light of the situation." Her pulse was racing. "What the hell, Lucy?"

"It's not what you think."

"Fantastic. Because what I think is that Miss Hotshot Cop there"—she pointed sharply toward the door—"is your ex. And I'm pretty sure she was here to get you back."

Lucy let out a heavy sigh but couldn't meet her eyes. "It's not quite that simple."

"Come on, Luce." She heard defeat in her tone as she pressed the base of her hands against her forehead. She took a minute to try to gain her composure but she just got angrier. "Fuck, I want to be wrong. I want to believe that my girlfriend would not escort her ex into the back room right in front of my face." She tapped the base of a fist on the edge of the counter. "I also want to believe there was a real good reason you didn't bother introducing me to any of your old friends. They think I'm your employee, by the way. That's an awesome feeling," she added sarcastically. "You know the worst part?" She stood and started backing away. "I actually believed I was more to you than just some person you're sleeping with." She bumped into a chair and almost knocked it over. "I guess not," she said righting it quickly. "Because that, the way you treated me just now? That's how you treat a fuck buddy. Believe me, I would know. But let me just say this." Her hand was on the door handle but she made eye contact from across the room. "Even when I'm away on business, I go out of my way to stay away from my project manager after hours." She rolled her eyes at her own foolishness. "God, these days, I don't even go out for drinks with my team, just to avoid any uncomfortable interactions or *anything* that could be misconstrued as flirting. I do that out of respect for you, Lucy. And you're not even there." She shrugged as she stood in the open doorway. "I guess we're just not on the same page."

Sam waited for a second. Whether she was hoping for Lucy to ask forgiveness or beg her to stay, she wasn't sure. It hardly mattered, because Lucy said nothing.

❖

It was almost nine. Sam tossed the controls aside and pushed off the leather couch in her parents' finished basement. She'd purposely let herself fall down the rabbit hole playing *Outback Outlaw* on her nephews' gaming system that was hooked up to the gigantic flat screen. The constant shoot-outs made it easier to avoid Lucy's texts that had been coming through steadily since she left the shop. They were all apologies and were probably heartfelt, Sam thought, even though texting dulled any emotion that might actually be present.

Sam knew this wasn't an end-of-relationship kind of fight, but she hadn't yet responded because she was still raw. Only now, hours later, was she finally coming down. She should probably send a message. At least answer one of the texts. Padding across the floor she searched behind her father's bar hoping for something to take the edge off as she figured out what she wanted to say. She'd tried a beer earlier but couldn't get past the first sip. Behind the oak bar, the selection was expansive but still nothing appealed. She leaned her elbows against the smooth bar surface and rested her head in her hands. Today sucked.

She heard her phone vibrating across the room, and when she looked over saw that it was Lucy. A phone call. That was…direct. Without taking time to overthink it, she walked over and answered.

"Hey."

"Hi." Lucy's voice was sweet and she sounded relieved Sam had answered. "I'm so sorry, Sam."

"Luce—"

"Please, listen to me for a second. I know you're ignoring me. And rightfully so, I guess."

"I just needed a minute. That's all."

"I want to give you as much space or time as you want. Honestly." She heard a siren in the distance echoing through the phone. "But I need you to know...what you said today, it's not true." The siren got louder and sounded close by. "That's not how I think of you."

Sam nodded even though Lucy couldn't see her. "I know." She sank into the couch and put her feet on the edge of the coffee table.

"You have to believe me." Lucy sniffled a little and Sam wondered if she was crying. "Can I see you?"

She wanted to say yes and race right over to Lucy's apartment, kiss her face, forgive her on the spot, but it seemed pathetic. Plus she was wearing beat-up sweats and a worn-out baseball tee. She could use a shower, a change of clothes at the very least. She found her dignity. "I'll come by in the morning, before I go into the city."

"I don't want to wait that long to talk to you."

She almost caved, but resisted. "We're talking now."

"I want to see you. I need you." There was a pause. "I get it if you don't want to be with me tonight. You need a break. I respect that. Can I come inside? Or, better yet, just come out for a minute."

"What?"

"I'm kind of outside your house."

"You are?" Sam took the stairs in twos, making it to her front door in under thirty seconds. Peering out the glass storm door she caught a glimpse of Lucy's Nissan Rogue across the street. She pushed the door open, not waiting for an answer. "Come here, park in the driveway."

Sam ended the call without saying good-bye as Lucy pulled in behind her Tahoe. She opened the passenger door and sat down next to Lucy.

"Sorry I'm a mess," Lucy said, smoothing her hair back off her face.

Sam fanned over her sweats and tee. "Right there with you."

"I'm not stalking you, I swear." Lucy shifted in her seat, and the glow of the gold streetlight framed her beautiful face. She let out a nervous laugh. "Okay, maybe I am a little." She rubbed her palms against her jeans. "Are you still mad?"

"It's not that I'm mad." Sam faced forward, her eyes glued to the back of her truck. Was that a scratch? "I don't understand why you would treat me like that." She pressed her head into the headrest and turned to look at Lucy. "You didn't even introduce me. Not that I really care, but then when your ex came"—she dropped her gaze—"I just felt like a jerk."

"Babe, I don't know what I was thinking." Lucy moved closer in her seat and placed her hand on Sam's forearm.

"What happened today?" Sam asked.

"It's not what you think."

"She's not your ex?" Sam's voice was full of disbelief.

"No, she is, but it's more than that." She looked out her own window and let out a heavy sigh. "It's complicated."

"Luce, you're here. I'm here. Talk to me."

"There was a moment"—Lucy's mouth hung open and she was clearly choked up—"more than a moment, when she could have saved my police career." She jutted her chin. "She didn't."

"Lovely woman."

"The incident at the police department, the accidental discharge, well, I was with her when it actually happened. I told you I wasn't in the room where it happened. I was with Dani. She could have admitted that."

"Why didn't she?"

"She was off post. There would have been repercussions to her career, for one. Also, she was married." She tilted her head to the side. "I can't imagine that would have gone over well at home either."

"Instead, you lose your job. That's fair."

"She apologized today. That's why she wanted to talk to me. She knows she screwed me over."

"A little late, no?" Sam's question was snide and she waited a beat before asking what she really wanted to know. "What else did she say?"

Lucy's expression told her that she didn't need to be more specific. She didn't even try to sugarcoat it. "She's divorced now."

"I knew it."

"It doesn't matter." Lucy reached for Sam's hand. "I'm with you. I told her that."

Sam raised her eyebrows. "She didn't seem convinced."

"That's just Dani being Dani." Lucy's voice was flippant. Sam wondered if she was downplaying their relationship for her sake.

"But you loved her." It was a question, even though she didn't phrase it as one.

Lucy smiled and curled her lips. "No, I didn't." She tapped the bottom of the steering wheel with one finger. "That might make it worse," she added. "But it's the truth."

"You took her in the back." Sam crinkled her forehead, knowing her distress was on display. "God, Lucy. It killed me."

"I know." She hung her head in defeat. "I was thrown off by all of it. The guys. Dani," she added. "It's no excuse. I shouldn't have done that." She gripped the steering wheel at ten and two, chewing her cheek. "I am so, so sorry. Please forgive me. I can't lose you over this."

"You're not." Sam shook her head. "I'm just...it hurt."

"I never want to hurt you." She looked at Sam and touched her face, her hands stroking her cheekbones and jaw. "I love you, Sam." She leaned forward and kissed her gently. "I am sorry. For everything today."

"I know."

"Come home with me." Her finger traced Sam's lips. "I need to be near you. I want to fall asleep in your arms."

"Okay." She didn't need convincing. She wanted those same things. "Give me ten minutes. I have to go grab a suit and stuff—I have a big presentation tomorrow." Sam opened the door but Lucy grabbed her forearm.

"Wait." She looked nervous and her voice caught in her throat. "Can I ask you something?"

Sam pulled the door shut, meeting Lucy's serious tone. "What's the matter?"

"You said something today. Earlier. It's been on my mind all afternoon."

"What is it?"

Lucy looked down at her short fingernails. "This woman you had a thing with." She looked out the window. "From your job." She paused again. "Is she always with you when you're away?"

Sam let out a long slow breath. It was a question she wasn't expecting. "A lot, yeah." She thought about it for a second. "Not always. But probably ninety percent of the time, these days."

"Ouch."

"Babe, there is nothing there. Trust me."

"I know. You don't owe me an explanation."

Sam reached across the center console and took Lucy's hand. "I'll give you one, though." She rolled her head against the headrest searching for the best way to put it. "It has nothing to do with anything other than we work well together. We have good click. Professionally, I mean."

"Stop." She squeezed Sam's hand. "I trust you."

"You should." Sam rubbed Lucy's hand with her own. "There was never anything there. The thing with me and—"

Lucy put her hand up stopping the conversation. "No. I don't want to know. I can't." She waved both hands frantically. "I can't know the details. I'll harp on them." She whooshed her hands through her hair. "Let's just leave it alone." She blinked long and hard. "I know myself. If I know too much, just trust me, I won't let it go." She turned, looked right at Sam, and frowned pathetically. "It's a character flaw."

"It's okay." Sam let out a half laugh.

"I probably sound crazy. Look, I know you've had a life before me. I get that. I just don't need to know the specifics. God, I have no idea how Lexi does it."

"What do you mean?"

Lucy shook her head. "Being with Jesse. Seeing Mary around all the time and knowing they were together. You know, like that." She widened her eyes. "Like the way she is now with Jesse. I couldn't do it. No way."

"I'm surprised you know that story."

"Lexi and I talk. She really went out of her way to include me when I moved here. Make me feel part of the community." Lucy's face softened at the recent nostalgia. "She knew my story, a lot of it anyway. I filled in the gaps for her." Her mouth twisted to the side in a small smile. "She confided in me too. Probably just to make me feel comfortable."

"She is one of a kind."

"My point is, I couldn't handle what she deals with on a daily basis."

"No worries, there."

"Sam, I know it's your job to be around this woman. I respect that. Just promise me, okay?"

"Luce, look at me." She waited until Lucy turned, and was silent for a second, hoping Lucy could see how deeply she felt about her. "You're it for me." She felt her mouth tweak up to one side. "I love you." She flicked Lucy on the leg with one finger making an attempt at light humor in spite of the seriousness of the conversation. "Even if I have to beg you to hang out with me outside of your store or your apartment."

"You don't have to beg me."

"I'm teasing," Sam said, even though there was an air of truth to her comment.

"In a year or so I'll be in a better place with the shop, I'll have less overhead, make more profit. Hire more staff so I can keep better hours. Probably not in the mornings," she added offhandedly, "but certainly I'll be able to get away more."

"Lucy, I'm not going anywhere. You're stuck with me."

Lucy reached for the bottom of Sam's shirt to pull her close, but Sam resisted, casting a look at the façade of the house.

"Is that not okay to do here?" Lucy asked, looking from the house and back obviously trying to assess the situation.

Sam rolled her eyes. "It's fine. I mean my parents know. Obviously." She indicated her body with one hand. "They're just...not great about it." She grimaced. "We have more of a don't ask, don't tell thing happening here." She picked a piece of lint off the glove box. "It's ridiculous, but it's their house and I'm living here for free." Rolling down the window, she let the fabric go in the warm breeze. "I hope you're not mad I didn't ask you to come in. It's not that they'd be outwardly mean to you or anything. They would just judge you silently. Like they do me." She zipped the window back up. "I have to endure it. You don't need that nonsense."

Lucy squeezed Sam's hand. "I didn't know."

"It's not tragic. They're not bad people. They just can't deal with me being gay. Actually, that's not even it. They're fine with the fact that I'm gay, in theory anyway. I mean, they are total libs, my parents. On paper, anyway. What they can't handle is that I'm butch. It bothers them. They used to ask why I wasn't more like Lexi. They thought I was trying to prove something." She winked at Lucy. "You'll do okay with them. The long hair helps." She was hoping her situation came off not as dour as she knew it sounded.

Lucy frowned. "I shouldn't have just shown up here."

"How did you find me anyway?"

"You mentioned that your parents live across from the country club." Lucy hid her smile. "I've seen your car just about every day for months. I know your plate. Force of habit," she said lifting one eyebrow in explanation. "I was a cop for almost ten years."

"You tracked me down?"

"Don't make it sound all creepy."

"It actually just sounds like a lot of work."

"Not really. I knew the general vicinity. I drove around until I saw your truck." Lucy picked a frayed fiber from the rip in her jeans. "It didn't take me long at all. I spent more time around the corner trying to work up the nerve to call you."

"Don't ever do that again."

"Come here? Okay," she said, answering her question before Sam could.

"No." Sam shook her head, smiling. "You can come here whenever you want. I told you that stuff just so you'll know what the vibe is here. But you are always welcome." She held Lucy's hand and looked at her seriously. "Never, ever be nervous about talking to me," she said, giving a little squeeze. "Promise me."

"I promise." She nudged Sam's shoulder. "Now go get your clothes for tomorrow, so I can take you home and rip these ones off. Okay?"

"Sounds like a plan."

CHAPTER SIXTEEN

Meg bounced along Ninth Avenue, basking in the feel of the warm morning sun on her face. Making the early boat put her ahead of schedule, so she stopped at the small café she passed every Saturday on her way to the rescue mission. There was no denying she was basically a volunteer in her own right at this point. The store's long line gave her time to reflect on that truth. While she had initially come there to hang with Sasha—build a friendship, she told herself—she had come to find working at the no-kill shelter beyond rewarding. The staff couldn't be nicer, and pairing sweet animals with loving families? No better way to start a weekend.

She balanced her bag of goodies in one hand as she waited for Sasha on the corner of Forty-Fourth Street. She was still way early, so she reached for her phone to do a quick social media scan when she heard a sharp wolf whistle from halfway down the block. Without lifting her head, she looked up to see Sasha walking toward her.

"Did you just catcall me?" Meg asked, grinning as she slipped her phone into her back pocket.

"I might have," Sasha responded with a devious smile.

"Interesting."

"More interesting that you looked."

Were they flirting? "Well it's six forty on Saturday morning. Can't help it if my interest was piqued. It's pretty much me and the street cleaners awake at this hour."

"And me." Sasha swayed back and forth. "What's in the bag, sexy?"

"Sexy?"

"Hey. I haven't even had coffee yet and I'm talking to a hot girl on my corner. No point in mincing words." She nodded with her chin. "Whatcha got there?"

This was definite flirting. Meg was surprised at Sasha's boldness and didn't bother masking it. She gave a long dramatic blink and shook her head, owning her shock. "Sorry, not used to so much attention this early in the day. Or ever, really."

"Well, get used to it."

What the hell? Not that she was complaining, but this seemed a new level. Perhaps Lexi was right. Well, that or she was completely overthinking it. Damn if she knew. "I bought us breakfast."

"Megan." Sasha dragged her name out, leaning forward and completely surprising Meg with a peck on the cheek. "You are so sweet."

"It's just coffee and croissants." She heard herself stutter and hoped Sasha didn't notice. "Don't get too excited."

"Still. Thank you."

It was a little awkward to eat and walk so they divvied up the provisions with Meg holding both drinks as Sasha took the bag of pastries. They took their time getting to the mission, Sasha pausing to take sips of her coffee here and there while she pulled pieces of almond croissant from the paper bag, alternately passing bites to Meg and feeding herself. She filled Meg in on the details of her Friday night—watching old episodes of *Miss Fisher's Murder Mysteries* on BBC while doing schoolwork. Meg's night hadn't been much more eventful. Without giving herself a chance to talk herself out of it, she blurted out, "So, next Friday, Lucy's showing *Thongs of The Undead* at the coffee shop. Want to come?"

"What?"

Sasha looked confused, so Meg explained. "You know that zombie movie people are obsessed with?"

"No, I know it."

"Or not." Meg felt suddenly embarrassed at her invitation. "I just thought, I don't know, she did it once before. Hosted a movie night. She got a nice crowd and it was fun. Different." Meg shrugged. "I know, dumb movie, but still."

"You obviously haven't seen it."

"No. Don't tell me." Meg shook her head slowly, making fun of Sasha on the spot. "Of course, you love it. I forgot about your penchant for ridiculous movies."

"*TOTU* is a metaphor. For life. You'll see," she said, with a playful bump to the shoulder.

"*TOTU?*"

"*Thongs of The Undead.*" Sasha counted out the words on her fingers. "*T-O-T-U.*"

"Oh my God." Meg looked to the sky. "What did I just get myself into?"

Sasha's smile was laced with something deeper as Meg held the door to the rescue mission open for her. They held eye contact and there was something there, Meg was sure of it, but the moment was broken when Beau, the shelter's hipster director, hooked Sasha's arm with a loud, "I need you," as he whisked her across the room.

Goddamn it. They were just on the verge of something. *Maybe.* She shouldn't care this much and she knew it. She took a deep breath trying to regulate her pulse as she watched Beau lean into Sasha's space. Fucking Beau. Even his name was annoying. He was nice enough but his type got under her skin. Maybe it was jealousy. He was insanely good-looking with his longish hair always a calculated mess and his dark facial scruff, more than a five o'clock shadow but not quite a beard, contrasting perfectly with his light eyes. He probably survived on kale and green tea. And he totally just ran interference on her. Did he just touch Sasha's arm? He was leaning in and whispering, looking serious as he spoke. No fucking way. No. She was wrong, she had to be. Sasha was just flirting with her less than a half hour ago. Or maybe she wasn't. And they had planned a date. Okay, maybe not officially. But Friday night. Movie. The two of them. Arguably a date.

Her blood pressure dropped a few points when Sasha looked over at her and smiled reassuringly. God, she must have been staring. She went down to the main area to clear her head and busy herself with the morning chores.

It was a hectic day at the shelter with more visitors than previous weeks. With the onset of summer, the shelter was busy as people were more inclined to adopt and the hours zipped by, filled with prospective pet owners and their myriad questions. It wasn't until almost noon when she got a minute with Sasha alone.

"Crazy today, huh?" Meg said.

"I know. Listen, Meg—"

But she didn't have a chance to finish before Beau was there. Again. "They need you for paperwork at the desk, Sash."

That was twice now. She didn't know what Sasha was going to say and it probably wasn't deep, but still it drove her crazy. She didn't have time to dwell on it before Beau gave her an assignment of her own. Before she knew it, she was done for the day. Sasha was nowhere in sight, so she found her backpack and started to pack up.

"You're not going to Irish good-bye, are you?"

"I looked for you."

"Is your phone dead or something?"

"No, why?"

"If you don't know where I am, you should text me."

That was a weird statement, but she brushed it off. "I figured you were busy."

"What time is the movie on Friday?"

"I think eight. I'm not sure." She bent down to tie her shoe, even though the knot was still in place. "What's up with you and Beau? You guys seem…chummy." She hated the way her voice squeaked out the word, making her sound every bit as petty and jealous as she felt.

Sasha's face held an expression Meg couldn't quite read. It was nerves or guilt or confusion. Maybe all three. "Nothing at all," she said finally. "He's into Jane-Anne. We hung out a couple of weeks back, a few of us and his friends. He asked me to see if I could orchestrate a redux for tonight. Any chance you would come?" She stuffed her hands in her pockets and let her shoulders drop. "Please?"

Even though she felt like a bit of an afterthought, Sasha's sweet expression told her it wasn't the case. And God, did she ever want to go, but the reality was she had a commitment she couldn't escape. "Ugh, I wish," she said, hoisting her backpack over one shoulder. "I have a birthday party to go to." She checked her watch. "I should get going, actually."

"Your party is tonight or…" Sasha lifted her eyebrows as her voice faded, clearly waiting for Meg to explain.

"No, sorry. It's this afternoon. In Ditmas Park. I'm not even really sure which subway to take." She frowned as she voiced her mild frustration out loud. "I feel like by the time I get there, sit through the party, and then make it home, it'll probably be late."

"Whose party is it that you are so completely unexcited about?"

Meg smiled at Sasha's perfect read of her sentiment. "Ezra. My cousin's kid. He's turning six."

Sasha responded with a nod. "Ah."

"With my parents living in Florida, my sister and I are expected to represent at family functions. I don't mind usually, but Shannon is tied up with her kids' stuff today, so I'm on my own." She shrugged.

"No, you're not." Sasha reached down and grabbed her bag. "I'll go with you."

"Shut up," Meg countered playfully until she met Sasha's eyes and saw she was serious. "Wait, really?"

"Is that okay?"

"Of course. But—"

"No buts." Sasha held up one hand stopping her. "I'm going to brave a kiddie party with a pile of six-year-olds hopped up on sugar. And then to return the favor, you keep me company tonight, probably at the straightest bar ever"—she added an exaggerated eye roll—"where we will try to orchestrate a love connection for Beau and Jane-Anne. Deal?"

Meg smiled. "How can I say no to an offer like that."

❖

A full four hours later, Meg strolled along Ocean Avenue unable to keep her smile secreted as Sasha walked next to her. She felt a surge of hope and angst race through her when Sasha's arm brushed against her own.

"So what'd you think?" Sasha hooked her hand through Meg's arm just above her elbow.

"Of the party?" Meg asked trying not to overthink Sasha's casual touch.

"Mm-hmm." Sasha peered into her goodie bag. "I give it a full ten. The food was great. Cake, spot-on. And that piñata—gold mine." She shook the bag in her hand, shuffling the contents inside. "Also, your family was super sweet to me."

"They're pretty great people." Meg didn't have the heart to tell Sasha that she was certain her relatives simply assumed she and Sasha were a couple. She also didn't reveal that she hadn't bothered to set the record straight, choosing instead to enjoy the fantasy of being girlfriends for a few short hours. She wondered if that made her pathetic, but the truth was she didn't care.

Sasha pulled out a Tootsie Pop before trading it for a Bit-O-Honey. "Ooh, look at this. Old-school," she said, twisting it between her fingers as she examined the wrapper before opening it. "Want half?"

Meg shook her off. "It is a miracle you have any teeth left."

"I know, right?" Sasha laughed at herself.

Meg shook her head in mock judgment, turning them toward the direction of the subway as she checked the time.

"Do you want to go home?" Sasha's voice was sincere and it caught Meg off guard. "I don't want you to feel like you have to come into the city tonight if you don't want to."

Meg narrowed her eyes. "We made a deal, I thought."

"I know, but I sort of squirmed my way in."

"You were in it for the candy all along." Meg's response was coupled with a fake grimace. "I should have known," she teased.

"Well, that is a bonus," Sasha started, but her voice lost its lilt as she got momentarily serious. "The truth is I wanted to spend some time together. I miss being around you."

What exactly that meant, Meg had no idea, but she felt her heart race and knew she was blushing at the mere possibility that Sasha was hinting at something beyond platonic. She hoped her voice held steady when she responded, "Sure, I could go home, I guess. But fair is fair." She shrugged. "Also, I'd be lying if I said I wasn't mildly intrigued to see the dynamic between Jane-Anne and Beau. I would never have put the two of them together." She reached for her MetroCard as she waited for Sasha to pass through the turnstile first. "I guess I figured Jane-Anne would go for the Wall Street type. Maybe even a jock. Definitely not a composting tree-hugger like Beau," Meg raised her eyebrows dramatically at her good-natured teasing. "I'm genuinely curious to see how this plays out."

Sasha smiled but her eyes were serious and Meg thought for sure she was about to say something deep, but the train rolled into the station breaking the moment. The subway car was jam-packed and they had to squeeze in just to let the doors close. Meg felt Sasha's body pressed against hers, and when the train jerked forward, Sasha grabbed her hand. "I may need to hold on to you for balance," she whispered.

Even though Meg was sure it was unintentional, being this close and feeling Sasha's breath in her ear made her heart ache, to say nothing of what it did to the rest of her body. She wondered if Sasha felt the same. Right at that moment, as if reading her thoughts, Meg felt Sasha give her hand a small squeeze. It sent her libido into overdrive. *How could this ever be friendship?* she wondered, swallowing her feelings as she relished the remaining alone time before they joined the rest of Sasha's crew.

❖

Sasha had arranged for her friends—Jane-Anne and a few other girls—to meet up with Beau and some of his buddies at Bar Nine, a relaxing spot with a super chill vibe on the West Side. After introductions were made, Meg grabbed a seltzer and headed to the outdoor area to enjoy the warm evening.

"Ooh, it's gorgeous out here." Jane-Anne's voice cut through the quiet breeze. She sat next to Meg on the wooden bench seat. "How have you been, Meg?"

"Good. How about you?"

"Really good, thanks." Even though Meg had spent a fair share of time with Jane-Anne when she and Sasha were together, they'd never been especially close and Meg wondered what they would talk about without the others to buffer, but Jane-Anne dove right in. "Sash says you got a cat. Do you have a picture?"

Meg unlocked her phone and pulled up a series of Spencer, handing it over so Jane-Anne could peruse at her own pace.

"Oh my God, Meg, she's really precious." She took a sip of her cocktail. "It's nice to see you and Sasha spending time together," she said changing the subject altogether. "I haven't seen her like this in ages. Happy, I mean."

Meg was sure Jane-Anne was going to say more, but Beau and one of his friends approached and changed the dynamic completely. They were followed shortly by Sasha and the rest of their small party. Sasha took the seat across from Meg and with one look inquired if she was doing okay. Meg smiled in response. She loved that they could communicate wordlessly like this. It made her feel connected and in sync and longing for more.

Hours later, when the group had mostly moved back inside, Meg found a vacant seat on a couch in the corner and rested her head against the backrest. She could do nothing to stifle her repeated yawns.

Sasha squeezed in next to her, half leaning over Meg to be heard over the music. "You're tired," she said.

"I am," Meg admitted. "It's been a long day."

"Great day, though."

"Definitely." She saw Sasha look at her mouth and wondered if she wanted Meg to kiss her. Meg was dying to make a move but there were so many people around, and even though the whole day had felt like an extended date, she still wasn't a hundred percent sure if she was simply projecting her feelings onto the situation. She broke eye contact to check the time.

"You want to go?" Sasha asked.

"It's not that I want to. It's just late and I'm beginning to lose the battle."

"I know." Sasha flicked her eyes over toward Beau and Jane-Anne deep in conversation in the corner. "I wish those two would wrap it up already. I want to go over there and tell them that it's confirmed. They are definitely into each other." She let out a small laugh.

"Oh, don't ruin it for them," Meg teased. "The beginning is the best part."

"I don't know. Beginnings can be scary. Sometimes it takes some time to be comfortable and really relax, you know?"

Meg smiled softly and nodded, for the moment convinced they were talking specifically about their past relationship. Sasha smiled back and reached for her hand, intertwining their fingers as she spoke.

"Come on, I'll walk you out."

Meg let her lead the way, not bothering to say good-bye to anyone else. When they reached the sidewalk in front of the bar, Sasha pulled her in for a long hug. With her arms tight around Meg's shoulders, she breathed in her ear, "I had the best day."

"Me too." Meg pulled away and then leaned forward again, placing a small kiss on Sasha's face so close to her mouth that their lips touched slightly at the corner.

"I'll see you Friday," Sasha said. "I really can't wait."

"Good night, Sash."

Meg backed away and watched Sasha re-enter the bar, already counting down the minutes until next weekend.

CHAPTER SEVENTEEN

M eg could tell herself all she wanted that she was rebuilding a friendship with Sasha, but she didn't have to dig deep to know she was kidding herself. On Thursday afternoon when she was supposed to be updating the Dillinger proposal, she found herself completely caught up in a fantasy about tomorrow night's movie event. What would she wear? Was it a date? It had to be. After last Saturday there was no denying they still had a connection. Should she invite Sasha back to her house after the movie? Of course she wanted to, but maybe it was too soon. Then again, Sasha would want to meet Spencer. She rubbed her hands hard against her face. She didn't have time to stress about this. Not now, when she needed to be focused on her client and thus secure the promotion she more than earned on a daily basis.

What was happening between them anyway? The chemistry had been building steadily, but should it be? This was the problem with Sasha—when she was with her, it felt right, but once she stepped away, Meg was able to think clearly about the past and remember their relationship as it actually had been. Then again, Sasha seemed different now. More chill than when they had dated. She was even completely fine with openly dating women, it seemed. Even if that was the case, it didn't change their past. Sasha had strung her along for months and ultimately cheated on her. But she seemed so different. The same, but different, if that made sense. She tipped her head back, letting her hands fall forward with a thud onto the pile of work waiting for her on the pressed-wood credenza. Now was not the time. For the moment, her head belonged to Dillinger Pharmco. After she landed the senior associate spot, she would allow herself to consider the possibility of something more than friendship with Sasha Michaels. Maybe.

In spite of her self-imposed mini-lecture, she needed to use all her willpower to buckle down for the next twenty-four hours. She allowed herself a few brief exchanges with Sasha, learning that Beau and Jane-Anne would be joining them for the *TOTU* event. That was interesting. Kind of double date-y, if she did say so herself.

❖

Lucy brought out extra seating for nights like this but real estate was still key. Meg arrived early and secured a nice table in the back that was perfect for the four of them. She put her phone down on top of it claiming the spot as she paced the back wall. She offered Lucy a hand, but everything was taken care of, so she kept her eye on the door and tried to keep her pulse in check. She was leaning on the bar talking to Lucy and actually did a double take when she saw Reina enter the store. In addition to her cousins Teddy and Rose who lived at Bay West, Reina was also accompanied by Melinda.

Meg kept her composure. "Hey, Reina," she said, kissing her politely on the cheek, following suit with Teddy and Rose. She gave a small wave in greeting to Melinda. "Hello, again."

"It's good to see you, Meg," Reina offered.

Meg nodded toward the screen. "I didn't know you were a fan."

"Not really me." Reina obviously felt bad admitting the truth that she was here for Melinda.

Wow. This was happening. Even though she shouldn't have been surprised, she was. She found her manners anyway and smiled supportively. She exchanged a look with Reina and thought she saw something of an apology in her eyes. It wasn't necessary and Meg wanted her to know it. "You guys should grab a spot. It'll fill up quick in here. I put my stuff on the table in the corner, but I'm pretty sure the one next to it is free."

Reina smiled and Meg saw gratitude in her eyes before she walked over to claim the space. Meg tried not to stare. She and Melinda doted on each other sweetly and she was happy for Reina. Inwardly she acknowledged her stomach muscles tightening. It wasn't jealously. It was something else—a sudden longing, a need—she couldn't wait for Sasha to arrive, so she could kiss her soft cheek, feel her body in her arms when she hugged her in greeting. Lost in her fantasy, she missed Sasha's entrance altogether and was jolted back into the present when she felt a hand on her back.

"Hey, stranger." Sasha's voice was soft in her ear but when she turned around to greet her she was met with not one, not two, but three smiling faces. "This is Evan," Sasha said, introducing a guy she had never seen before. "He's Beau's friend."

"Oh. Nice to meet you." Meg hoped the irritation she felt at the unknown addition to her group didn't show. She stuck out her hand to make nice and guided them to the table she had reserved. Deep breath, she told herself. This was going to be fine. But she had to scurry to find an extra chair to drag over, and when she did, she had to jam it in between Sasha and Jane-Anne, inevitably pushing Sasha closer to Evan and his man bun. She expected Sasha to say something, whisper an explanation as to why she hadn't informed her that she was bringing someone else. She wanted to hear that his presence was a surprise to her too. Instead, Sasha was deeply engaged in a spirited four-way conversation about the existential message embedded in *Thongs of The Undead.* Meg rolled her eyes and scanned the room. As if things could get any worse, less than two feet away she caught Melinda slide her hand along Reina's thigh. How the fuck was this happening?

Thirty minutes into the ridiculous film, her blood was still boiling when she got a message from her sister. Bingo. She didn't have to endure one more minute. No one would ever need to know that Shannon was simply texting to say hi. Meg excused herself quietly and slipped behind the counter, past Lucy, and through the door into the kitchen.

Heading straight for the back door she ignored the sting in her throat and was so focused on bolting that she nearly bumped into Sam who was just arriving.

"Hey, Meg." Sam grabbed her by both arms to steady them both. "You leaving?"

"My sister needs me," she lied.

"Isn't Sasha here?"

"It's okay," she said, hoping her voice didn't crack. "She brought her friends. I'll shoot her a message. I'm sure she'll understand."

"Whoa, Meg." Sam folded her arms and looked her right in the eye. "You okay?"

"Yeah, yeah." She coughed to cover the hitch in her voice. "I really gotta go." She backed away. "Have fun."

Something was up. Sam could tell right off that Meg was upset but she was so determined to leave that she wasn't going to stop her. Sam crossed to the sink in the kitchen and helped herself to a glass of water before spotting Lucy leaning on the counter as she watched the zombies philosophize.

"Hey, baby," Lucy whispered as Sam came up behind her. She put her hands on top of Sam's as they circled her waist. "How was your trip?"

"Fine. I missed you." Sam kissed her ear. She checked out the sizeable crowd, seeing the situation at Sasha's table and shaking her head as she put the pieces together on the spot. She held Lucy tighter and kissed the top of her shoulder.

"I'm surprised you stopped home first," Lucy said. "I know how you feel about *TOTU*."

Sam smiled against her neck. "There was something I needed there."

Lucy arched to look at her, her eyes narrowing in unspoken question.

Sam didn't leave her in the dark. She held her tighter, nuzzling her face into her neck and slowly moving her pelvis against Lucy's body. It took a second—but only a second—before Lucy registered the bulge in Sam's pants against her backside. Sam was exactly sure when it happened. She saw Lucy's mouth drop open and felt her simultaneous sharp intake of breath.

They had used the strap-on several times in the weeks since their initial conversation and one thing was certain—Lucy was a fan. But this was new. Sam usually assembled herself just prior to the act. She liked to think of what she was doing right now as functional packing, being ready to go right away, and she believed it would take the experience up a notch.

She rocked against Lucy slowly, loving her instinctual response as she matched the rhythm. Lucy grabbed her hand and pulled her into the kitchen. "How are you doing this to me?"

"What?" Sam answered playfully.

Lucy pulled her in for a long deep kiss and Sam obliged willingly. She backed Lucy up against the aluminum counter and felt Lucy's hand on her cock over her jeans. Lucy moaned low and deep before breaking them apart. "How much is left in this stupid movie?"

"*TOTU* is not stupid." Sam was aware of the ridiculous amount of seriousness in her tone before she chuckled, adding, "Like forty-five minutes."

"Fuck. Then I have to clean up." She leaned her head forward onto Sam's chest. "Torture. This is going to be torture."

"We don't have to wait," Sam said, lifting Lucy onto the counter swiftly as she filled the space between her legs. "Everyone is completely entertained out there. I'll be so fast," she whispered. Sam was mostly kidding but Lucy seemed to almost be considering it when the door opened.

"Yowza." Raven's eyes widened at their compromising position. "Don't mind me. Just getting some sugar. Apparently, you guys are too," she said winking and giggling at her own joke before grabbing a full dispenser and disappearing again.

"And that's why we have to wait," Lucy said with an exaggerated whimper.

"Good." Sam kissed her cheek and let her lips trail to her ear. "I want to take my time with you anyway."

"I hate you," Lucy said with a needy pout.

"No, you don't," Sam responded, unable to keep the sass out of her voice. She kissed her sweetly and patted her ass as Lucy led the way into the main room.

When the movie finished and the crowd dispersed, Sam watched Lucy and her staff clean the store with an unprecedented amount of zip. As she pitched in, snapping up extra folding chairs and storing them in the back, she almost wondered if Lucy had bribed the two girls. Whatever the case, she was thrilled to be on the road before eleven following Lucy to her apartment in expectation of what lay ahead.

They pushed through the front door and raced up the stairs, Sam's hands on Lucy's hips the entire time as they headed right for the bedroom. Sam let Lucy take control for the moment, swallowing a smile as she did so. She had come to love these little instances when Lucy took charge. It was something about the way her eyes got dark and heavy at the acceptance of the temporary power shift. Sam sat down on the edge of the bed and Lucy climbed on her lap, the weight of their bodies pushing them to the mattress.

Through her jeans, Sam could feel the base of her cock press against her clit when Lucy sat upright and writhed on top of her. Sam held her in place and moved with her, loving the sense of anticipation, the buildup of almost being together. For a second, she got lost in the excitement of the moment and she let out a little sound at the feeling it gave her. Lucy's breath was heavy and ragged as she shifted forward and met Sam's mouth with her own. The kiss was wild and intense, and Sam held the back of Lucy's neck as she pushed her tongue in deep, her desire for Lucy almost insatiable. Lucy moaned loudly in response before breaking them apart to kiss her way down the front of Sam's body, unbuttoning her shirt with unrivaled speed.

At her waistline, Lucy slowed down, and Sam noticed her hovering for a second as though she was considering something. She wondered if she should take over but Lucy met her eyes and answered her with a look that was just slightly naughty before she snapped back into action, undoing her belt and pulling her jeans off as she knelt between her legs. Sam felt Lucy's hands drift up her legs, her lips brushing the skin along the inside of her thighs. Sam propped up on her elbows to watch the action and saw Lucy caressing her cock through the tight fabric of her boxer briefs before tracing the outline with her open mouth. She teased her for a second only, lifting her boxers over the shaft and removing them completely.

Sam wasn't a hundred percent sure how far this was going to go, but her pulse raced at the possibilities. Her answer came one second later when Lucy ran her tongue along the shaft, reached the tip, adjusted for girth, and took it in her mouth.

Lucy's hair spilled forward and Sam reached for it gathering it up in her hand and holding it back so she could watch. Lucy moved her head slowly, allowing a little more in each time, occasionally stopping to run her tongue along the sides. Sam was so turned on she couldn't keep from moving her hips, and when she heard a moan from Lucy, she pulled back a little, worrying that she had gone too far. Thankfully, Lucy's expression told her it was okay.

This was completely new territory for Sam and the effect it was having was unbelievable. She felt her body jerk beyond her control and was suddenly afraid she was going to come just from watching. She rubbed her thumb softly on Lucy's cheek.

"Come here," she said in a low voice. Sam guided Lucy toward her smoothly, but with a firm hand, bringing her close and kissing her possessively. She lifted off Lucy's shirt and removed her pants quickly as she moved her mouth along Lucy's lithe body.

"Turn around," she whispered, helping Lucy into position in front of her. Reaching over from behind, Sam slid a hand along Lucy's breasts and stomach, pulling her upright to kiss her. She moved Lucy's hair off her neck and trailed her lips down Lucy's back as she bent her over again. She slid two fingers inside, but Lucy was so wet Sam took them out right away, reaching for her cock and guiding it in gently.

"Oh my God, I love that," Lucy said at the contact.

Sam tried to go slow but she was ready to explode. She kept her hands on Lucy's waist struggling to hold back.

"More," Lucy said between gasps.

"I don't want to hurt you," Sam managed.

"You never hurt me," Lucy said. "Please, baby."

Sam almost lost it at Lucy's pleading, but she listened, letting herself go completely as she fucked Lucy hard and fast. Lucy moaned loudly, finally dropping her shoulders and pressing her head against the mattress as she squeezed the fluffy pillows at the top of the bed. Sam was right there with her. The orgasm started at her center and surged through her entire body, synapse by synapse, until the tingle reached all the way to her fingertips. It was almost as though she was high, and she collapsed forward, her head sweaty as it fell between Lucy's shoulder blades, exhausted and content in her release.

She had nearly drifted off into a light sleep when Lucy turned to face her. She felt her soft hand on her lips a millisecond before Lucy kissed her and asked, "You okay, babe?"

"Mm-hmm." Sam opened her eyes and smiled. "That was… unreal."

"Yeah?" Lucy snuggled in. "You liked it okay?" she asked with an impish grin.

Sam raised one eyebrow. "Uh. Yeah." She moved Lucy's hand away from where it hovered near her crotch. "No way. I'm too sensitive still."

"Wow." Lucy nodded, clearly impressed with herself. "That must've been good."

"Babe." Sam licked her lips. "I can barely talk." She brought Lucy closer. "It was incredible." Her fingers skimmed up Lucy's back finding the ends of her hair and touching it gently. "No one has ever, ever done that for me before."

Lucy perked up on one elbow. "Really?"

"I'm sort of embarrassed to admit how much I liked it."

"Why?"

"I don't know. It seems…a little ridiculous, I guess."

Lucy just smiled. "I don't think it's ridiculous. I think it's hot." She leaned in and placed a soft kiss on Sam's lips. "Even hotter that I'm the only one." She made small designs on Sam's chest with her short nails. "I like knowing there's something that's only mine. It makes me feel special."

Sam kissed her forehead and waited for Lucy to look up. "Luce, you are way beyond special." She held her close as she spoke. "You know I love you." Rolling onto her back, she pulled Lucy with her, their bodies touching everywhere. "What you don't know is that I've never felt this way before. About anyone."

Lucy crinkled her forehead.

"Too much?" Sam winced a little, covering her eyes with one hand.

Lucy pulled her hand away. "No, babe." She brushed Sam's hand against her cheek before she kissed it. "I'm just surprised. What about Julie?"

Sam shook her head. "Nah. Julie was…a crush at first. Then kind of a challenge, which I know makes me sound like a dick." She blew out a long breath. "With Julie, I guess I thought I could be in love with her. See, it's like this," she started, moving a pillow into position behind her head. "I just never thought I would be *in love.*" She tucked a strand of Lucy's dirty-blond hair behind her ear. "The things other girls talked about feeling"—she shrugged—"I never felt it." Her fingers traced Lucy's face as though she was trying to memorize it by touch. "I just figured I wasn't wired like that. But then, you…" She blinked slowly, mimicking an explosion sound with her mouth and hand at the same time. "All at once. Boom."

She opened her eyes and Lucy was looking right at her.

"God, I love you."

"You do, huh?"

"You know I do." Lucy dropped a kiss on her. "You are never allowed to be with anyone else again."

"You know I won't."

"Great. Now we just have to go back and delete everyone from your past," she added with a shy smile. "So it's only me."

"It is only you, Lucy. Always." Sam leaned forward and her kiss was filled with sweetness and desire and passion and an endless amount of love. All the things she had never believed were in the realm of possibility for her were suddenly here, present in her every day. She turned Lucy around so she could hold her until they fell asleep. Life was fucking fantastic.

CHAPTER EIGHTEEN

With a sigh, Meg dropped into her favorite leather chair in the corner of Lucy's coffee shop in need of something supremely caffeinated to pull her out of her slump.

"I'm shocked you wanted to meet this early." Lexi's voice caught her off guard.

"Early? It's ten thirty." Meg looked past Lexi and waved hello to Sam and Lucy at the counter. "How did I not see you when I walked in?" she asked more to herself than anything.

Lexi answered anyway. "You're in your own world." She touched Meg's shoulder. "What do you want—I'll get it for you."

"Just coffee, but it's fine, I'll get it."

"Do you want to talk about it?" Lexi asked, settling into the spot across from Meg.

Meg looked out the storefront window and shook her head. "Nothing to talk about."

"Bullshit, Meg." Lexi tucked one leg under the other and paused for a second as she sipped her drink. When Meg still didn't respond, she pushed. "No mission today?"

"Nope."

"So you're just done with that now?"

"Third degree much?"

"I'm sorry. I thought we were friends." Lexi's voice was loaded with spirited snark as she punched Meg's knee. "Hey, when I'm upset, I talk to you. When something's up with you, you talk to

me. That's what we do, Meg. If you're not ready yet, that's fine."
She leaned all the way forward keeping her hand on Meg's jeans.
"You've been off the radar for over a week now, so you know I'm
going to make sure you're okay. You would do the exact same
thing for me."

"I know." She patted Lexi's hand. "I'm sorry," she said,
settling in to the worn chair. "I'm all over the place."

"This is because of Sasha and the movie thing?" When Meg
looked at her with an obvious question in her eyes, Lexi fessed up.
"Sam filled me in."

"But how did she—"

Lexi raised her shoulders. "She saw you there that night. She
said you were a mess and that you left in a hurry with some bogus
story about your sister needing you. Then she spotted Sasha and
her friend and the two guys. Not that hard to put together."

Meg rolled her neck and looked at the ceiling. "It's not just
Sasha. I mean, it is. But that is my own stupid fault for letting
myself get caught up again." She leaned forward and touched
the edges of her short hair for comfort. "I know what she's like. I
should have seen it coming."

"Meg, don't."

"Don't what?" She looked right at Lexi. "Admit the truth?
Sasha just wants attention. She'll take it anywhere she can get it."
Meg let out a nasty smirk. "Even better if she can have it from
everyone at the same time."

"Come on, Meg. I don't think that's true."

"Oh no?" Her voice was filled with anger and hurt and she
knew Lexi heard it. "What's the truth, then?"

"She wants to be with you, Meg."

"Yeah, okay," Meg said with a dismissive laugh.

"Look at me." Lexi waited until Meg gave her her full attention.
"I'm not guessing or surmising or anything like that. Sasha wants
to be with you. She told me, Meg. She's still in love with you."

"What?"

"You heard me."

"What are you talking about?"

Lexi let out a deep sigh. "Look, she came to me. I don't know, months ago, now." Lexi chewed her lip. "She asked for my help. She told me she'd made a huge mistake with you. And she wanted to win you back, essentially."

"Why didn't you tell me before?"

"Because she wanted to prove it to you herself. Which was the right thing to do, I think." Meg tried to interrupt, but Lexi stopped her. "Wait." She held up her hand. "I don't know exactly what happened during that stupid zombie movie, but I know she's upset about it and I know you've been blowing her off."

"Part of that is because of work." Meg held her head in her hands. "I need to get my head on straight if I'm going to get this promotion."

"Well, you should tell her that. The fact that you won't talk to her"—Lexi twisted the ceramic mug in her hands—"it's really hurting her."

"Lex—"

"Don't get all full of pride." Lexi rolled her eyes. "You love her. I know it. You may be able to BS everyone else, but I know the truth. And so do you. So stop being a baby and talk to her."

Lucy arrived with a fresh cup of coffee and Meg thanked her, wasting no time before taking a huge sip of her drink.

They watched Lucy return to Sam's side. "Now, moving on," Lexi said.

Meg laughed a little. "I know, I know. We have to get on the planning of the summer carnival idea we tossed around in the spring."

"Forget that." Lexi waved her off. "Sam and I figured it out." She shook her head. "We bailed on doing the carnival." At Meg's surprise, Lexi broke it down. "A carnival would be really expensive, and in the summer"—she shrugged—"we just don't get the numbers to make it profitable." She pushed her hair off her shoulders. "Maybe next year if we do it early and really promote it, but now, it's just too late in the game. I feel like in August everyone's away on vacation or running out to Fire Island to get their last shot at the beach."

"So we're just dropping it altogether?"

"Well, I think it's better to put more of our effort and resources to the singles event we talked about for the fall." Lexi tucked one leg under her. "But in the meantime, Sam and I hatched a plan to do a luau."

"A luau?"

"Yep." She tossed her hair lightly over her shoulders. "Think about it. Right off, the vibe is much lower key than a traditional social. We'll do tropical drinks and traditional food, like a pig roast but without the pig actually being here. Because, gross." She laughed at her own squeamishness. "Sam already has a local restaurant on board."

"All right. I can see it."

"Set up tiki torches all around. Throw down a makeshift dance floor. Keep the pool open. The whole thing will be outside. Unless it rains. Then we're fucked."

"It sounds really nice."

"It's different. Kind of chill. I think it will be a hit."

"Did you run it by Kam?"

"Not yet, but she'll go for it. Particularly once she hears how cost-effective it is. Even if the turnout is low, we won't lose money."

"I feel bad that you guys did all this without me. I suck."

"Not at all." Lexi rubbed her stomach gently with both hands. "Once this little peanut comes out, you'll be picking up the slack." She smiled at her friend. "We're a team."

"Thanks, Lex." Meg stood and kissed Lexi's forehead. "I'm going to go thank Sam too."

"When you're done with that, will you please call Sasha?" Lexi called over her shoulder. Meg didn't say yes, but she certainly allowed herself to consider the possibility.

❖

Meg wasn't able to commit to a phone call but late in the afternoon on the following day she sent a text to Sasha. She apologized for missing out on her volunteering duties for the past few weeks and cited work as the culprit. She couldn't bring herself to ask about Evan or the movie, and when Sasha attempted to bring it up, she dodged the subject. They kept it light like this for the next two weeks, and while Meg knew she was being purposely distant she justified it to herself as something she would deal with after the promotion had been announced. Truth be told, she needed the next three weeks to blow the roof off the Dillinger Pharmco folks to land the spot.

The week of the LOL—Ladies Only Luau—Meg worked her ass off at Sullivan. Finally coming through the door to her condo at ten p.m. Thursday night, she scooped Spencer up in her arms and cuddled her at the base of the staircase. She felt Spencer's sharp claws knead into her legs as she scratched behind her ears.

"You love that, don't you," Meg said.

Spencer answered with a loud purr and a turn of her tiny head as she touched Meg's nose with her own. Meg couldn't help herself. She reached for her phone and snapped a pic of Spencer's sweet face. Without spending a half hour overthinking her word choice, she threw it in a text to Sasha with the comment: *Come to Bay West's luau on Saturday. I really want to meet you!*

It wasn't the warmest invite, but she hoped the exclamation point made it less awkward.

Sasha's response was immediate. *Yes! I look forward to seeing you, adorable Spencer.*

Her text was followed immediately by more bubbles, so Meg waited to see what else Sasha had to say.

One question. What does one wear to a luau?

Duh. The corner of Meg's mouth curled into a tiny grin as she typed. *A coconut bra, of course.*

LOL. Got it. See you Saturday, Spence. She punctuated her comment with a heart emoji and Meg felt her own heart beat faster in response.

CHAPTER NINETEEN

The day of the luau boasted record-breaking temperatures. Factoring in the humidity, the heat index was in the midnineties by nine a.m. At three, Meg met Lexi and Sam to prep the grassy knoll area next to the pool and meet with their food and drink vendors, one of which just happened to be Lucy's Coffee Bar supplying sugary treats and nonalcoholic fare. They stocked Bay West swag at a makeshift merchandise stand, along with floral and kukui nut leis, and ensured that all the tikis were filled with burn oil. Just under a half hour before the party officially kicked off, Meg announced she was running home to grab a quick shower. When Lexi rolled her eyes in obvious disapproval, Meg mimicked the gesture in playful response, citing her level of perspiration and promising to be back in fifteen minutes.

Just as she was exiting the party setup, she saw Sasha sauntering toward her in a short, breezy cotton dress.

"Party's this way, I thought?" she said with a lazy smile.

Meg felt her cheeks pinch with a big smile. "You're early."

"I might have been hoping for some one-on-one time with a particular host," she said in a lyrical tone.

Meg felt herself blush and looked down at her clothes, slightly disheveled from hours of work in the blistering heat. "Well, this host is a disaster at the moment." She swiped at her damp shirt pulling it away from her body before snapping it back in place. "I was setting up all afternoon. I'm kind of a sweaty mess."

Sasha gave her a complete once-over and ticked her head to the side. "I think you look hot. As in, like, hot-hot. I mean sexy-hot, not, you know, because of the temperature." She covered her face with both hands. "Gah, talk about butchering a line."

Meg laughed as she pulled Sasha's hands away from her face. "You are cute, but I stink. I'm just going to shower quick. Go in," she said, nodding over her shoulder. "Lexi is there and Sam. I'll be right back."

She got ready fast enough, toweled her hair dry, keeping it a shaggy mess with extra pomade, and threw on clean shorts and a fresh tee. She felt good and clean and ready for the night ahead. But just as she approached the luau's entrance, Kam Browne pulled her aside.

"Meg, run up to the office in the Commons and get some change. We're low on small bills already. If there's nothing there, then hit the main business office in the rental section, that's definitely stocked. Here's the keys," she said handing over a gigantic key ring. "They're all labeled. I'm going to text you the safe combination now." It was not a *Please do this favor for me* kind of situation. This was an order from her boss. Good soldier that she was, she zipped to the Commons, but just as Kam suspected, the safe was low on singles and fives, so she was forced to trek to the rental section and back which took a good chunk of time. The second she got back, the beer vendor recognized her as one of the organizers and as he hooked her up with an IPA, he informed her that one of his CO_2 tanks was losing pressure. He had a backup in his van parked in the auxiliary lot, but with a busy bar and only one helper, he didn't have the staff to retrieve it.

Meg pounded her drink and took another as payment for her services as she hoofed it across Bay West's grounds to the overfill parking lot. Upon her return, she downed another drink, mostly from thirst, but as she watched the bartender fill her cup for the fourth time she remembered that she had hardly eaten all day. She should probably slow down. Taking the drink anyway she was about to turn around when she felt a hand on her shoulder.

"Hey, you." The familiar voice came from behind her and she turned, meeting Reina eye to eye.

Meg smiled, genuinely happy to say hello to her old girlfriend. "Reina. It's good to see you."

"Same, Meg." She reached forward and pulled Meg into a nice embrace. "Teddy tells me you're running things here at the development these days."

"I wouldn't say running them."

"The way I heard it, you're responsible for this party."

"That's kind of true, I guess."

Reina raised her mostly empty drink. "Nicely done, Meg. Really." Her smile was sincere. "This is a nice night."

"Thanks, Reina."

"You're truly in your element here, Meg. I'm happy for you."

Across the crowded bar, Meg saw Melinda eyeing them suspiciously as she fought to get her order in.

"Yeah, you too," Meg said with a nod. "Speaking of, I should let you get back to your girlfriend," she added.

"And you to yours," Reina said with a wink as she gestured into the distance. Meg followed her eyes to the edge of the dance floor where Sasha was talking to a tatted-up andro chick. She didn't bother to correct Reina's assumption. Her tone was completely earnest and Meg didn't know how to explain the state of in-between-ness that described her current relationship with Sasha.

She walked away, beer in hand, as a mix of emotions flooded through her. Trying to focus on the positive, she acknowledged that she was happy to have peace with Reina. Not that there had ever been any real fallout over their breakup, but it was still nice to feel completely content with the way it had all played out.

As she made her way toward Sasha, she couldn't ignore how much it irked her to witness the blatant flirting that was going on. Sasha didn't stop, even as Meg got closer. Fully annoyed, Meg continued walking right past, hoping to find Lexi or Sam or even someone who might give her another errand. She was almost at the Porta-Johns when Sasha caught up to her.

"Meg. Hey, Meg," she repeated when Meg ignored her. "Wait." She reached for her arm. "Are you avoiding me?"

"Sorry," she said coolly. "I had stuff to do." She looked past Sasha to the lines forming to use the facilities. "You seemed to entertain yourself okay." She took a sip of her drink. "No surprise there."

"What does that mean?"

Meg frowned keeping her eyes in the distance. "I'm gone for a few minutes. Working, by the way. And you've already moved on. Same old, same old." She raised her cup in an odd toast to her sentiment, before taking another long swig.

"Look at me," Sasha demanded.

"Excuse me?"

"I want you to look at me."

"You want everyone to look at you. Me, Beau, Evan, that chick over there." She gestured roughly with her cup and some beer spilled over the side landing with a splash on her foot. "That's sort of the problem."

"You're mad that I was talking to a girl?" Sasha shook her head like she couldn't believe it. "Meg, you've been gone for hours. Your friends are busy doing party stuff. Like you. When you didn't come back, I just felt"—she fingered her floral lei—"a little in the way."

"I'm so sorry to have inconvenienced you."

"Stop, Meg." Sasha touched Meg's forearm. "That's not what I meant."

She withdrew her arm, crossing it over her chest. "Fine, whatever, Sasha. It doesn't matter."

"Why are you being like this?"

Meg laughed obnoxiously. "I'm not being like anything. Go." She flicked her away with a dismissive wave of her hand. "Go back to your new friend, whatever her name is."

"Meg, I'm here for you. I want to be with you." She had tears in her eyes and her voice cracked a little. "You know I do."

"That's the problem, Sash. Even when you're with me, I mean, who knows?" She shrugged. "I disappear for a second and boom." She snapped her fingers. "Replaced, immediately."

"That's not true."

"It is though. I mean, cheating on me with Scott last year was the ultimate betrayal but I'm not even talking about that. Or tonight when you decide to pick up a random while I'm doing my job." She stuffed her hand into the pocket of her shorts, gripping her keys tightly. "Christ, even the fucking movie event at Lucy's. I actually thought we had a date planned, but no. You were on a date. With Evan, apparently."

"Meg, I didn't even know about that. Honestly."

"Sure you didn't."

"Really, I found out five minutes before we got there."

Even though she was a little tipsy, Meg heard truth in her own words. All the fears she hadn't wanted to own were suddenly impossible to ignore. It was as though her slight intoxication had lifted the lock of the dam and she was instantly flooded with the clarity to see her feelings and the courage to verbalize them.

"I can't keep being your doormat." She sniffled in spite of herself. "I won't do it."

"Gah, Meg." Sasha held her forehead with one hand. "I get it. I know you have every right to doubt me because of what happened with Scott. And even before that when we were together"—she shook her head—"I was a jerk. Selfish and stupid. So worried what everyone thought. But then I lost you and none of that mattered. Like, at all."

Sasha paused, and Meg waited. Sasha must have realized Meg wasn't going anywhere because she took a deep breath and continued. "You don't have to believe me. Honestly, I get why you're scared. I am too. I watched you talking to your ex just now at the bar. Hugging her. Was I jealous? Heck, yeah. That's life. I have spent the last, I don't know, year?" She held her hand up, not bothering to calculate exactly as she continued. "Trying to figure out how to get you to talk to me, to look at me like you used to.

I was thrilled when you asked me to watch *TOTU* with you. Not because it's a sick movie, but because I thought, *This is it*. This is my moment. And then the second we get there Beau springs it on me that his friend is coming and is, like, down the street. I tried to explain all of this to you over text but you kept shutting me down. So I let it go. And then you texted and told me to come tonight and I was so relieved and excited because, once again, I thought, yes, it's finally going to happen."

Sasha turned back and forth in a small semicircle, her nerves clearly getting the best of her as she spoke. "But I can see you're not ready. And it's okay. It's fine. But know this: I'm not giving up. Because I know in my heart you're it for me." She hugged herself, gripping both elbows. "Deep down, I think you feel the same. I could be wrong, I guess." She wiped away the tears that slid down both cheeks.

"What we had"—she shook her head—"it's not a given. Some people never find this connection." She gestured back and forth between them. "Every song I hear reminds me of you. When I watched *Game of Thrones* this season, the whole time I'm thinking, gah, is Meg watching right now? I had to keep myself from calling you just to hear what you think is going on with Jon Snow. And, you know, whether I have a great day or a crappy day, you're the one I want to talk to about it." She let out a heavy sigh. "It sucks that I blew it last time. I hate myself for that." She looked up at the stars. "I am so sorry for hurting you."

Waiting a half a second, she met Meg's eyes. "You have my word that nothing like that will ever happen again." She crossed her arms and nodded, losing the fight to maintain her composure. "I understand that my promises probably don't count for much, but I will prove it. But you have to give me the chance." She pursed her lips, obviously still upset. She took a step forward and put her hand on Meg's chest. "Don't shut me out, okay?"

Meg nodded once, truly unable to find her voice as Sasha took a step away.

"I have to go," Sasha said looking at the ground. "Not because I'm trying to be ultimatum-y or dramatic. It's just too hard for me to stay right now." She rubbed delicately at her face again, undoubtedly brushing away more tears. Her voice cracked desperately as she spoke. "Call me this week, Meg. Please?" she added as she backed away and out of Meg's sight.

Meg tipped her head back and stared at the dark sky, trying to process what was happening. She was angry and sad and kind of confused, if she was being totally honest with herself. While she hadn't quite admitted that getting back together with Sasha was what she wanted, she knew it was the truth. But she'd just let her go, when she could have asked her to stay.

The truth hit her right then, doubling her over, and she thought she might puke. Sasha was right. After all this time, the months of friendship and buildup to something more, a simple fact remained.

She wasn't ready.

CHAPTER TWENTY

"Wow, it's like we're not even in New York." Lucy stood with her hands on her hips as she took in the varied landscape, a mix of trees and hills, the fall foliage displayed in vibrant reds and yellows all around her.

"That's because we're not. We're in New Jersey. Remember?"

"You know what I mean."

"Spoken like a true New Yorker."

"Hey, what's that supposed to mean?" Lucy used two fingers to poke at her muscular back playfully.

"Nothing." Sam looked over her shoulder to make sure Lucy was doing okay on the rocky trail. "Just, you know, New Yorkers, we think we're the center of the universe."

"In our defense, we kind of are."

"Don't get me wrong. New York City is amazing. It's not like I want to live anywhere else. We can just be kind of uppity about it. The rest of the country has a lot to offer too. I mean, look around." She held her arms out to her sides and did a full three-sixty. "All this, and we only had to drive, what? A half an hour," she said, answering her own question. "And it's beautiful and peaceful and quiet. With tons of plants and wildlife, hundreds of different species of birds…" Her voice trailed off as she headed down a steep incline.

"You're adorable when you get all serious and outdoorsy."

Reaching level ground Sam turned around. "I thought I was always adorable." She waited for Lucy to step into her space before she looped her arms around her. "I thought"—she dropped a kiss on her lips—"that was my most endearing quality."

"You might have a few other selling points." Lucy grinned.

"Like?" Sam asked, hoping Lucy would expound. But when Lucy did open her mouth to speak, Sam covered it with her hand, shushing her. She turned Lucy around and held her close, leaning in to her ear. "Look right over there," she said, steering her body to the right. "There's a doe and her fawn behind that tree."

They stood together quietly for a good few minutes watching the deer graze less than twenty feet away until they were spotted, and the mother and baby dashed off into the forest of trees.

"That was awesome. They were super close." Sam released her hold on Lucy's waist, but Lucy held on to her hand, lacing their fingers as they moved along the trail. "I used to see elk a lot in Oregon when I went hiking. Spectacular animals." Sam pushed a fallen branch off the path with her foot.

"What did I do to deserve you?"

Lucy's question was out of left field and Sam stopped and turned around, chuckling heartily as she responded. "What?"

"You're all business suit one day. Which is"—she bit her bottom lip dramatically—"well, don't even get me started on what that does to me." She seemed almost shy as she continued. "And then here you are, rugged trail guide, with your sexy worn-out boots and insane knowledge of the great outdoors." She leaned in, resting her arms over the top of Sam's shoulders. "How am I ever supposed to resist you?"

"You're not." Sam folded her in her arms and kissed her sweetly. "Ever. Deal?"

"Deal," Lucy said with a smile.

They walked a few more feet, crunching the acorns beneath them as they worked their way up a formidable hill.

"So," Lucy started, hesitating a little as she caught her breath. "Are you guys squared away for the singles social or whatever it is you're calling it?"

"Mix and Match." Sam sighed. "Not that creative," she said with a shrug. "Should be a good night, though." Wow, was that a bald eagle? "We partnered up with Ladies First, you know, the dating app. They've been promoting it pretty heavily and we've been doing our part, so I'm expecting a good turnout." She continued to walk as she talked. "We sort of broke it down like this: We'll use the Commons as a meeting point for anyone who has been scoping each other on the site and wants to meet in a public place. That will start at around seven." She held back a bit of shrub that jutted out onto the path. "Then we'll open the doors to the social at nine, like regular, but the place will already be stacked with people who are single and looking." She checked a look at Lucy to gauge her reaction. "Honestly, for a single lesbian, it's a fantastic opportunity to meet someone who's in the same boat." She watched a chipmunk scurry off in the low brush. "Obviously, we're hoping to capitalize on that too. Financially, I mean."

"Sounds like you have it all worked out."

"Sorry, I'm going on and on. Did you have a question about it?"

"Not really. I was just curious what else you have coming up. Weekend-wise. At Bay West." Sam stopped walking and turned around, intrigued. Lucy answered her unspoken question immediately. "Columbus Day weekend my parents are celebrating their fortieth wedding anniversary."

"Wow. Forty years. Impressive."

"I know. They didn't want a big to-do. Just a small dinner party at their house on Saturday night. My sisters and their families will be there of course, and a few aunts and uncles and cousins who live nearby." She reached for Sam's shirt. "Emily is going out there the night before. And I talked to Kate the other day. She and Luke are flying in from Chicago on Friday too. I'm sure Beth will stop by for a little bit." She worried one side of her lower lip with her teeth, appearing almost nervous. "Would you be willing to come with me for the weekend? I know it's a lot of family time." She winced a little but looked hopeful. "It would mean a lot to me."

"Come here," Sam said pulling her in for a hug as she kissed the top of Lucy's head. "Why do you look nervous about asking me?" She leaned back and looked into Lucy's gray eyes. "Of course I'll go." She pulled Lucy along next to her until they reached a narrow wooden bridge and were forced to proceed single file. "So what will you do with the store?" Sam called over her shoulder. "That weekend, I mean?" She checked the sturdiness of a rock with one foot before putting her body weight on it. "I'm actually surprised that you're willing to leave for that long."

"I know. But my amazing girlfriend has been convincing me to leave for little bursts of time. And it's been working out okay."

"Your girlfriend sounds like a genius."

"In all seriousness, these little outings, like this one today, they have really helped, Sam." She held her hands out to the side for balance as she climbed. "Even before, when Raven called, she asks the right questions. She doesn't call for silly stuff. Her level of responsibility astounds me. And relaxes me."

"Look at that. A breakthrough." She held a wayward branch aside so Lucy could pass by, openly gazing at her ass as she passed.

"I think that was gratuitous," Lucy said.

"Gratuitous, chivalrous. Tomato, *tomahto*, as they say."

Lucy rolled her eyes but smiled. She obviously loved Sam's attention. "To answer your question, I know it's still weeks away, but I figured I'd close the store early that Friday. Let Raven go home since she'll be running the show Saturday and Sunday. Would you be able to head out around four-ish? This way we don't get completely destroyed in the traffic heading out east."

"Easy. I will make sure I don't have to go into Manhattan that day. Unlikely anyway, it being the start of a three-day weekend."

They walked in comfortable silence for almost a full minute. "So assuming everything goes well at the store Columbus Day weekend," Lucy said, breaking the silence, "which I'm sure it will, I could theoretically get away for a real vacation one of these days."

Sam turned all the way around, the confusion at Lucy's vague statement surely apparent in her expression. "What are you getting at?"

"I was thinking. In the spring I could take a long weekend. Get the girls to cover the store or even close up shop for a few days depending on the timing." She picked a leaf off the ground and examined its colors. "Have you ever been to Yellowstone?"

Sam smiled ear to ear. "Never."

"Look, I can't get down with the camping. That's still beyond my comfort zone at this point. But there's tons of quaint and reasonably priced cabins, hotels, lodges. All sorts of options really, depending on how rustic you want to get."

"Are you serious? You've actually researched this?"

"Yep." Lucy wore an impish smirk that she didn't even try to hide. "The only hitch is there don't seem to be any direct flights." She scrunched her nose. "I could get past that, if you can."

"Uh, yeah."

"I didn't book anything, because, well, I didn't know your work schedule or if you'd even want to go there."

"You weren't sure I'd want to go to freaking Yellowstone National Park? With you?"

"Well, I thought you'd be into it." She smiled. "I didn't want to be presumptuous." She pulled at the strap of her light backpack. "If there's somewhere else you'd rather go..."

Sam stepped toward her. "Lucy, I want to go everywhere with you." She brushed Lucy's face with the pad of her thumb as she brought their lips together. "Let's start at Yellowstone. It's perfect." She kissed her again. "Come on, let me get you back to the store. I just scored not one, but two weekends with you. I will push my luck no further," she said with a huge smile as she led the way to the trailhead.

CHAPTER TWENTY-ONE

Meg rested against the chain-link fence that enclosed Bay West's tennis courts watching the paint crew work their magic on the exterior of the Commons. She had come out to check the status of the job per a directive from Kam Browne, but after a few minutes she found herself soothed by watching the long smooth strokes of the roller brush spreading glossy paint that both cleaned and covered the blemishes of the old building.

"Everything okay over there?" Jesse's voice came from the path a few feet away. "You look extraordinarily deep in thought," she said walking over to hang with Meg.

"Actually, I'm not thinking about anything at all."

"Just watching the guys paint?"

"It's oddly relaxing." She broke her stare to look at Jesse. "Reminds me of when I used to watch my mother iron growing up. Anyway"—she shook herself from the memory—"what brings you over this way, cowboy?"

"I went for a run down on Bay Street, near the Alice Austen house." She pointed off into the distance behind them.

"Beautiful day for it." Meg looked up at the clear blue sky. "Better get all your running in now before your sole exercise is changing diapers."

Jesse laughed low and soft.

"So are you ready?" Meg asked, her eyes still fixed on the workers.

"For?"

"Parenthood."

Jesse smiled. "I wonder if anyone's ever ready for parenthood," she mused. "I'm excited, a little nervous."

"Please, you guys will be great," Meg said, affectionately bumping Jesse's shoulder with her own. "Still not going to tell me if it's a boy or a girl?"

"Sorry, kid. You'll have to be surprised like everyone else."

"Nah, I'll break you before then."

Jesse laughed at Meg's slight air of confidence. "Congrats on your promotion, by the way. Lexi told me last night."

"Thanks."

"You really have been working like crazy. Chicago, Phoenix, and Seattle in the last two weeks. That's a lot of jetting around." She stretched her arms over her head. "I'm glad it paid off."

Meg spotted a leaf falling from a tree and kept her eyes on it until it touched the ground in front of her. "Yeah, me too."

Jesse waited a minute before she spoke. "How's things with Sasha?"

"Haven't seen her," Meg responded, locking her eyes squarely on the scaffolding. "Busy, you know."

"Sure, yeah. Of course." Jesse toed a rock with her sneaker. "Think she'll show tomorrow night at Mix and Match?"

It was a reality Meg hadn't considered. Since their face-off a few weeks back, her communication with Sasha had seriously declined. Sasha had reached out to her several times early on but she'd been traveling steadily for work, and had used that distraction effectively as a stall tactic, keeping all her responses brief and generic. It had actually been a few days since they'd communicated. It was entirely possible Sasha had given up on Meg after all. But geez, would she really come to a singles event at Bay West?

"I doubt it." She met Jesse's serious expression. "I mean, maybe," she said, reversing course immediately before shrugging her shoulders. "Who knows?"

"Why are you doing this, Meg?"

"Doing what?" Meg said sharply.

"Don't get mad at me," Jesse said. "I'm on your side." She pushed her sweaty hair off her forehead. "You should let yourself be happy."

"Was I really happy with Sasha?" she countered bitterly. "All the head games, the uncertainty. Living in the closet. Not to mention the cheating episode." She picked up a fallen sycamore ball and whipped it at the tree a few yards away. "Doesn't sound like bliss to me."

"This self-imposed torture, woe-is-me routine doesn't appear to be a blast either."

"I'm just telling it like it is."

Jesse shook her head. "No. You're telling it like it was." She folded her arms across her chest and bladed her body, putting all her body weight on one shoulder against the fence so she was looking right at Meg. "You can't fake it with me. I know you love her. It's blatantly obvious when you're together. And kid, I understand your fear. Believe me, I do. Because yes, all that stuff happened. And it was terrible." She touched Meg's forearm, demanding her attention. "Even then, you didn't stop caring about her. You shut her out. You moved on. Or tried to, anyway." She put one hand on Meg's shoulder. "Meg, I commend you for your willpower, your inner strength, your commitment to your own sense of self-worth. It's truly admirable."

Jesse gave her shoulder a small squeeze. "Look, I get it. Settling down, committing to one person, it can be daunting." She smiled. "It's the part that no one talks about. And you and Sasha are both so young. I can imagine how scary it is for you." She looked over at a squirrel scampering down the long branch of a tree. "You want some advice?"

"Um, do I have a choice?"

"No." Jesse laughed, before getting serious again. "When it's right there in front of you, don't push it away."

"What, like, girls?"

"No, Meg. Love." She let out a heavy sigh as though she was about to reveal an age-old secret. "You don't know when, or if, it will come around again. I know you want a guarantee that it's all going to be perfect and smooth and easy—"

"I don't," Meg jumped in, cutting her off. "I get that it's hard and you have to work at it. But yeah, forgive me for wanting some assurance that it's worth the risk. Is that really too much to ask?"

"Yes."

"Yes, that's too much to ask?"

"Yes." Jesse nodded in support of her statement. She must have read the distress on Meg's face because she continued. "Meg, we all want guarantees." She held her hands up in a kind of surrender. "None of us gets them." She dropped her shoulders. "That's life, kid."

Meg shook her head in disbelief. "But you and Lex, it's different. You don't worry about it not working out, do you?"

Jesse cast her eyes over at the maintenance crew still working away. "I suppose I don't stress about breaking up." She rubbed her chin as she considered Meg's question. "It's because I love her. And I believe in us." Her hand brushed through the short waves atop her head. "I don't think there's anything we couldn't get through." She stretched her arms over her head. "That's what I'm trying to tell you," she said, putting her hands on her hips and rocking from side to side. "You love Sasha. She loves you. Figure out how you can trust her again. And just do it. Be happy." Pulling each leg up one at a time, she worked her hamstrings, the final step to her cool-down. "I have to head home. You sticking around to see this project through?" she asked, nodding at the painters.

"For a few more minutes. They look to be almost done and it's strangely comforting."

"Kam Browne knew what she was doing when she singled out you and Lexi as the new show runners here. Can't fault her there."

"What?"

"Meg, she's grooming you. Both of you. It's almost endearing." She grinned. "You know how I *love* giving her a compliment. But in this one particular case, I believe she made two excellent choices. So I can swallow my pride, I suppose."

Meg smiled at Jesse's meager humility. "I don't know that you're right about the grooming stuff."

"Oh, I'm right," Jesse said, her voice loaded with signature confidence. She started to turn away, but Meg saw an enormous smile spreading across her face. "Kid, I'm right about this. I'm right about Sasha. I'm pretty much right about everything." She winked. "It's funny, you're just like me in so many ways. Pragmatic, logical. It's why we're successful." She bounced off the fence and squared her body. "But Meg, relationships?" She looked up at the sky. "They're not neat and orderly. And love, forget it. Makes no sense most of the time. Not to me anyway. And yet it's amazing. The best feeling in the world. There really is no explaining it. But you know I'm right." She pointed at Meg as she backed away. "Even if you don't, you should just trust me," she said, turning around and heading in the direction of her house. "And trust yourself. It will be worth it. You'll see." She waved over her head and disappeared into the distance as Meg got lost in the long, lean brushstrokes while she silently contemplated her future.

❖

Just over a day later, Meg stood inside the door of the Commons, a hint of the fresh paint coming in with the slight breeze reaching her post near the entrance. There was kind of a lull at this odd hour, just before eight o'clock, with most of the Mix and Match participants having already arrived and the regular social not slated to get under way for another hour. Meg watched the single women skirt each other, the room characterized by an energy that was a mix of hope and angst. In a little while the vibe would change completely when the room filled to capacity with lesbians from all across the spectrum—single, married, partnered, young, old, in between. Would anyone find love tonight? She sighed, knowing she would never know. But the thought filled her soul with optimism as she kept her eye on a cute pair that had been chatting steadily for the last thirty minutes. It was cheesy, she knew it, but the idea that this event or tonight's social might have a hand in changing someone's life forever gave her a sense of satisfaction that it was a possibility, however remote. Meg smiled, truly proud to be part of this night, this community, something so much bigger than the sum of its parts.

"That is a great smile."

Meg recognized Sasha's sweet voice before she turned to face her. She met her deep blue eyes and felt her heart pound as she tried to keep her voice steady. "Sasha." She took in all of her, from her dark wavy hair, down to her tiny ballet flats. Her skinny jeans highlighted her slim figure, and the cowl-neck sweater perfected a casual, sexy look. She had to stop herself from staring. "Hi," she managed, with a subtle shake of her head.

"Hi."

"You're early." Meg stuffed her hands into her pockets. "The social doesn't start for another hour or so." Sasha's face fell a little, and Meg realized her gaffe immediately as she stuttered out the words. "Shit. Sorry." She swallowed past the sting in her throat. "You're here for Mix and Match." She reached for a name tag and started writing out Sasha's name in black Sharpie.

"Meg, stop." Sasha put her hand on top of Meg's, momentarily stilling her action. "I'm not here for the dating thing." She pulled her hand away and clutched her purse. "I wanted to see you. I thought we might get a few minutes alone before things got crazy."

"Oh."

"We haven't talked at all since the luau."

Meg put the cap back on the marker. "I've been busy with work," she said, even though she knew the explanation was weak.

"I heard you got promoted. Congratulations." Sasha's smile was genuine and Meg felt her guard immediately soften.

"How did you know?" Meg asked, suddenly curious.

"I had lunch with Anne earlier this week. She told me all about it. She's so proud of you, Meg."

Meg knew she was blushing, but figured the dim lighting saved her. She looked at Sasha still standing in front of the table. "Why don't you come in," she said, tipping her head to the side as she waved her through. Despite their last interaction, Meg couldn't resist the urge to talk to Sasha. Also, she thought an apology was probably in order. "I'll get you a seat," she said, trying to come up with the right thing to say, when something occurred to her. "Unless, I mean, you could go mingle if you want." Meg shrugged as she sat down. "There's no rules."

Sasha sat down next to Meg, crossing her legs lazily. "No, I'm good."

"Do you want a drink? I can text Sam to bring one from the bar. Or I could grab you one if you watch the door." She started to get back up but Sasha put a hand on her thigh.

"Meg, stay." She kept her hand where it was, giving her leg a gentle rub. "I just want to see you." She licked her lips and smiled. "I missed you."

Meg almost echoed the statement, but Lexi and Jesse appeared next to them, sliding into extra seats they brought with them, breaking the moment as they gave Sasha an enormous welcome. Sasha asked Lexi how she was feeling and Lexi took her hand in response, placing it on her belly so she could feel the baby bouncing around. For the next few minutes they made small talk about babies, and parenthood, and the holidays just around the corner before Jesse turned the conversation to Meg's ascension up the corporate ladder at Sullivan & Son.

"Did you hear the kid here is now a senior associate?" Jesse said with a squeeze of support on Meg's shoulders.

"I heard," Sasha responded with a sincere grin. "Are we really surprised, though?" She pushed her hair off her shoulders. "You forget. I got to see her in action for over a year. She was basically running Sullivan back then." Her eyes twinkled and Meg felt her pulse quicken at Sasha's obvious affection.

"Here too," Jesse said, taking a quick sip of her drink before she continued. "Between her and this one"—she winked at Lexi—"they're set to take over this place."

"Watch out, ladies, we're just getting started." Lexi clapped enthusiastically at her own statement. "I'm just kidding. It is fun though, isn't it?" she crinkled her nose at Meg.

"It is," Meg answered with a smile.

They were joined immediately by Sam who came equipped with a fresh bankroll of cash as they prepared to open the doors for the nine p.m. surge. The crowds came right away and both Sasha and Jesse stayed to help process the early rush of partygoers. Almost an hour had passed before there was a break at all, and Meg took the opportunity to secure the initial profits in the makeshift office downstairs in the Commons.

After counting out the cash and updating Kam's old-fashioned ledger, Meg locked the money into a small gray box and put it away in the bottom right-hand drawer. She rolled her chair back from the desk, checked that the drawer was locked, put the keys in her pocket. She'd gotten up to return to the social when she saw Sasha in the doorway.

"Hey, you," Sasha said with a small wave.

"Hi," Meg said with some question in her tone. Why was Sasha here?

"I just thought I might steal you for a minute." She leaned on one shoulder holding onto the doorway, almost lolling her body halfway in.

"You look exactly like when you used to come by my office at Sullivan before we'd cut out for lunch," Meg said, her voice full of nostalgia at the memory.

Sasha met her smile. "Those were good days," she said dropping her gaze to the floor.

"They were."

Sasha nodded as she ran a finger along the metal door latch. "The party seems to be a success. Pretty crowded up there."

"Definitely a good turnout." Meg stepped around the desk but instead of leaving the tiny office, she leaned her butt against its front edge, less than two feet from Sasha. "Sam's really on top of the marketing stuff, which is half the battle. Plus she had an in at Ladies First. She put me in touch with her connection and we got the whole thing off the ground. I think it's going really well."

"I'll say." Sasha turned her body so her back was flush against the door frame as she leaned on her hands. "I was watching some of the action upstairs though." She sighed heavily. "When we were all chatting." She fixed her eyes on a ceiling tile.

"How come you didn't want to participate tonight?" Meg toyed with a pen from Kam's desk. "In the Mix and Match." She knew why she was asking. Something deep inside her needed to hear Sasha say it.

Sasha arched her eyebrows dramatically and waited a beat. "Are you really asking me that?"

Meg shrugged. "I don't know. Maybe?"

"I guess I could have." She perched one foot on the back wall. "Technically, I am single." She slid her hands in the front pockets of her dark jeans. "But I'm not on any dating apps. Because"— she lifted one shoulder—"what would be the point?" She smiled a little. "I came here for one reason tonight. One." She held up her index finger in support of her statement. "So I'm not going to waste my time, or anyone else's, going through the motions or pretending to be interested. I can't fake it anyway." She puckered her lips and shook her head. "I don't want to. All my friends know. All yours do too. Probably half the people upstairs can see it. But in case it isn't clear, Meg"—she looked right at her—"I choose you. Every time." She tipped her head and smiled, seeming confident in her words even as she continued. "I remember the exact moment I was sure of you."

"Yeah?" Meg managed, hearing her own voice crack with emotion.

"The day we walked along the West Side together. From my apartment all the way down to Battery Park City."

Meg felt the corner of her mouth hitch upward. "After our first night together?"

"Yes." Sasha's cheeks reddened at her confession.

"You walked me almost to the ferry."

"I begged you to come back and stay another night."

"You didn't have to beg," Meg corrected her.

"I didn't want you to leave." She hooked her body inside the room and pressed her head against the wall. "God, I knew. I just knew. I felt it." She smiled, almost to herself. "I was so in love with you already. It scared me half to death. I didn't know how to deal with any of it. So I self-destructed. I ruined everything." A small laugh escaped her as she bit her lip. "I want a do-over."

"Sash—"

Sasha put both her hands up as she swallowed a smile. "The funny thing is I keep waiting, hoping almost, for, like, a hero moment. A chance to swoop in and save the day, really show my level of commitment. So you would actually see how much you mean to me. I imagine something big and grand gesture-y, like in the movies. But, no luck." She squinted one eye closed. "I'm assuming both your kidneys are in good shape?"

Meg couldn't help but laugh in response.

"Fine, have it your way." She shrugged playfully. "You'll just have to deal with me being around, then. Because Meg, I love you. I have for a really long time. And I'm not going to stop. I know, well I don't know, but I truly believe that you love me too." She pushed off the wall with her foot and her face wore an expression that was a little defiance mixed with hope. "I take it back," she said. "I do know it. In here." She covered her chest with one hand. "It's you, Meg. You're my person."

She turned to leave, but Meg didn't let her go. She reached out for her hand but caught her forearm. She let her fingers drift all the way down until they touched Sasha's and she guided her forward.

Meg said nothing, she simply leaned in and kissed Sasha gently over and over, until their lips parted and the kiss was real, and deep, lovely and emotional, brimming with the promise of more. Meg brought her hands up to Sasha's cheek, touching it softly. She smiled, bringing their foreheads together, her lips grazing Sasha's as she spoke.

"I love you."

Sasha rushed both hands through Meg's thick hair, grabbing on to the short top with a tug. "Thank fucking God."

"Stop it," Meg teased her with a kiss. "You knew it all along."

"The hell I did." Sasha raised her eyebrows and drew in her lower lip. "I wanted you to. I love you so much." She shook her head emphatically. "I'm still sorry, Meg. For everything." She peppered Meg's face with baby kisses. "I'm going to spend forever making it up to you." Her mouth brushed against Meg's cheek.

"Starting now," Meg said, turning ever so slightly so their mouths met in perfect accord.

They stayed right where they were, holding each other, as they made up for a year of lost kisses until an affected cough got their attention. When Meg opened her eyes, Kam Browne was at the door, so close that Meg could only wonder how much she had witnessed and heard.

"Sorry, girls," she said through clenched teeth. "Just wanted to lock up some more money." She kept her head down as she opened the desk. "This event is a huge success, Meg. The room is packed. Excellent work," she added as she whipped out her ledger. She reached for a pen to make her notation as she talked. As if reading Meg's mind she grinned. "I suppose now I'm going to have to give in to you girls and go electronic with my record keeping too." She shook her head playfully and snapped the book closed. "I'd say we're pretty squared away here. Lexi and Sam have things under control, if you want to cut out early." She returned her pen to its holder and returned the book to its drawer.

"Thanks, Kam," Meg said as she took Sasha's hand and led her through the door. She tossed a look of gratitude over her shoulder as she exited and was genuinely touched by the sentiment in Kam's smile and wink in response.

Despite their plans to leave, Meg and Sasha were met by their friends the second they reentered the main room. They dutifully made their rounds, and Meg checked in with all the girls to make sure they were settled before they finally made their way back to her house.

❖

"Are you sure you're ready for this? It's a big moment," Meg said, sliding her key in the front door. "Make it or break it, some might even say." Registering the slight trepidation in Sasha's eyes, Meg smiled as she called out, "Spencer. Oh, Spencer," but the cat didn't come. "Cats," Meg said with a huff as she closed the door behind them.

"Where's her favorite spot?" Sasha asked. "I'll go to her."

"My room."

Sasha headed up the stairs and Meg followed her into the bedroom, where Spencer was sprawled out across the spread, lazily stretching her legs as they entered.

"Look at you, gorgeous." Sasha crouched down next to the bed and held out her hand for Spencer to inspect.

Spencer nosed her fingertips for a fraction of a second before pushing her jaw directly into Sasha's hand. Sasha responded with ample petting and cooing as she moved to lounge next to Spencer on the bed. "I think I passed," she said to Meg.

"What?"

"The test. Make it or break it?" Sasha added with a shift of her eyebrows. "I think I'm getting an A."

"Oh, you think so?" Meg said, kicking off her shoes as she lay down in the spot next to Sasha. She moved her long hair and kissed the back of her neck, moving her hand under Sasha's sweater to feel the smooth skin against the palm of her hand. Sasha turned onto her back and Meg leaned down over her. She kissed her, intending to be sweet and go slow, but Meg's whole body got hot at once as she grazed her fingertips over the flesh of Sasha's belly and watched her mouth drop open in response.

Sasha must have felt it too because she pulled Meg's shirt over her head and her hands were already working on her belt. Meg leaned back and stood up off the bed, taking Sasha's hand and lifting her up too. She slid her hands under Sasha's shirt taking it off and letting it drop to the floor. She kissed the curve of her breasts above her bra and unbuttoned her jeans, watching them fall around her ankles as she kissed along her collarbone, her neck, and up to her lips. She unhooked Sasha's bra and took it off, covering both breasts with the palms of her hands before she bent down to kiss them generously. Then she finished taking her own pants off, stepping out of them, and pulled back the bed covers. Thankfully Spencer got the hint and sprang off the bed and into the hallway. Meg shut the door behind her and slipped into bed next to Sasha.

"You okay?" she asked, running her hand along the curve of Sasha's side.

"Of course," Sasha responded. "Better than okay."

"Good." Meg leaned forward and kissed her. It was deep and intense and before she knew it, she was on top of Sasha, the center of her body between Sasha's legs, their remaining clothes scattered somewhere in the sheets. Everything was both familiar and fresh at the same time. Sasha's scent, a sweet mix of expensive soap and pure desire, the little noises she made when they kissed, the baby moans she let out as Meg slipped the first finger inside which increased when she added another, and finally the loud moans she'd nearly forgotten about when Sasha climaxed. It was followed softly, so softly it was almost inaudible, by Sasha breathing out her name.

When Sasha whispered, "I love you," it was new, completely welcome, and it made Meg gush with excitement and need.

When Meg flipped onto her back, Sasha went with her, her cool lips kissing the soft spot between Meg's chest and shoulder.

"I love these freckles." She nuzzled in and Meg could feel her smiling against her skin. "I missed them."

"What freckles?" she said, recycling an old joke. "I barely have any."

"Right, I forgot," Sasha answered, going along with Meg's denial. She traced her lips along Meg's chest and abdomen, and lower, tipping her head up as she teased, "I'm just going to check if you have any new ones."

Meg answered with a suggestive eyebrow raise.

"You don't know," Sasha said, playful as she continued her way down Meg's torso. Meg didn't stop her, she wouldn't dare. She'd been fantasizing about this moment for a full year. Now that it was finally happening she hoped like hell she would last more than thirty seconds. Feeling her hips arch uncontrollably as Sasha's mouth reached her, she knew it would be fast. It didn't matter, she reminded herself with an indulgent smile. Suddenly, they had forever.

❖

"We should get some sleep." Meg's speech was slurred with exhaustion as she held Sasha from behind, dropping light kisses on her bare shoulder.

"But look at that sunrise," Sasha said watching the sky change colors through the bedroom window.

"One of these days, you know, when we can actually walk again, we'll go down to the beach and check it out for real."

"That sounds perfect."

The whole night was as easy as this. Cuddling and caressing one another and talking with ease about their future. They rehashed some of the past too, dissecting mistakes they'd both made and coupling them with promises of open communication and a level of commitment that felt honest and new. When they were together, insatiably gratifying one other all night long, it was intense and sweet and perfect. The road ahead likely wouldn't always be as smooth as the last twelve hours, but Meg was sure of one thing: Sasha was her person. She hadn't ever really thought about it in those terms before Sasha had said it so simply, so succinctly, the night before.

Sasha took Meg's hand and rubbed her lips over her knuckles. The gesture was sexy and comforting and Meg could almost feel her heart rate slowing as she started to drift off.

"Before I forget," Meg said, "we're meeting the girls at Lucy's at ten thirty."

"Fun. Should I set an alarm on my phone?" Sasha asked, reaching for it off the end table before Meg answered.

"Mmm, yeah. Probably," she muttered, losing the battle to stay awake.

"Good night, babe. Or, technically, good morning," Sasha corrected herself as she put her phone down and curled her body into Meg's, nestling in for sleep. "I love you."

"I love you, too." Meg smiled soundly as she fell into a world of dreams that didn't hold a candle to her reality.

CHAPTER TWENTY-TWO

"Thank you so much for driving," Lucy said from the passenger seat of Sam's immaculate SUV. "You're too good to me."

"I don't mind at all."

"You may feel differently after a weekend with the Weston family."

"Well, at least I have a getaway car, if necessary." Sam tossed a wink across the console. "In case all you girls get to be too much for me."

"You joke now, but after an hour with my sisters, your ears will be bleeding."

"Never." Sam switched lanes, taking advantage of some movement in the dense traffic. "Emily will be there, right?" She settled her hand over the top of the smooth steering wheel. "She'll look out for me."

"She does love you."

"And can you really blame her?" Sam teased.

She grinned when she caught Lucy sticking out her tongue. "You're so cocky," Lucy said. "I don't know what I see in you."

"You love me."

"I do." Lucy checked a text that had just come through. "Speak of the devil," she said, her eyes still locked on the screen. "It's Emily. She's headed to the LIRR now." Lucy shook her head. "By herself. With two fucking kids."

"Why is she taking the train? We would have picked her up." Lucy jutted her chin out. "She's taking the Long Island Rail Road because her fucking wife was supposed to be with her, but now Frankie's stuck at work so she's not coming until tomorrow."

"Things still aren't good there, I take it."

"Frankie's an ass."

"Did Emily ever determine if she was cheating? I know that was a concern a while back."

Lucy looked out her window at the ocean that bordered the highway. "I don't know. She only ever mentioned it that one time. But I know she worries about it. I can tell." She gave her phone a quick glance. "Whether her concern is warranted or not doesn't change the fact that she deserves better than what she is settling for."

"Agreed." Sam rubbed Lucy's forearm. "Why doesn't she leave?"

Lucy shrugged, reaching for Sam's hand. "I don't know. They've been together forever. But Em's not happy. I wonder, sometimes, if she isn't just scared." Her voice got lower as though she was considering the possibility for the first time. "You know, two kids and everything."

"But Frankie barely helps her, you said."

"Emily depends on her financially."

"She has a job, though." Sam looked over as the traffic stilled. "How old are the kids?"

"Hannah's six, Liam is four. They're sweet."

"She works at a day care, right?"

"She runs it actually. She has a degree in early childhood education."

"Babe, tell her to ditch Frankie and move to Bay West. Christ, she could probably open a day care center there. Or at least somewhere nearby. And you could give her shifts at your place if she needed. Plus, I'm sure she would get child support from her wife. What is it that Frankie does?"

"She's an ad executive for some big company. I forget the name."

"See." Sam rubbed her fingers together. "Money."

"But where would she live?" Lucy looked unconvinced. "Even if she was down with this plan we're so graciously working out for her without her consent or knowledge"—she chuckled at their harmless meddling—"it's not like there's an abundance of open apartments at Bay West."

"You bring up an excellent point." Sam tried to hide her grin as she spoke. "What about Seventy-Two Vista? Top floor?"

"Jerk." Lucy whacked her playfully. "That's my apartment. I love Emily, but that place is not big enough for four of us."

"You could stay with me."

"At chez Miller, up on posh Todt Hill?" She raised her eyebrows. "The digs look sweet from the outside, but I have it on good authority that Mom and Pop Miller are not super cool with their daughter bringing the ladies home."

"Mmm. Good point." Sam scratched her chin. "I guess we could stay at the new three-bedroom I just bought at the end of Crescent Street."

"What? Crescent Street, as in Bay West? Why didn't you tell me?"

"I wanted to see if they would take my offer first." She smiled big. "Which they just did this morning. We're already in contract."

"That's fantastic. What number?"

"Twelve." Sam put on her turn signal to switch lanes again. "It's not the place I was originally looking at. It's way farther down where the street kind of bends. Almost in the back of the development. Near the softball field."

"That's even better. Kind of private. Secluded." Lucy shook her head, but a smile came through. "I can't believe you kept this from me." She leaned over and kissed Sam's cheek. "Congratulations, babe."

"So you stay with me. Emily and her kids crash at your place until something opens up for them at the development. They would need something bigger than a one-bedroom anyway. But it could do in a pinch." She muscled her way into the left lane even though it was barely moving. "Maybe, with real options, she'd consider it."

"Emily would totally love Bay West."

"Who doesn't?"

"True, but she would be so into all of their activities. She is a true joiner." Lucy tapped her own chest. "We are complete opposites in that regard."

"Why don't you mention it to her if you think she's really not happy." Sam reached for Lucy's hand. "Bonus, you can help me design my new kitchen, since it needs to be completely gutted."

"Well, that sounds fun." She squeezed Sam's hand, getting serious for a moment. "Sam, you're sweet to think of my sister."

"I love you." She shrugged. "And I want to help Emily out. This would be a win for me too. I'd get to spend all my nights with you."

"I still can't believe you held out on me." She shook her head but clearly wasn't upset.

Sam made sure anyway. "I wanted to make sure I got it first. You're not mad, right?"

"Not even a little. I'm excited." Her hand drifted up between Sam's legs. "I may make you pay for withholding the info though."

"Is that right?" Sam looked pointedly at Lucy's futile stretch across the wide center console as she tried, and failed, to reach Sam's crotch. "Looks like an empty promise."

"There's always later," Lucy said.

"At your parents' house?" Sam opened her eyes wide. "Yeah, I think I'm all set," she said with a slight laugh.

"Aw, what happened to my girlfriend's signature swagger?" Lucy teased.

"It fizzled at the thought of having sex next door to your mom and dad."

"First off, my room is down the hall. Secondly, you will change your mind. Third, it's going to be fantastic." She reached for Sam's hand again. "So quit being a wuss."

They spent the remainder of the ride bumper-to-bumper, talking about Sam's new house and her plans for it. Lucy gave a brief rundown of the relatives who would be in attendance at tomorrow's celebration and the family that would be at her parents' tonight—just her sisters and their families, keeping it informal and intimate.

Ninety minutes later, they pulled into Lucy's parents' driveway at the same time as a massive pizza delivery.

The Weston family gave Sam a warm welcome complete with hugs all around. Lucy's dad thrust a beer in her hand and gave her a clap on the shoulder as he talked about Staten Island's role in the Revolutionary War. He was a sweetheart and had clearly done his research on the small borough. He obviously cared about his girls and wanted to connect with their partners—she could tell by the way he made her feel as welcome as Beth's and Kate's husbands who had been in the picture long before she had. In fact, both of those guys—John and Luke, she thought their names were—were super friendly as well. Lucy's mom, and of course Emily, doted on her all evening, making her feel like she was already part of the family. It was a great night, but Lucy didn't lie. It was loud. Beth's three children and Emily's two accounted for some of the racket, but the Weston core themselves were a force to be reckoned with. They were boisterous, funny, and competitive as they one-upped each other with outrageous and embarrassing stories from the past.

Well after the children were put to sleep, Lucy's parents called it a night and were followed shortly by Beth's and Kate's spouses. Sam took the cue to give the four sisters bonding time and she happily trekked up to Lucy's room at the end of the upstairs hall listening to the girls cackle away.

It was a good while later when Lucy finally came to bed, her energy still high from a night filled with laughter.

"It was a good night?" Sam asked as she sat up.

Lucy pulled her shirt over her head. "I love my sisters," she said, still beaming. "And you...you were so charming." She slid her pants off and folded them on the dresser. "Beth and Kate can't say enough about you. And I think my dad about fell in love with you himself."

"He's nice. Steve," she said with a wink. "We're buds." She added a grin as she watched Lucy take off her bra, step out of her panties, and pull back the covers. "What are you doing?"

"Getting into bed."

"Um, naked?"

"Um, yeah," she echoed, teasing with her tone. "Like always."

"Your parents are three doors away." She turned her cheek when Lucy attempted a kiss. "And one of your sisters is right next door."

"It's Emily," she said, undeterred. "And who cares?"

"I do."

"Sam, relax." Lucy guided her face back and kissed her gently, slipping her hand underneath the waistband of her boxers. She smiled when she heard Sam's breath catch even as Sam reached down to stop her. "Babe, it's okay. I'm just touching."

Sam knew exactly where this was going, but her resistance melted away when she felt Lucy's hand move lower. Without thinking she let out a groan that was both frustration and desire.

"Shh." Lucy whispered in her ear. "It's okay," she repeated, kissing along the sides of Sam's face and down her neck before she turned around slowly. She swung her leg over Sam's body and kissed the area below her belly button as she pushed her boxers down.

Sam couldn't help but reach for Lucy's beautiful body inches from her face. She spread her legs open for Lucy at the exact same time she brought Lucy down to her mouth. She loved sex like this, maybe because it reminded her of their first time, maybe just because it was hot. Either way, she knew Lucy knew it.

The feel of their bodies touching everywhere, moving in time, plus the fact that it typically resulted in simultaneous orgasm— everything about it was perfect. Being together like this had come to symbolize precisely how Sam felt about their relationship: together, equal, connected, loved beyond measure. In this single moment, she was as happy as she ever remembered being and she gave all credit to her amazing girlfriend. And why shouldn't she?

Just hours ago in the car, Lucy had predicted this very moment and it really was about to be fantastic.

❖

The party got rolling around two o'clock. Sam and Lucy had enjoyed a lovely walk early in the day in a nearby park. It wasn't quite hiking, but Sam relished the solitude with Lucy and managed to steal several kisses before they returned to the house, and when the extended family began arriving Lucy never left her side. She made sure Sam met all her aunts and uncles, keeping the introductions sweet as she rubbed Sam's back and gently scratched her neck. When Sam slipped upstairs to charge up her phone, Lucy found her in the bedroom.

Lucy wrapped her arms around Sam's waist and kissed her between the shoulders. "You doing okay?"

"Of course. Your family is awesome."

"They love you."

"I love you." Sam turned around and dropped a kiss on Lucy's forehead.

Lucy kissed her lips before pulling back. "Fucking Frankie isn't here yet," she said with a scowl. "I may punch her in the throat when she finally shows." She pointed one finger at Sam's chest. "Do not try to stop me," she said in playful warning.

"Like I can stop you when you set your mind to something." It was completely true and they both knew it. Lucy's face was full of acknowledgment and love as she linked her hands with Sam's. "Come on. Back to the party. I don't trust myself with you in here."

A half hour later, when Lucy was tied up with her Aunt Suzie's millionth question about the coffee shop, Sam slipped away to grab a beer off the back porch. She was already entering the room when she saw Emily in a heated discussion with a woman whose back was to the door. Judging from the level of emotion on display it had to be Frankie. Sam lifted the lid on the cooler and reached her hand in, content with anything just to get out of the way. She tried to be silent, hoping to slip out unnoticed, but it was too late. As she made eye contact with Emily, she gave her a look that she hoped conveyed both apology for interrupting and the sentiment that it wasn't necessary to acknowledge her presence.

No dice. Emily gave her a small wave as she wiped away her tears. "You're fine, Sam," she said in response. "We were just finishing up here." Emily took a step toward her and the woman turned at the same time. "Sam, this is Frankie. My wife."

"Blynn." The name fell out of Sam's mouth as if she was in a daze. No time passed before her heart sank into her stomach as the realization of what was going on registered.

"Sam, what are you doing here?" Frankie asked through a snide snicker.

Emily jumped in to answer. "Sam is Lucy's girlfriend. I told you about her."

"You didn't tell me it was Sam Miller." Her smirk was completely self-indulgent. Sam recognized the look of smug satisfaction her colleague slash ex-fling typically reserved for the boardroom. What an egomaniacal bitch.

Emily's voice revealed her confusion. "I didn't know her last name. Sorry, Sam," she said, offering a weird apology. "I'm shocked you were even listening to me," she said, tossing out a barb of her own. She leaned back and crossed her arms looking between them. "Do you know each other?"

"Sam and I work together."

"For real?" She looked to Sam for an explanation. "How did we not put that together?"

Her mouth hung open a little as Sam shook her head from side to side. "I don't know. But Blynn, sorry, Frankie," she corrected, knowing her expression still held shock, "and I do work together from time to time."

"Sam's being modest. I routinely insist that she is my lead graphic designer. She's the best. And so am I. We have phenomenal chemistry. Am I right, Sam?" Her eyes were loaded with innuendo and Sam hated her for it.

"But *Blynn?*" she said, still hung up on her name. It was a ridiculous detail, yet she couldn't get past it.

"Frances is so formal. I was Frankie through high school but it's quite juvenile." She took her time before she met Sam's eyes. "Also, it's a touch masculine for me." Her smile was coy and vain. "I've gone by my middle name since I began in the advertising world."

F. Blynn Hughes. Mother. Fucker. Sam started to sweat.

"There you are." Lucy's voice at the doorway cut the tension, but also added to it. "I was getting worried. Hon, would you grab me a seltzer." She stepped out onto the porch and touched Sam's back as she sidled next to her. "Frankie, so nice of you to grace us with your presence today."

"Get this, Luce." Emily's voice still held bewilderment. "Sam works with Frankie."

"What?"

"They work together. Sam calls her Blynn and everything." Emily clucked her tongue as she rolled her eyes, clearly taking a jab at her wife's pretentiousness.

Question and concern covered Lucy's face as she turned to Sam. "You know Frankie?"

"No. Yes," she said, changing her answer on the spot. "I didn't know...I mean, I only know her as Blynn...not Frankie." She didn't mean for it to come out as an excuse or an explanation. In fact, she didn't want to own up to anything, not at this particular moment in time. But Lucy must have seen the confession in her eyes, because Sam read her recognition right on the spot.

"No." Lucy's protest came out as a kind of plea. "Sam," she said desperately, but it was a whisper barely heard by the others. "No." Quieter still this time, as she shook her head slowly, clearly using all her resolve to hold it together. "We should all get inside," she said through a terse smile. "Em, we have the toast and tribute to Mom and Dad in a few minutes." She turned quickly and bolted into the house. Sam raced to follow her, but just through the french doors Lucy's dad caught her arm to introduce her to his brother.

At the risk of being rude, Sam stayed for the mandatory hellos, escaping as quickly as she could, but it wasn't in time. Lucy was already at the front of the room, surrounded by her sisters, while Beth clinked a spoon against a champagne flute to solicit the room's attention.

The next thirty minutes passed in a blur. Sam watched the photo montage and listened to the girls' choreographed speeches, registering breaks of laughter as they pierced through her haze, but it was as though she was hardly present. She was still on the porch trying to make sense of what happened back there. Blynn was Frankie. But how?

When the homage ended, Sam tried to get Lucy's attention but she was flanked by family. Sam backed away and slipped up the stairs into Lucy's room.

She grabbed her phone and texted Lucy her location, spending the next fifteen minutes pacing and chewing at her short fingernails until the door opened.

"Lucy, I—"

"I'm not talking about this, Sam." She was trying to cover it but her voice held both anger and pain. "Not here." She leaned against the back of the bedroom door and covered her face with both hands. Despite her proclamation she asked, "How did this fucking happen?"

"I don't know."

"She's my sister's wife, Sam." Lucy spoke through her palms but Sam could hear rage and betrayal as her voice cracked. "My *sister*," she repeated. "I can't." She slid her hands up pulling at the front of her hair and Sam saw tears in her eyes. "No." She clenched her jaw fighting back her emotions. "We are not doing this now."

Sam couldn't take seeing her pain. She crossed the room and reached for Lucy, folding her in her arms as she kissed the top of her head. Lucy went willingly, crying in earnest against Sam's chest.

"It's okay," Sam whispered against her hair. "It'll be okay."

"It won't." Lucy's voice was tempered, even as it came out muffled against Sam's sweater. She pushed out of Sam's embrace and let her body weight rest on the door behind her as she rubbed at her wet eyes with the edges of her shirt. "I have to look like I'm not a fucking mess." Her voice was still full of fury and sadness. "I want to go home." Her eyes filled up again. "Can we just…go?"

Sam wanted to protest, to tell Lucy that she was making too much of it. Whatever ridiculous arrangement she'd had with Blynn had ended the second she thought she had a shot with Lucy. But even in her own head, it sounded pathetic. She nodded in response. At least the car ride back to Staten Island would give them time alone, a solid hour to flesh it out. But the traffic was unusually light and they flew along the Belt Parkway, making it to Bay West in just under forty minutes. The entire journey Lucy stared out the passenger window, never uttering a word. When Sam heard a sniffle as they zipped past JFK, she tried to touch Lucy's shoulder, but Lucy moved away. Finally pulling into Bay West, Sam parked in front of Lucy's unit and cut the engine.

"You can't come in," Lucy said through heavy tears.

"Luce, we need to talk about this."

"No." She looked straight ahead. "I need to think."

"We weren't together, Lucy. You have to believe that."

"That's not the point." She looked off into the distance, letting out a measured breath as she clearly tried to keep her composure. "She's married to Emily, Sam." Her eyes seemed steeled on tiny droplets of rain beginning to land on the windshield as she continued. "Emily, who thought she was cheating. Which she was." Her face fell as she spoke the truth. "With you."

Sam shook her head in silent protest but it was pointless. Lucy pulled the door handle.

"Lucy, wait," Sam implored, almost reaching her but it was too late. Lucy slipped out of the car, letting the door close with a sad click as she walked away.

❖

For the next few days, Sam busied herself with work. She did everything from home, of course, having no idea how she was going to handle Blynn when she saw her. Mostly she didn't care, but she hated that her colleague had obviously enjoyed a kind of rush over the situation the other night. Fuck her, she thought, closing her project immediately. She could be a crappy wife to Emily all she wanted, but Sam wasn't about to let her screw up her chances with Lucy. She fired off a quick email to one of the headhunters who was always trying to poach her for other firms. Shutting her laptop with a click, she stood up and got moving.

She set the shower water temperature to a toasty 110 degrees on the digital display and stepped in, letting the hot water wash over her body. She ached from lack of sleep over the last seventy-two hours and the steady hot pressure rejuvenated her. Although she didn't really have a plan, she knew she needed to see Lucy. It had been three full days of zero contact. She'd acquiesced and given her space and time to think. Forget waiting any longer. It was time Lucy heard her out.

Warm light poured out of Lucy's Coffee Bar as she pulled into the dark lot. Sam couldn't help but remember the first time she'd come here so many months ago, the night eerily similar to this one. Back then she'd had hopes of finding a simple dessert. She smiled now, thinking about how far they had come. First coffee, then the lunch dates disguised as friendship. The whole time she was slowly, sweetly, slipping into love. It happened so seamlessly Sam couldn't identify the precise moment she'd known. Suddenly her life was divided into the time before Lucy and now.

The bell above the door jangled and Lucy looked up from her chore at the counter, doing a double take at the sight of Sam walking to the bar.

"Hi," Sam said, noticing the heaviness in Lucy's eyes right away. "I was hoping we could talk."

Lucy put her hands on her hips as though she was bracing for something, but when she spoke, her voice cracked and Sam heard nothing but sadness. "Not here, Sam. I'm at work."

"A few minutes. Please?" She didn't even care that she was begging. "Lucy, come on?" Her voice wavered and it was perhaps her obvious emotion that made the difference. Whatever the case, Lucy gave in. She turned for the kitchen signaling with her eyes that Sam should follow.

"Raven, give us a minute, would you?" Lucy's voice was as serious as ever and Raven asked no questions as she breezed past Sam with an uneasy smile.

Sam touched the countertop with one finger, her other hand stuffed in her pocket as she contemplated what to say. Despite her plea for a moment with Lucy, she hadn't given the content of their conversation much thought. On the spot, she decided to go right from the gut.

"I miss you."

Lucy blinked slowly, seeming pained by Sam's small sentiment.

"I know this situation is..." She paused. "Not ideal. I don't know what to say about it, really."

"*Not ideal* is a bit of an understatement, I'd say." Lucy's voice had some zing to it—a combination of anger and resentment.

"Okay," Sam said. "Like I said, I don't know what to say." She shrugged. "I don't think it's worth throwing in the towel over." She looked up and hoped her eyes conveyed the level of emotion she felt. "I love you, Luce. I never felt this way about anyone. Ever. Tell me what to do to make it better. Please?"

Lucy braced herself against the countertop and tipped her head all the way back before meeting Sam's eyes. She was clenching her jaw over and over. "I don't know if there's anything you can do."

"But Lucy, we weren't even together, you and me. When all that happened. Honestly."

"I know, Sam. I believe you."

"I had no idea she was married, Luce. For whatever that's worth. Maybe that's stupid or I was believing what I wanted, or just not thinking about it at all. But trust me when I tell you I didn't know."

"I believe you, Sam. I do." She clenched her jaw and fought back the tears. "It's more complicated than that."

"I know," she said, even though she didn't quite know why. "I just can't stop picturing you with her. With Frankie."

"Don't." Sam looked right at her. "There was never anything between us. Honestly. It was purely..." Her voice faded, knowing the admission did nothing for her cause.

"Physical," Lucy finished for her. "I know. That doesn't help, actually."

"I just meant that I never had any feelings for her."

"I hate that you were with her like that. I hate it." She wiped a tear before it fell, her voice getting more agitated by the second. "I hate that I can't stop thinking about it. I hate that obnoxious, selfish Frankie got to experience you the way *I* do. When you are vulnerable and shy and sweet." She balled her fists but released them right away, rubbing her palms on her worn-out jeans. "I hate that anyone else besides me ever got to see that side of you. I know that makes me sound jealous and greedy in my own right, but I want to be the only person who does that to you."

"But you are."

Lucy shook her head. "I'm not. And I hate it." She breathed out audibly. "More than anything, I hate that I have to tell Emily about it," she said.

It was the answer to a question she'd been too uncomfortable to ask, but the knowledge still shook her to her center.

"Don't look at me like that, Sam. I have to tell her. You know I do."

Sam nodded and then shook her head, the conflicting emotions she felt on display.

"Just don't let it define us." The words were out of her mouth before she had a chance to filter them. Lucy was about to talk but Sam stopped her. "Babe, I get it. I don't like it but I get it. I know she is your sister and you are close, and Emily deserves to know that Blynn, ugh, Frankie," she self-corrected, "is not being straight with her." She took a step forward and put one hand delicately on Lucy's waist. "I'm sorry for my part in all of it. I'm embarrassed by it," she admitted. "But even still, I'm not willing to lose you over this." She put her other hand on Lucy's side. "I love you, Lucy. More than I ever loved anyone in my whole life." She looked up at the stained ceiling before meeting Lucy's eyes. "I know you love me." She kissed Lucy's forehead. "That has to count for something."

Lucy leaned forward, pressing her head into Sam's chest, her hands drifting along the lean muscles of Sam's upper body. Her body language said it all. She wanted to be held, she needed it. Only a few days had passed but she clearly missed Sam's touch. Lucy tilted her head up and Sam kissed her softly, the small moment taking over, making it seem as though everything might be okay.

"I can't, Sam." Lucy's voice was so low Sam wasn't sure she heard her correctly.

"What?"

"I'm not saying it's over." She paused. "I don't know what I'm saying."

"Then don't say anything." She ran her hands the length of Lucy's arms hoping for a positive response.

"I just need some time. To process. To talk to Emily. To get these awful images out of my head." She worried her lower lip. "Give me a few days. A week. Maybe more. I don't know," she muttered with a shake of her head.

"Take whatever time you need, Lucy. I'm not going anywhere." In a bit of irony lost on neither of them, Sam stepped backward toward the rear door. "I mean, technically, I'm going home, but"—she channeled her best charm and hoped she looked irresistible—"you know what I mean."

Lucy answered with a smile that was sad but sweet, and Sam was sure she saw love in it. She could only hope it would be enough.

CHAPTER TWENTY-THREE

"I hate Sundays." Meg let her head fall gently against Sasha's bare back, groaning a little in her dismay.

Sasha turned in her arms, touching Meg's face as she kissed her cheeks and her eyelids, her lips brushing her face as she nestled her body closer.

"No, you don't. In fact"—she found Meg's lips—"you love them." She gave her attention to Meg's freckled chest. "Because we're about to do this. Again." Her expression was as coy as ever. "And at ten thirty we're going to meet the girls at Lucy's like we do every Sunday." She dropped a kiss on Meg's collarbone. "When we come back, we're going to veg all day, curl up on the couch, read the *Times*, work on the puzzle." She licked her lips almost laughing as she continued, "Then you'll find a ridiculously cheesy movie."

"Which you will pretend to hate, but secretly be infatuated with, even though you will make fun of it the whole time."

"I have no idea what you are talking about," Sasha cooed.

"Mm-hmm." Meg played along. "Sure, sure. Cut to three hours later when you can't stop talking about how cute the old couple was or the puppy or the kid sister or something else completely secondary, so I'll know you were totally invested. Newspaper prop or not."

"Shut up." Sash punctuated her words with a series of light finger pokes to Meg's biceps. "I do not do that."

"You completely do." Meg caught her index finger and brought it to her lips. "It's adorable."

Sasha smiled. "You are making my point."

"Which was what again?"

"You love our lazy Sundays."

"I do." Meg kissed Sasha's forehead. "I could use some coffee right now," she said, glancing over at the clock.

"We could shower and head to Lucy's a little early. Lexi beats us there every week. She could be there now for all we know," she said through a laugh. "Hey." Sasha pushed Meg's hair off her forehead gently. "Any chance we'll see Sam today at the coffee shop?"

Meg scrunched up her nose, all but saying *no* even though she wasn't a hundred percent certain. "She and Lucy are still on eggshells, I think."

"Did you ever find out what exactly happened?"

"I didn't really ask." Meg drifted her fingertips along the tops of Sasha's soft shoulders. "Lexi didn't say, and I didn't want to push it. But obviously it's pretty serious."

"Serious enough to break up over? For good?" Her voice was full of genuine concern as she stroked Meg's belly. "I thought they were talking things out," she said with unmistakable hope. "That's what Lexi said the other day."

"They are. But it's still dicey."

"Meaning what?"

"I don't know." Meg's answer was starkly honest. "I want to believe they'll work it out. Babe." She tipped Sasha's chin up with her thumb. "You don't even know what Sam was like before. She was *the* player." Meg shook her head. "Seeing her with Lucy, witnessing her transformation, I mean, girls check her out all the time. Still. At the socials, even at the coffee shop, they just approach her and, like, throw themselves at her. The old Sam would have been all over it." Meg frowned. "I'm telling you she hasn't given a single second glance to anyone. She is completely in love with Lucy. That's all I know."

"Well that's something."

"The thing is, I get the gist that it's Lucy who's the holdout. I mean, Lexi basically told me as much."

"And Sam just bought the house. She had to have plans on being with Lucy in it. Even if it was down the line." She pouted. "It makes me sad."

"Don't write them off. It could still work. Look at us."

Sasha looked right at her and her eyes held an emotion Meg couldn't quite identify. "You're right," she said with a nod. "But I lost you for a whole year almost. I missed you so much. Every single day." She punctuated each word with a tiny kiss. "I'm never letting you go again."

"Promise?"

"Promise." Sasha spread her legs wide enough to straddle Meg. She leaned forward for a kiss but Meg stopped her.

"I don't want you to leave."

"I wasn't planning on it," Sasha whispered, her tone holding the mood.

"That's not what I mean." Meg put her hand on Sasha's face. "I want you to stay." She saw Sasha's brow furrow and knew she needed to explain. "Sash, you're right. I love Sundays with you. But lately," she admitted, swallowing her feelings, "they stress me out." She rubbed the top of Sasha's thighs. "It's because of this. We spend all this time together on the weekends and it's perfect. But then, eventually, Sunday night rolls around and you go back to Manhattan and I have to wait three days to see you again." She saw the edges of Sasha's lips curl upward. "I know sometimes it's only two," Meg said. "Still. Too many."

Sasha looked like she was about to say something but Meg didn't give her the chance.

"I want to spend every night with you. I want to come home from work and see your gorgeous face when I tell you about my day. I want to hear the crazy things your students did, listen to you make lesson plans, talk to you about your grad classes. I know we do that now over the phone, but it's not the same." Her hands drifted up to Sasha's hips, holding her in place as she continued. "I want to come up behind you when we're cooking dinner, sit next to you every night when we eat. Hug you and kiss you and see your beautiful eyes when you get all animated over *Little Dorritt*."

"It really is Dickens's most underappreciated work."

"See." With one finger Meg made a small circle an inch from Sasha's face, finishing it with a tiny touch to the tip of her nose. "I need to see this face. All the time."

Spencer leapt onto the bed interrupting Meg's moment, but she went with it. "See, even Spencer agrees." She reached over and let the cat's body brush against her hand. "You're right," she said, bringing Sasha's face to her own. "No more lost time." Meg leaned forward and kissed her. "Stay." She tucked a lock of Sasha's hair behind her ear. "For good." She shrugged a little. "Just stay."

Sasha's face was full of emotion and Meg knew she was going to say yes.

"I love you so much, Meg." Sasha looked over at Spencer. "You too, Spencer Carlin," she added before giving her attention back to Meg. "Yes."

"Yes?"

"Yes, I want to stay. Every time I leave here, I'm sad." She kissed Meg. "No more." She glanced around the bedroom. "Truthfully, Meg, I would live anywhere with you. My apartment, here, somewhere we don't even know yet. But this"—she swallowed, clearly absorbing the weight of their conversation— "this place feels like home. It's where I always picture our life together." She bent down and kissed Meg over and over. "Can we swing by my apartment later?" she asked. "I just want to grab a few things to bring back. My lease is up in December, but I don't want to wait another minute." Her mouth hitched up to the side, a gorgeous smile emerging.

Meg responded with a sweet kiss that turned passionate almost immediately. She repositioned them, rolling over on top of Sasha so their bodies touched everywhere, the moment sexy and tender at the same time. Meg felt her entire life click into place. For all the time she had spent looking for *the one*, the perfect match, pursuing women she knew were wrong for her, trying like hell to make the right ones work out, here, true love had snuck up on her when she'd least expected it. It was cliché and corny and so unbelievably true.

She let her mind drift back over the last few years and acknowledged a truth she knew to her very core. In her mind, there wasn't a moment that passed when Sasha wasn't the first person she thought of when she had news to share. Whether it was mourning, celebration, or complete nonsense, it was Sasha every time. She didn't need to ask—she knew Sasha felt the same. The days and years ahead wouldn't always be this easy and carefree, she knew that. Life wasn't simple like that, nor should it be. Meg knew the future would be characterized by ups and downs, ebbs and flows, years filled with joy and hardship and sorrow and bliss. And Sasha. Forever, Sasha.

CHAPTER TWENTY-FOUR

Sam leaned against the wooden framework of her redesigned kitchen countertop, half watching and listening to the contractors as they put the finishing touches on her overhauled downstairs bath. She peeled the plastic lid off her coffee and braved the steam to snag a taste.

"Knock-knock." Lucy's sweet unmistakable voice came from the open front doorway, and Sam did her best to cover her enthusiasm at the surprise pop-in. "Are you busy?"

"Not at all." Sam felt her heart pound even as she tried not to read too much into this impromptu visit. Their communication had been on a steady incline. They talked once a day, texted all the time, sometimes they even flirted. Sam wasn't sure if it was deliberate, but it didn't matter. It still counted in her mind, and as a bonus, for the last week and a half they'd spent a solid few minutes every night wishing each other sound sleep and pleasant dreams. It had to mean something. Friends didn't do that, right?

Now at their first face-to-face in over a month, Sam searched for a sign, but Lucy's tempered demeanor gave nothing away.

Lucy ran her hand along the smooth Sheetrock as she made her way inside. "Wow, big changes, huh?"

"Just upgrading mostly," Sam answered casually. "A couple of fixes too." She pointed her coffee in the direction of the freshly hung drywall. "I was thinking—"

"Oh my God," Lucy interrupted her. "Are you drinking Starbucks?" Her mouth dropped open in mock horror.

Sam clenched her teeth and lifted her eyebrows in a kind of apology. "Sorry?"

"You should be." Lucy was obviously teasing, but Sam still felt bad.

"What can I say?" She shrugged her shoulders trying to explain. "I was tired. I needed a boost."

"Why didn't you come into the store?" Lucy sounded almost hurt.

It broke Sam's heart and she took a second to find the right words but nothing came to her. She went with the truth.

"I needed coffee. You need space. It's a dilemma."

Lucy blinked slowly, shaking her head. "You come to me. No matter what. That's what you do. I'm telling you this for future reference." She made her way closer to Sam's spot near the makeshift counter. "I didn't even know you were back from San Francisco."

"My training ended sooner than I thought so I jumped on an earlier flight. I wanted to check on things here."

"I was surprised when I saw your truck outside," she said. "How's the new job panning out?"

"Good," Sam said with a nod. "My boss seems like a decent guy. There won't be a ton of travel. Which means I can do everything from right here." She let her eyes drift around the half-finished space. "That will give me a lot of opportunity to take on more freelance, which I'm pretty amped about."

The two construction workers emerged from the bathroom, making a small racket as they packed up their tools for the day. They showed Sam their progress before consulting with her on tomorrow's schedule. Sam shut the door behind them, ready to give her full attention back to Lucy.

"You should go with marble," Lucy said. She rubbed her finger along the wooden bones. "For the countertop."

"Not granite?"

"Granite is nice. Marble is nicer. It would look great with these gorgeous floors."

"I thought there can be a staining issue with marble."

Lucy furrowed her eyebrows in disbelief. "Sam, you don't cook."

"Yeah, I know." Sam hung her head, shielding a tiny smile. "What if my girlfriend cooks? What if she bakes?"

Lucy's face registered the playful banter. "There are things you can do to protect the surface."

"Is it sturdy, though?" Sam tried for eye contact. "I mean what if there were things I wanted to do on it. Like, say, the baker?"

Lucy rolled her eyes, but her smile and her body language told Sam she liked the attention. "Stop it, you."

Her voice was lively in a way that Sam hadn't heard in ages and she couldn't filter her emotion. "I miss you, Lucy."

"I know, Sam." Lucy was suddenly serious. "I miss you too."

"How's Emily?"

A small laugh appeared to escape beyond Lucy's control. "She's great, actually."

"Really?"

Lucy answered with a nod. "Frankie moved out. Emily put their condo on the market. They both have lawyers, but honestly, it's progressing very smoothly. They should be officially divorced in no time."

"Wow. Fast."

Lucy chewed the inside of her cheek. "It's almost like this was the validation she needed to end things and move on with her life. It's unbelievable."

"That's fantastic." Sam took a sip of her drink, nervous about the response to her next question. She found her courage and asked, "How are things with you two?"

"Me and Emily?" She bobbed her head back and forth. "Things were awkward…for about one second." She shrugged and smiled at the same time. "Ems and I, we can't stay mad at each other. It's just not how we function."

"I'm glad to hear that." Sam fiddled with the top of a screw, sweeping sawdust off its head with the pad of her finger. "Does she hate me?"

"Who could hate you?" Lucy's mouth turned into a kind of frown but her voice was oddly jovial.

"Um, your sister, for one."

"Nah, you're too sweet to hate. Plus you love me—that works heavily in your favor."

"I do, you know. Love you."

"I know." Her voice was serious and sweet as she continued. "Emily knows it too. The thing about Emily is that she is sweet and kind and forgiving. She wants me to be happy and she knows I was happy with you."

"You were, right?" Sam asked the question but didn't wait for an answer. "I was too. More than I ever even knew I could be." She heard the hitch in her own voice and tapped her finger on a two-by-four. "What do we do now?"

"Well, my therapist says I should go slow." She touched Sam's finger with her own. "Protect myself so I know exactly what I'm getting into. Set up boundaries so I don't get hurt."

"Okay."

"But"—she let her hand cover Sam's—"I don't want to."

Sam's heart was pounding and she was useless to stop the smile from spreading across her face. "No, huh?"

"Nope." Lucy moved closer and slipped between Sam and the counter. "I don't think you'll hurt me."

"I won't. Ever." Her hands went to Lucy's hips out of habit and desire. "You know that."

"I do. In my heart, I do."

"Good." Sam leaned down and kissed her lips lightly. "Because it's the truth."

When they kissed, it was long and slow and deep. Weeks of separation were made up for in several moments of passion and honesty and love beyond measure. Sam wanted it to go on forever, but the sun was starting to set, and in minutes they would be surrounded by complete darkness.

"We should go," she said, kissing her way down Lucy's neck. "Wait a second." She interrupted her own actions. "Shouldn't you be working right now?"

"Yes," Lucy whispered. She found Sam's lips again. "I don't know if you know this." She breathed the words in Sam's ear. "I'm the boss. I come and go as I please."

"Is that right?"

"It is. And"—she stroked Sam's cheeks—"there happens to be a full moon tonight. Did you know that?"

Sam didn't bother to verbalize her response, relying instead on the look of pure disbelief she was sure was all over her face.

"Of course you do," Lucy said answering her own question. "I do have to go shut down and lock up the store. But after that, I was wondering if you might take me somewhere to see it."

"You're going to close? Now? It's not even six o'clock."

"Can you imagine, closing shop early for a date." She opened her mouth dramatically, teasing Sam outright. "I guess I must love you or something." She rushed her hands through Sam's hair, bringing her in for another kiss. "Come on, let's go."

Sam stepped back and grabbed her keys from her front pocket. "Lucy, you don't have to. It's an incredibly sweet gesture. Closing the store early, I mean." She glanced around the barren room, making sure she had all her things. "But it's not necessary. For real. The moon won't be in the right spot for hours."

"Oh, Sam," Lucy said, with a lively lilt to her tone. "So naive you are sometimes."

Sam's laugh was completely honest. "What?"

"We have hours of catching up to do before that moon viewing." She let her eyes run the length of Sam's body, her intent on display as she backed toward the front door. "If you haven't eaten in a while, I suggest you load up now." She raised her eyebrows and bit her lip suggestively. "Lots of carbs. You're going to need your energy."

Sam felt a rush of happiness, desire, and pure love come to the surface but she kept her response simple. "Yes, ma'am."

CHAPTER TWENTY-FIVE

M eg stood in front of her front door, turned the lock to the left and listened to the bolt slide securely into place.

"No Sasha?" Lexi's voice behind her came out of nowhere and it made her shriek in surprise. "You're kidding me with that ridiculous scream, right?"

"Well, don't sneak up on people. I could have a heart attack."

"Sneak up on you? It's the middle of the afternoon, broad daylight." With both hands she made a grand gesture around her for effect before narrowing her scope and pointing directly at her big belly protruding through her open winter jacket. "And I'm the size of a house. So hardly tiptoeing around over here."

"I just didn't expect you to be right here." Meg nodded toward her door. "Did you want to come in for a few minutes?"

"No," she said with a laugh. "I want to get this over with."

Meg's voice shook a little. "Meeting the contractor, you mean?"

"Meg, you are a terrible liar." Lexi hooked her arm through Meg's. "I know we're going to my baby shower."

"Fuck." She stomped her foot. "Who told you?"

Lexi's dimples came out when she smiled. "No one told me. I put it together on my very own."

"But we were all so careful not to slip."

Lexi rolled her eyes. "My moms have been completely weird about today for weeks. First making sure I would be around. Then not allowing my brothers to commit to any sports activity the whole weekend." She grinned. "Kam was all over me too. Making sure I was definitely available to meet with the nameless *vendor*." She threw some air quotes around the word for emphasis. "On top of that, Lucy has been baking nonstop, Sam hasn't made eye contact since Thursday, and Sasha froze when I asked her what she had going on this weekend." She lifted her shoulders. "I'm no fool. I knew something was up."

Meg hung her head in laughter and disappointment. "You have to act surprised." She pointed at the Commons. "These people are really excited for this."

"I know." Lexi's voice was full of enthusiasm. "Believe me, I'm excited too. I love a party, you know that." She tapped Meg's forearm. "I just want to get through the beginning. I know I have to look shocked. I don't want to let anyone down. It makes me nervous."

"We still have a few minutes to kill. They'll have my head if I bring you there one minute early."

"But weren't you just leaving when I got here?"

"Yes. I was coming to your house to stall and make sure you didn't pull a fast one. Like try to meet me over at the Commons or something." Meg gestured at her front door, getting ready to reopen it. "Do you want to sit down?"

"Not really. I know it's cold out but it's still kind of nice." She looked up at the clear blue sky. "Let's walk for ten minutes."

Meg nodded and they headed in the opposite direction from the Commons, taking up the whole sidewalk as they strolled.

"How's living with Sasha?" Lexi asked.

"Amazing."

Lexi smiled. "I do love you guys together."

"I know. I do too." She took a quick step ahead and moved a branch out of Lexi's path.

"Look at you, so gallant." Lexi paused to tilt her head and flutter her lashes playfully at Meg.

"Don't be a dick. I don't want you to fall." Meg offered a hand at Lexi's elbow for support. "Besides the fact that I care about you"—she thumbed behind them—"there's a line of people that will kill me if I don't deliver you to that party in one piece."

Lexi huffed in disdain but hooked her arm through Meg's as they continued walking, circling the block and coming up on the opening for the rental section. "I wonder if Lucy will move in with Sam," she mused idly.

"I bet they do. My guess, spring."

Lexi nodded in agreement or consideration, Meg wasn't entirely sure. With still a few minutes to spare, they wandered over by the empty dog run and the gazebo, which was looking a little run-down in the bright afternoon sun.

"We should probably have this painted after the winter," Meg said matter-of-factly.

"Look at you." Lexi bumped her with her hip. "Spoken like a true board member."

Meg laughed. "Except I'm not. Neither are you. We're the Bay West lackeys."

"Stop it." Lexi shook her head. "You know that's not true."

"I know. I'm just playing around." She tipped her head to the side. "You know me, anything to get a laugh."

"Oh, before I forget." Lexi rubbed one hand over her stomach. "There's a new girl. She just passed her board interview. I think she's moving into her unit next week."

"Cool."

"Riley is her name, I think. She's like you were when you got here."

"Meaning what, exactly? She's awesome and sexy and single?"

"Well, yes." Lexi let out a little laugh. "But what I meant was…she's super shy and she doesn't know anyone at all." She pushed a wayward curl off her face. "Kam wants us to make sure we look out for her. Introduce her to people, include her when we can. She's like a scared kitten right about now."

"That does sound vaguely familiar." Meg laughed at herself. "God, I remember that feeling." She threw her arm over Lexi's shoulders as she looked up at the bare trees. "You saved me that very first day."

"Jesse too. We made sure you had people." Lexi smiled, obviously proud of their joint kindness. She reached up and touched Meg's hand at her shoulder, squeezing it a little.

"Only a few years ago, and it feels like a whole different life," Meg mused.

"Crazy."

"And just think, things are about to change again for you." They were steps from the Commons door and Meg reached for the handle. "You ready?" she asked, covering a lot of ground with her simple question.

Lexi bounced her shoulders up and down seeming to psych herself up or brace herself for what came next. She smiled wide and both her dimples came out. "I guess so," she said. "Hey, Meg." She placed one hand on Meg's forearm, the other on the center of her belly. "It's a girl."

"Isn't it always?" Meg said with a sly smile.

"True that, sister," Lexi responded, meeting Meg's grin with her own before reaching out and pulling her into a hug.

They stayed there for a second, hugging each other tightly, before Meg broke them apart. She held Lexi at arm's distance, one hand squarely on each shoulder.

"Here we go," Meg said.

Meg opened the door, and boisterous cheers of surprise and excitement spilled out and carried her forward, almost as if on air. The room was full and Meg's eyes met Sasha's immediately, their deep affection for one another communicated wordlessly across the crowded space. Surrounded by her friends, her family, the love of her life, Meg felt her entire life falling perfectly into place. Whatever the future would bring was, as life is, a complete mystery. But Meg was more than ready. In fact, she could hardly wait.

About the Author

Maggie Cummings lives in Staten Island, New York, with her wife and their two children. She has degrees in English, theater, and criminal justice. She works in law enforcement in the NYC metropolitan area.

Books Available from Bold Strokes Books

A Date to Die by Anne Laughlin. Someone is killing people close to Detective Kay Adler, who must look to her own troubled past for a suspect. There she finds more than one person seeking revenge against her. (978-1-63555-023-8)

Captured Soul by Laydin Michaels. Can Kadence Munroe save the woman she loves from a twisted killer, or will she lose her to a collector of souls? (978-1-62639-915-0)

Dawn's New Day by TJ Thomas. Can Dawn Oliver and Cam Cooper, two women who have loved and lost, open their hearts to love again? (978-1-63555-072-6)

Definite Possibility by Maggie Cummings. Sam Miller is just out for good times, but Lucy Weston makes her realize happily ever after is a definite possibility. (978-1-62639-909-9)

Eyes Like Those by Melissa Brayden. Isabel Chase and Taylor Andrews struggle between love and ambition from the writers' room on one of Hollywood's hottest TV shows. (978-1-63555-012-2)

Heart's Orders by Jaycie Morrison. Helen Tucker and Tee Owens escape hardscrabble lives to careers in the Women's Army Corps, but more than their hearts are at risk as friendship blossoms into love. (978-1-63555-073-3)

Hiding Out by Kay Bigelow. Treat Dandridge is unaware that her life is in danger from the murderer who is hunting the woman she's falling in love with, Mickey Heiden. (978-1-62639-983-9)

Omnipotence Enough by Sophia Kell Hagin. Can the tiny tool that abducted war veteran Jamie Gwynmorgan accidentally acquires help her escape an unknown enemy to reclaim her stolen life and the woman she deeply loves? (978-1-63555-037-5)

Summer's Cove by Aurora Rey. Emerson Lange moved to Provincetown to live in the moment, but when she meets Darcy Belo and her son Liam, her quest for summer romance becomes a family affair. (978-1-62639-971-6)

The Road to Wings by Julie Tizard. Lieutenant Casey Tompkins, air force student pilot, has to fly with the toughest instructor, Captain Kathryn "Hard Ass" Hardesty, fly a supersonic jet, and deal with a growing forbidden attraction. (978-1-62639-988-4)

Beauty and the Boss by Ali Vali. Ellis Renois is at the top of the fashion world, but she never expects her summer assistant Charlotte Hamner to tear her heart and her business apart like sharp scissors through cheap material. (978-1-62639-919-8)

Fury's Choice by Brey Willows. When gods walk amongst humans, can two women find a balance between love and faith? (978-1-62639-869-6)

Lessons in Desire by MJ Williamz. Can a summer love stand a four-month hiatus and still burn hot? (978-1-63555-019-1)

Lightning Chasers by Cass Sellars. For Sydney and Parker, being a couple was never what they had planned. Now they have to fight corruption, murder, and enemies hiding in plain sight just to hold on to each other. Lightning Series, Book Two. (978-1-62639-965-5)

Summer Fling by Jean Copeland. Still jaded from a breakup years earlier, Kate struggles to trust falling in love again when a summer fling with sexy young singer Jordan rocks her off her feet. (978-1-62639-981-5)

Take Me There by Julie Cannon. Adrienne and Sloan know it would be career suicide to mix business with pleasure, however tempting it is. But what's the harm? They're both consenting adults. Who would know? (978-1-62639-917-4)

The Girl Who Wasn't Dead by Samantha Boyette. A year ago, someone tried to kill Jenny Lewis. Tonight she's ready to find out who it was. (978-1-62639-950-1)

Unchained Memories by Dena Blake. Can a woman give herself completely when she's left a piece of herself behind? (978-1-62639-993-8)

Walking Through Shadows by Sheri Lewis Wohl. All Molly wanted to do was go backpacking...in her own century (978-1-62639-968-6)

A Lamentation of Swans by Valerie Bronwen. Ariel Montgomery returns to Sea Oats to try to save her broken marriage but soon finds herself also fighting to save her own life and catch a murderer. (978-1-62639-828-3)

Freedom to Love by Ronica Black. What happens when the woman who spent her lifetime worrying about caring for her family, finally finds the freedom to love without borders? (978-1-63555-001-6)

House of Fate by Barbara Ann Wright. Two women must throw off the lives they've known as a guardian and an assassin and save two rival houses before their secrets tear the galaxy apart. (978-1-62639-780-4)

Planning for Love by Erin Dutton. Could true love be the one thing that wedding coordinator Faith McKenna didn't plan for? (978-1-62639-954-9)

Sidebar by Carsen Taite. Judge Camille Avery and her clerk, attorney West Fallon, agree on little except their mutual attraction, but can their relationship and their careers survive a headline-grabbing case? (978-1-62639-752-1)

Sweet Boy and Wild One by T. L. Hayes. When Rachel Cole meets soulful singer Bobby Layton at an open mic, she is immediately in thrall. What she soon discovers will rock her world in ways she never imagined. (978-1-62639-963-1)

To Be Determined by Mardi Alexander and Laurie Eichler. Charlie Dickerson escapes her life in the US to rescue Australian wildlife with Pip Atkins, but can they save each other? (978-1-62639-946-4)

True Colors by Yolanda Wallace. Blogger Robby Rawlins plans to use First Daughter Taylor Crenshaw to get ahead, but she never planned on falling in love with her in the process. (978-1-62639-927-3)

Unexpected by Jenny Frame. When Dale McGuire falls for Rebecca Harper, the mother of the son she never knew she had, will Rebecca's troubled past stop them from making the family they both truly crave? (978-1-62639-942-6)

Canvas for Love by Charlotte Greene. When ghosts from Amelia's past threaten to undermine their relationship, Chloé must navigate the greatest romance of her life without losing sight of who she is. (978-1-62639-944-0)

Heart Stop by Radclyffe. Two women, one with a damaged body, the other a damaged spirit, challenge each other to dare to live again. (978-1-62639-899-3)

Repercussions by Jessica L. Webb. Someone planted information in Edie Black's brain and now they want it back, but with the protection of shy former soldier Skye Kenny, Edie has a chance at life and love. (978-1-62639-925-9)

Spark by Catherine Friend. Jamie's life is turned upside down when her consciousness travels back to 1560 and lands in the body of one of Queen Elizabeth I's ladies-in-waiting…or has she totally lost her grip on reality? (978-1-62639-930-3)

Taking Sides by Kathleen Knowles. When passion and politics collide, can love survive? (978-1-62639-876-4)

Thorns of the Past by Gun Brooke. Former cop Darcy Flynn's heart broke when her career on the force ended in disgrace, but perhaps saving Sabrina Hawk's life will mend it in more ways than one. (978-1-62639-857-3)

You Make Me Tremble by Karis Walsh. Seismologist Casey Radnor comes to the San Juan Islands to study an earthquake but finds her heart shaken by passion when she meets animal rescuer Iris Mallery. (978-1-62639-901-3)

Complications by MJ Williamz. Two women battle for the heart of one. (978-1-62639-769-9)

Crossing the Wide Forever by Missouri Vaun. As Cody Walsh and Lillie Ellis face the perils of the untamed West, they discover that love's uncharted frontier isn't for the weak in spirit or the faint of heart. (978-1-62639-851-1)

Fake It Till You Make It by M. Ullrich. Lies will lead to trouble, but can they lead to love? (978-1-62639-923-5)

Girls Next Door by Sandy Lowe and Stacia Seaman eds. Best-selling romance authors tell it from the heart—sexy, romantic stories of falling for the girls next door. (978-1-62639-916-7)

Pursuit by Jackie D. The pursuit of the most dangerous terrorist in America will crack the lines of friendship and love, and not everyone will make it out under the weight of duty and service. (978-1-62639-903-7)

Shameless by Brit Ryder. Confident Emery Pearson knows exactly what she's looking for in a no-strings-attached hookup, but can a spontaneous interlude open her heart to more? (978-1-63555-006-1)

The Practitioner by Ronica Black. Sometimes love comes calling whether you're ready for it or not. (978-1-62639-948-8)

Unlikely Match by Fiona Riley. When an ambitious PR exec and her super-rich coding geek-girl client fall in love, they learn that giving something up may be the only way to have everything. (978-1-62639-891-7)

Where Love Leads by Erin McKenzie. A high school counselor and the mom of her new student bond in support of the troubled girl, never expecting deeper feelings to emerge, testing the boundaries of their relationship. (978-1-62639-991-4)